Other books by LESLEY CHOYCE

SHORT STORY COLLECTIONS
Eastern Sure (1980)
Billy Botzweiler's Last Dance (1984)
Conventional Emotions (1985)
The Dream Auditor (1986)
Coming Up for Air (1988)
Margin of Error (1992)
Dance the Rocks Ashore (1997)

NOVELS
Downwind (1984)
The Second Season of Jonas MacPherson (1991)
Magnificent Obsessions (1991)
The Ecstasy Conspiracy (1992)
Republic of Nothing (1994)
Trap Door to Heaven (1996)

POETRY
Reinventing the Wheel (1980)
Fast Living (1982)
The End of Ice (1985)
The Top of the Heart (1986)
The Man Who Borrowed the Bay of Fundy (1988)
The Coastline of Forgetting (1995)
Beautiful Sadness (1996)

NON-FICTION
Edible Wild Plants of Nova Scotia (1977)
An Avalanche of Ocean (1987)
December Six: The Halifax Solution (1988)
Transcendental Anarchy (1993)
Nova Scotia: Shaped by the Sea (1996)

World Enough

A NOVEL

LESLEY CHOYCE

GOOSE LANE

Published by Goose Lane Editions with the assistance of the Canada Council, the Department of Canadian Heritage, and the New Brunswick Department of Municipalities, Culture and Housing, 1998.

Edited by Laurel Boone.
Cover photograph by Sterling Keays. Reproduced with permission.
Book design by Julie Scriver.
Author photograph by Jason McGroarty. Reproduced with permission.
Printed in Canada by Transcontinental Printing.

10 9 8 7 6 5 4 3 2 1

Canadian Cataloguing in Publication Data

Choyce, Lesley, 1951-

    World enough
    ISBN 0-86492-246-9

I. Title.

PR9199.3.C497W67 1998   C813' .54   C98-950178-7
PSS8555.H668W67 1998

Goose Lane Editions
469 King Street
Fredericton, New Brunswick
CANADA E3B 1E5

For my good friend, Professor Malcolm Ross

One

There is a boy who lives in an old house somewhere along a forgotten shoreline of a vast expanse of water. He wakes in the morning when it is still dark. He puts on his clothes, sneaks down the creaky wooden stairway and walks barefoot across the wet morning grass. By the time he reaches the shore at the farthest edge of his back yard, the sky is a blue-grey fuzz of light.

The boy finds a large, cold, damp boulder and sits down on it, waiting for the sun to come up. The boy is me, twenty-some years ago. The scene is either real, true to life, the way it really happened, or it never happened at all and I imagined it, then shuffled it out of my imagination into the cascade of images that is the memory of my childhood.

The boy is very daring and adventurous to sneak out into the world so early, all alone. He wants to see the sun at the very instant it rises out of the bay. He's wanted to see this for a long time. For this, he will break his parents' rules. He will be punished if he's caught.

The sky finds many different hopeful, muted colours to show him, and soon all the grey has disappeared except for a pale mist with threads of clouds dancing above the mirrored surface of the water.

Then fire suddenly rears up out of the sea. The boy stares straight into the morning sun as it boils up from the deep. He closes his eyes and feels its warmth, and when he opens his eyes again he is amazed at how quickly the sun is flooding the world with light. He shivers once and then braces himself on the large bare rock.

Suddenly he hears the footsteps of someone running towards him from the house. Small bare feet slapping the grass. He turns just as his little sister leaps towards him and throws her arms around his neck. She's breathing very fast and laughing. He has to hold onto her quite tightly to keep her from falling from their perch.

"I told you not to follow me," he says.

"I know. But you didn't mean it."

Together they watch as the water goes red, then gold and then the sun pulls itself out of the water and begins to climb into the sky. A lone osprey appears and lets out a loud shriek, dives deep into the bay and surfaces with a fish. It flies back into the sky and shakes itself once before flying off to the east.

Every stone on the shoreline, every scrap of seaweed on the sand seems illuminated from within. The boy holds his breath, waiting for something to happen next. Or pretending he can freeze time and make this last forever.

Two

Henry Sinclair had a PhD in psychology, and he was the author of dozens of articles about the frailty of the human condition. He had ideas that were either way ahead of or far behind the times, yet he had an uncanny ability to persuade government bureaucracies that his "rehabilitation workshop" deserved all the funding it could muster. He had friends in high places because the high-placed friends saw an advantage to having a man of Sinclair's calibre on their side. Nonetheless, he sucked up to no one, he despised politics, and his only interest was in the betterment of society and the improvement of the lives of those lucky enough to become "clients" of New Dawn.

"There are no limits, really," Dr. Henry Sinclair instructed me on the day of my interview. "There are obstacles and impediments but always solutions, alternatives and possibilities. For you, for me and for them. What do you think?"

"I agree. The only true barriers are the ones we set up for ourselves. And those can be deconstructed." I was a chameleon. I wanted a job. My own philosophy was a warped and twisted doctrine of limitations. Sinclair was a man out of my league, brilliant and much more energized than all the psych profs who had cudgelled me through graduate and undergraduate school in New Brunswick.

"Tell me about yourself," he said finally.

It wouldn't matter that much what I said next. Sinclair would hire me because he liked me. The truth was this: I wasn't at all qualified academically or otherwise to be a rehab counsellor working with the likes of Dr. Sinclair. As a graduate student in psychology at UNB Saint John, I had been average at best, and that was probably flattering myself. I had been assigned to teach a section of freshman psych and did a miserable job. I stumbled through my teaching, ever uncomfortable with my class. I hated standing at the front of the room and speaking to thirty university students, most of whom, I was sure, were smarter than me. I was a lousy teacher and a wretched student in my own field of study. After failing the orals for my master's degree, I quit. I was tired of university, tired of who I was and who I had been. I wanted to experience something else, something beyond university that I called "the real world."

The real world, I was certain, was either south of Saint John in the States or west, in Nova Scotia. I was twenty-two years old and as insecure as any thirteen-year-old. If I could have pinned down exactly what I was afraid of, I might have been able to reconstruct a new identity right there in my home town. But I didn't know the cause of my fears and anxieties. So I would run away to someplace else and start over.

I went as far as Calais, Maine. I walked up and down the main street and asked myself if I wanted to live in Maine or any other part of the United States of Ambition. I walked on out of town until I came to a McDonald's on US 1. Studying a road map of America over a cup of coffee and a Big Mac, I suddenly felt terribly homesick. Yet I wanted very badly to be brave, to be adventurous.

I studied the ganglionic mess of interstate highways on the map before me. The cities all looked choked and strangled by the roads. The entire east coast seemed coloured green with interstate asphalt. I wondered how people found room to live between all those roads. Big, lonely, crowded country, I concluded. I traced my finger along the St. Croix River and the border of New Brunswick. I traced the infinitesimally short route on Highway 2 back through St. Stephen and on home to Saint John. Saint John, New Brunswick, city of despair. No fond memories there. Why the hell would I want to run back? I scraped my thumbnail further on.

Up the Saint John River through Loyalist farms to Fredericton. That would never do. No Fredericton. No more UNB, no more academics. I turned my thumbnail east on the Trans-Canada and ran my finger off the map. I knew that Nova Scotia was there. I could clearly picture it on the laminated top of the McDonald's table. And I knew it had to be better than this. As a kid, the "Nova" and the "Scotia" of that neighbouring province had sounded foreign, exotic, not just Latin for "New" and "Scotland," but "Nova" for "New Worlds" and "Scotia" for, well, just for its sibilant, enchanted sound.

So I walked out of McDonald's and took refuge in an Irving station, where I drank another cup of coffee before walking back through town and across the St. Croix River to my native land. A bus took me home to Saint John and that dingy row house down the street from the big ugly hospital that dominated that city, a hospital so ugly and obtrusive it would be abandoned for years, left to become an eyesore, then dynamited before hundreds of onlookers who applauded its demise. It took me another month to build up the courage to leave again, this time following Plan B to Nova Scotia.

I guess I was too slow to respond. Sinclair repeated the request. "Tell me about yourself. Please."

"I'm looking for challenges," I said quickly. Blank, heroic, generic.

"You are, aren't you? Are you willing to forget anything

you ever learned out of a textbook about people with special needs and so-called abnormalities?"

The question caught me off guard. Was it a trick? I needed a job desperately. If this one didn't work out, I was destined for a return trip to Saint John. I would have to move back home with my mother. Death, another option that sometimes had the appeal of a long holiday in the Bahamas, was a consideration, but I was too timid. I didn't have the nerve for such dramatic action.

"I think the ideas put forward in the textbooks are interesting as . . . reference points . . . but only that. Look at Freud."

Sinclair smiled. "Yes, look at Freud. A genius. But mostly, well, mostly wrong. Intoxicated with his own wrongheadedness. But he gave us a good kick in the pants."

"And then proceeded to set psychology in the wrong direction for, what, fifty years?"

"Something like that." Sinclair wore black-rimmed glasses that he would take off and study as if reading from his own sacred canon. As if answers to life's greatest questions were written in tiny print on the inside ridges of the frames. He was an intense but likable man. He said nothing else for perhaps a full minute. I thought that I had gone too far, said the wrong thing, but I was also amazed that he had pulled these words out of me. I had put myself out on a ledge. Not my style at all. Mr. Safety. Better safe than sorry was my motto. Better invisible that caught out in the open.

"Tell me what you know about human nature," Sinclair asked, now sounding like my dead-bolt UNB professor.

"I know that most people never live up to their abilities. I know that we lie to ourselves all the time. I know that compassion works better than coercion. I know that most people are afraid to admit that Christmas makes them truly unhappy."

Sinclair put his glasses on and looked at me with grave concern. I was sure I had said all the wrong things. The look in his eyes told me this. "You think people expect to be happy?"

"Yes. But they don't work at it."

"Happiness is a human right."

"Dignity would be preferable over happiness to most of us."

A lift of the eyebrow. Sinclair stood up. The interview was over. "Teach them what you know," he said. "Give them hope . . . of dignity if nothing else. Teach them one significant skill and do it to the best of your ability."

"I've got the job?"

He shrugged. "Minimum wage. Nothing to write home about. Connie will show you the ropes. She thinks the future for them is in hand-crafted jewellery. We're not giving up on shipping and handling, though. Basic but necessary stuff. Life skills. Don't expect miracles. Most of our clients have been in training programs and workshops all their lives. These are adults, not children. Looking forward to having you on board."

Sinclair got up and left the room without saying goodbye or shaking my hand. Perhaps he thought I'd balk at the minimum wage part. That aspect didn't bother me at all. All I knew was that I was spared the return trip home. I was a new man.

Three

My first real contact with a client was with a furtive man in the hallway who had the demeanour of a nervous shoplifter.

"Hey, how ya doin'? I'm Roger. Got a stick of gum?" Every conversation with Roger, I would soon learn, began with a request for something.

"Sorry, Roger. I don't have any."

"No Juicy Fruit? No Hubba Bubba bubble gum?"

"No."

"I'd settle for Dentyne."

"Sorry, man, I forgot to go to the store." Roger now looked hurt and sad beyond belief. He was a cute kid, a goofy eight-year-old boy inside the body of a forty-five-year-old man. An eight-year-old with sideburns and weight lifter's biceps. Dark, lustrous black hair combed to perfection. Women probably thought he was gorgeous.

"Sugarless gum is good for you. Then you don't have to floss."

"No gum. I'm really sorry, okay? What else is on your mind today?"

"Got a cigarette?" His eyes were piercing.

Then I remembered. I reached into my wallet and pulled out a single thin, desiccated slab of Cinnamint gum. Must have been in there for five years. Roger's eyes lit up like Christmas lights. I handed it over. I would make no deals for it. A gift, not a learning tool.

"You're way cool," Roger said. He carefully unwrapped the gum, folded the paper neatly and put it into his pocket. He slipped open the foil and closed his eyes, inhaled the stick of gum. I think he had goose bumps on his neck. Something near a religious experience was going on.

I watched as the gum entered his mouth and his head swayed slightly from side to side. "I'm gonna buy a lot of gum when I grow up."

"You have lots of time for that, Rog," I said. "What kind of work do you do here?"

"Taping boxes. I like the sound of the tape. You like the sound the tape makes when you stretch it out across the boxes?"

"It's a good sound, I bet."

"It's a great sound. I can tell from the sound if I'm doing it right."

"I bet you're a damn good worker."

"Damn good."

Roger was still in chewing-gum nirvana, standing there piously in the hallway. I could hear footsteps behind me and turned to see Henry Sinclair coming our way.

"How's the gum, Roger?"

"Like heaven," he replied.

Sinclair twisted sideways slightly to make eye contact with me. He smiled and tilted his glasses down. I couldn't figure out what it meant. Maybe I wasn't supposed to have given Roger the gum.

"Alex, some guy from the province is coming later today. Don't pay any attention to him. I said he could hang around as much as he liked."

"Funding stuff?"

"Nobody's saying, but we're always under the gun. Don't pay any attention to him. Do what you're hired to do."

Precisely what I was hired to do was still pretty vague to me.

"What about me?" Roger asked.

"You too, Rog. Do what you do, pal. I've seen your work. A-one."

Sinclair was gone. Just me and Roger again, like a couple of little kids hanging out on the sidewalk.

"A-one is good, right?"

"Near the top."

"I used to carry a gun at my other job."

"Stick with the tape gun, Roger. It's a whole lot safer."

"And it makes the tape do that neat sound."

"To work, comrade."

"Aye, aye, captain."

Later I would learn that Roger had been a Mountie working near Montreal. A good, honest Mountie, so they say. Twenty years. Clean slate. Wife and kids. Career man. Busted some bikers for drugs and prostitution. Their friends staked out an overpass and dropped a couple of concrete blocks through the windshield of his family car. His oldest kid, Ricky, was in the car. It was five a.m. and they were on their way to Ricky's hockey practice at the rink. Ricky was killed, bled to death before an ambulance got there. Roger suffered brain damage. When he woke up he knew who he was. He even remembered the concrete blocks, his kid screaming. He recognized his wife, he knew he was a cop and all the rest. But his thought processes were those of an eight-year-old. His wife moved him and their other son down to the Maritimes to start over. There was nothing, nothing anywhere for Roger but this. Shipping and handling in a sheltered workshop in the Burnside Industrial Park near the shore of Bedford Basin.

Before Roger walked away, he touched my sleeve. "If Jeff asks you to drive your car, say no."

"Who's Jeff?"

"He's blind. You'll meet him."

"I'm looking forward to it."

"You shouldn't let Jeff drive. He can't see."

"I guess that sounds logical."

"Driving without a license is against the law."

"I know that."

"Good. Cars are dangerous. Like weapons. Someone could get hurt. That's why they have laws, you know?"

"Roger, you're a good man. You don't want to see anyone get hurt."

The little safety lecture was actually his way of leading up to another request. "Can *I* drive. I've got a license. Used to have my own car. A Pontiac. Would you let me?"

"Sure. Why not. Do you remember how?"

"You turn on the key, right?"

"Got it." He gave me thumbs up, smiled, then nodded, pulled the gum out of his mouth and stretched it with his two hands. "Something about gum. I don't know what it is." Roger's blue eyes were so intense, as if he could drill right into my brain. He could have been a movie star, this guy with his classic dark good looks.

"Nobody knows. It's a scientific secret, I think."

Roger reminded me of what it was like to be a little kid, and that tripped some heavy memories. Memories of my parents, memories of my little sister, Karen. My father had always believed we were a very unlucky family. He felt that the world had inflicted all kinds of problems purposefully on us. We had lived at Point Lepreau, on the coast south of Saint John. The province decided to build the Maritimes' first nuclear power plant just down the road from our home, and they wanted to buy my father's land, our house, the homes of our neighbours. They said it would be the safest nuclear power plant on the earth.

That safe nuclear power plant was one of the most unlucky things that happened to us. It drove a wedge into our family. But it wouldn't be the worst thing to happen to us. Not by a long shot. After we were driven away from Lepreau and the coast and we lived in a row house in Saint John, my mother kept waiting for the next really horrific unlucky thing to happen. When things did go badly, she'd compare the minor disasters to the exile from the coast. "This wasn't big enough. This wasn't it. It's still out there waiting to happen." And it eventually did.

Four

Connie Gavin was already working at New Dawn when I was hired. She was very attractive in an urban, sophisticated way, and she came by it honestly. Her mother was a fashion model, her father a Halifax developer of shopping malls. She had grown up wandering around her father's malls as if their sterile, trendy halls were the natural playground for any child. Whereas I had been shaped by my father's overstated negative expectations of life, Connie had been fashioned by parents who gave her high but ultimately materialistic expectations. Her entire view of the world was formulated by money and the things it could buy.

Henry Sinclair had given her an office much larger and

nicer than mine. I don't fault him for that. Connie simply looked as if she expected something of distinction. I did not. Why she was a counsellor of special needs people is a bit of a mystery, but it would be a short-lived career. She had the intimidating charm of young, beautiful women who know they have power over men. Roger had, on occasion, let his gum drop from his mouth when she was in the room. He had a bad habit of staring, a man with the hormones of a healthy forty-five-year-old in a body to match but a mind stuck somewhere in the third grade. He also had a habit of giving Connie little presents like hockey cards (he only really wanted the gum anyway), plastic rings and rubber spiders from vending machines. Sinclair knew she was good for the diplomatic cakewalk needed to keep New Dawn afloat. She was an ace at flattering the right men at just the right time.

That first day on the job, after Sinclair's pep talk and chatting with Roger, I was shuttled into Connie's well-equipped office. She had provided her own accoutrements, ransacked the furniture stores and shopping malls of the metro area for the best of everything.

The first thing Connie did, once I had sat down, was lift her blouse. "Do you like it?"

I was caught off-guard.

"I just had it done yesterday. It hurt more than I expected." She was pointing toward her belly button. There was a ring there. She'd been pierced — professionally, of course — by the best.

"I didn't know you could do that," I said, a perfect country bumpkin, brought up on a diet of salt cod and dulse.

"And this was done last year." There to the left across her attractive midriff was a kind of infinity symbol tattooed into her delicate skin. "It's supposed to be a Celtic symbol meaning universal love, but I just like the way it looks."

"It's great."

Connie talked and I listened. She didn't have that much to say about the job. She mostly talked about herself. She was well aware of the fact that men felt honoured just to be in her presence, and this gave her a certain license to speak at length on anything that was on her mind. I soon learned about Boyfriend A and Boyfriend B.

"Greg lives in Calgary. He's in the oil patch. Charles is just another Halifax lawyer. But I like them equally, and someday I'm going to have to decide."

What followed was a description of what each of them wore, what sort of cars they drove and the types of restaurants where they took her to dinner. She commuted to Calgary at least once a month to be with Boyfriend A, Greg. To keep her occupied between junkets, there was Boyfriend B, Charles. Charles had his shortcomings because he had not grown up with money, but he was learning to come up to her expectations. Greg had cash and breeding on his side, and my money (what little I had of it) would be staked on him if I had to bet on who would ultimately win her favours.

"I needed a challenge, so I thought I would go into social work," she said at length. It was an offhand remark that required less enthusiasm than a story about buying her most recent pair of shoes. "I liked school, so I stayed on and took an MSW. Nobody ever thought I was stupid."

How wonderfully odd to meet my exact opposite. I almost wanted to ask her if her father had ever said to her, "Connie, there are two types of people in the world, and you know which type you are."

"I'm really glad Henry hired someone like you," Connie said, a sweet smile on her face as she sipped coffee from a mug with the inscription, "Virginia Is For Lovers."

I wondered about the "someone like you" part. I knew

that most people's first impressions of me were not very positive. I had a hard time with eye contact. I wasn't good at small talk. I had low self-esteem. My father had trained me well.

"I like the guy," I said. "He seems very sincere."

"A very sweet man. Brilliant, but not focused. No business sense."

"He sounded as if he hired me because he's expecting to expand. More funding, more clients. Something like that."

"We have fat and thin times here. Been up to fifty people in the workshop. Now we're down to twelve. It's a little like the stock market. Could bottom out at any time."

"But he wouldn't have hired me if he didn't expect some kind of expansion, right?"

"Henry Sinclair would hire you if he liked you. If a cow walked into his office and asked for a job and rolled those big dark cow eyes at the man, that cow would be on the payroll and have a pension plan. No offense."

"But I get the point."

"A lovely man. One of the reasons I took the job here was that it was obvious that he needed me. I'm good for New Dawn."

I don't think I really liked Connie very much at first. She seemed shallow, insincere about her work, work I was about to throw myself into. In New Brunswick I had no life. I had carved out an identity of loneliness, failure and insecurity. Now I envisioned a life, something with meaning. Connie and I had come from opposite worlds. Yet, even though I didn't like her, I was attracted to her and for all the wrong reasons, attracted in the same way I had been attracted to the two women I had loved while in graduate school — two women who both dumped me for someone more interesting. I had grown to expect nothing from a relationship except hurt and humiliation, but I was also a man in the process of re-engineering his whole identity. In Nova Scotia I would have a life, I would rage and kick my wasted ego up out of the dungeons of despair, and I would live.

"Connie, could I, like, buy you a drink or something, today after work? Just to get a chance to know you better." *Risk everything*. I didn't really care about Boyfriend A or B. I knew I did not want to fall in love with Connie. I just wanted to take the dare, to stick my neck out because it was so unlike me. *Fight the old instincts*, the voice would tell me. *Go with the new*.

Connie seemed more than a little surprised. She lifted her blouse again and studied the bruising by her navel where she'd been pierced. I almost laughed out loud. "Sure, I guess. But to tell you the truth, I think I already told you everything that's worth knowing about me."

I smiled. "No, that can't be true." I got up to leave. "Okay, after work. Lawrence of Oregano. I want you to tell me everything you know about loneliness," I said and I left.

Henry Sinclair's idea for how I would learn the ropes of my job was what he called "holistic and somewhat gestalt." In other words, aside from the little philosophical rap from himself and an introductory lesson in nothing at all from Connie, I would introduce myself to the people I was to train and figure out for myself what was going on.

Rebecca and Jules were both working on jewellery when I went into the workshop. Both were trainees, but Rebecca, I would soon learn, could handily run the shop when no staff members were around. Rebecca was deaf and had very bad eyesight. She wore a hearing aid and very thick glasses as well. I watched as she signed instructions to an uninterested male companion wearing a tattered name tag that read, "Hello, My name is Jules."

Neither looked up when I entered the room, and I studied their eyes. Rebecca, in her late twenties, had hyper-attentive eyes. She was teaching with her hands — talking with them and then using needle-point pliers to fit together small loops of copper wire that she then joined with a soldering gun. Sinclair had explained to me that his dream was to train everyone at New Dawn to make copper jewellery and quickly move up into silver, even gold perhaps, where the big money would be.

Rebecca kept touching Jules on the hand to re-establish attention. Jules had inward-looking eyes, other interests. The copper loops sat on the table in front of him, the soldering iron on its metal stand, an acrid thread of smoke racing up into the air. Jules looked older than Rebecca. He was partly bald, and what hair he had was flecked with grey. I don't think he was over thirty. Each time Rebecca patiently repeated touching him, getting his attention so she could show him how to solder the copper links, Jules watched attentively for about five seconds, then turned away, looked down at the flat table top in front of him, and began to move his fingers about on the table, performing some kind of mysterious personal ritual that I could not fathom.

I felt it unfair to stand there like an intruder without saying hello. I tapped Rebecca ever so slightly on her wrist once she had set the soldering iron back in its holder, and she looked up. I signed hello, the only sign language I knew. She smiled and signed back a long, complex message that I could not understand, and I was embarrassed that I had set her up.

"I'm sorry. 'Hello' is all I know."

"That's okay," she said slowly in an other-worldly monotone. "At least it's something."

"You read lips, too?"

"Yes, and I hear a little. Mostly noise, but a little is better than nothing." She touched her hearing aid and it gave off loud, almost symphonic feedback that Rebecca did not seem to notice.

"I'm Alex."

"Hi, Alex," she said. The X was very difficult for her so that she sounded as if she were clearing her throat. I didn't mind at all. "I'm Rebecca. This is Jules."

Jules did not look up. He reached further and let his hands dance over the edge of the work table. There was certainly purpose and pattern. "What does he see there?" I asked Rebecca.

"It's not what he sees," she said, pointing at her eyes, "but what he hears," touching my earlobe.

I watched without understanding, and then it clicked. "Music."

Rebecca nodded.

"My god, that's great. Can he play?" I was ready to jump up and down with joy. Not only had I landed a job and a date with a beautiful, conceited woman, but now I would be working with what I hoped was an *idiot savante*, a musical genius.

"You should hear him," Rebecca said. "He's good when he wants to be. I don't think he likes making jewellery. But it's better than packing plastic parts into boxes."

"Is he playing a song or just random notes?"

"I think it's called Rachmaninoff. I don't know much about it. I can hear people speak words but I can't hear music hardly at all."

"Rachmaninoff," I said very loudly. "Holy Christ."

Jules looked up and made the sign of the cross. "Sergei Vasilyevich Rachmaninoff," he said, looking not quite at me

24

but through me. Then he stopped moving his hands about and folded them in front of him, making a steeple with his fingers.

"What's wrong with *you*, Alex?" Jules asked in a very quiet, childlike voice.

Rebecca apologized for him. "He doesn't mean it that way. He just wonders what brings you to the workshop."

Of course, it wasn't obvious. I looked more like someone in need of help than someone there to help. "Oh. Well, I've been hired by Dr. Sinclair to work here." I was uncomfortable with the word counsellor or trainer, so I said, "I guess I'm the new teacher."

Jules didn't seem to hear me, so Rebecca touched his hand and then signed the news to Jules.

"What can you teach?"

Stumped, I wanted to say the right thing. "Life skills," I answered.

Rebecca laughed out loud, a laugh too loud and raucous for such a small woman. When the deaf laugh, the world takes note, I discovered.

"Life skills?" Jules noted, his voice not unlike that of a psychoanalyst with a patient on the coach. "Life skills, yes," he said with certainty, his eyes moving side to side. "Mickey Mantle, born October 20, 1931. Lifetime batting average .311 as of 1960. He was five foot eleven inches tall and weighed 198 pounds. Had 280 home runs in his career. Up to that point. I saw his baseball card in a shop."

"You like baseball, Jules?"

"Not really. Just the scores. The numbers. I like the numbers."

"He memorizes them from books. He likes the phone book, too. Anything with names and numbers."

"Now that's life skills," I said. "Jules, I think you might be able to teach me something."

"1960 to 1967. Anything that happened in the American League those years."

"I'm impressed."

Jules had already lost interest in me, though. He got up and walked away. Rebecca unplugged the soldering iron and blew onto the tip of it like a gunfighter on the streets of Dodge City.

"You don't seem like someone who needs to be here," I said to Rebecca. I was determined to avoid being condescending to the people I would work with. Rebecca was obviously very intelligent. She started to answer me by signing something, then stopped herself. "I like it here. If there was some other place for me to be, I would be there, but so far nothing has worked out. Three times Dr. Sinclair sent me to jobs. Each time something happened. When the time came to lay people off, I would always be first. Deaf people don't need as much money to live as those with hearing, apparently."

"I'm sorry."

Rebecca raised a finger. I saw defiance in her eyes. "I would appreciate it," she began, struggling to pronounce that word, "if you would not say that to me or any of us."

"I'm sorry," I repeated like an moron, then flinched and smacked myself in the head. Rebecca's eyes flared at me. She stood up and walked away to join Jules by the window.

Rebecca had taught me the first of many lessons. All my life I had appreciated the pity of others. The women who dumped me had both felt bad about their decisions, pitied me, and I had wallowed in their pity. But it went deeper than that, much deeper. I had fed off pity as if it were the closest thing to compassion and love I would ever discover in my life. Yet on my first day on the job at New Dawn, I had walked into a world where pity had no value, and I resolved to strip it from my own emotional register once and forever.

Five

Aside from my one social flub with Rebecca, I made it through the rest of the day just fine. Jeff, seventeen years old and blind, was working a tape gun, packing boxes that seemed to be filled with nothing but bits of Styrofoam. "I can stare straight at the sun and it would be like you trying to find your way to the bathroom in a totally dark house in the middle of the night" was the way he explained his blindness. Milton could not have done better. "I can't even hear that good. But I got a sense of smell you wouldn't believe. I wake up every morning around four o'clock 'cause I can tell when they put the coffee on at the coffee shop three blocks away. And my father says there's foxes out at Lawrencetown Beach that would be envious of my sense of smell. Connie's, like, sensory overload." Jeff was smiling. He wasn't complaining. He told me he was glad there was a male instructor now. He couldn't concentrate when Connie was around. She was way too distracting.

After saying too much to Rebecca, I had decided to get to know the others by letting them do most of the talking. That way I was less likely to say something stupid. "One more thing," Jeff said. "First day on the job, man, it's okay to be nervous. Go for the dry roll-ons. They work the best."

"Thanks for the advice."

"No problem." Jeff stared straight out into the empty nowhere in front of him. His hands worked automatically with the tape gun, sealing up cardboard boxes. "What'll I call you?"

"Call me Alex."

"No mister or doctor or nothing?"

"Nothing. Just Alex."

"Alex?"

"Yeah?"

"You own a car, man?"

"Yeah."

"What kind?"

"Nothing great. Dodge Shadow. 1990. Stick shift. Four cylinders. Nothing to brag about."

Jeff was smiling. "Fuel injected, though. Bet it's red."

"It is, how'd you know?"

"Dodge made a lot of red Shadows that year."

"You know cars?"

"I live and breathe cars. Can't drive though. If I could I wouldn't be sitting here doing this shit."

"Could be worse."

"It could be better. I could be out there driving across to Vancouver on the Trans-Canada in something like a Z28 Camaro with a babe sitting alongside of me."

"Maybe someday," I said stupidly. "Science and all that."

"Don't think so. I read about some kind of optical implants, but so far all they can do is sense infrared. Doesn't sound that appealing."

"Probably all you could do was see through walls and stuff like that."

"Nah. No superman stuff. Just night vision, red and black at best. I don't know if I'd even want to go for it. You couldn't drive or anything."

Rodney and Cornwallis were both in their late sixties. Why they were here for rehabilitation wasn't exactly clear to me, and I began to see that "rehabilitation" was a catch-all for anyone that Sinclair could squeeze into his workshop. Rodney had been a longshoreman all his life. Born and raised in Dumfries in Scotland, he had never fully lost his accent. Everybody called him Scotty, despite his own distaste for the nickname. But that was a battle he had fought and lost many times over. He was arthritic now, and Sinclair was "retraining" him to pour white chips of Styrofoam into boxes containing hollow computer CPU housings.

He shook my hand and winked. "Lots of useless wankers out there, lad," he told me. "Here inside this shop you got nothing but salt of the earth. Take Cornwallis, here."

"Pleased to meet you." Cornwallis Itwaru was a tall, very noble-looking black man, nearly seven feet tall but bent over in a way that took at least a foot and a half off his stature.

"Pleased to meet you, Cornwallis."

"Listen, brother," Cornwallis said. "Go over and try to cheer up Gloria over there, would you? She's in one of her dark moods. An old man like me ain't quite up to the job. A young, good-looking boy like yourself might do better."

Gloria Vincent sat by herself in a chair near the window. She wore glasses with milky plastic frames and a dress that was two sizes too big.

"Hi," I said, pulling up a chair to sit down. "I'm new here. Alex."

"Hello." She didn't look up at me. Her voice made me think of a fire that had gone out, leaving only a dull glow from the cooling ashes. At first it frightened me because it reminded me of something within myself. Her voice expressed the hollowness of someone who had given up on everything, and I knew that feeling very well. It was the voice of someone alone in a small, grey world without a family or a companion.

"Bad day?"

"Not really. I just have a hard time with the energy patterns. Sometimes I'm on, sometimes off."

"More off than on?"

"Yeah, I guess." She looked up at me now, gave a half smile. I was shocked to realize that she was young, perhaps twenty-five, four or five years younger than me. And there was beauty in her face, but it was diminished by whatever malady was draining the life out of her. She held out a closed fist and looked guilty.

"What?"

Gloria opened the fist. There was a pill inside. "Guess I should have taken this."

"Does it help?"

"It does, but I don't always feel like me. I become what the drug wants me to become."

"And that is?"

"Sometimes I'm happy. Sometimes I don't care."

"I can see why you don't always want to take it."

"Alex, why are you here?"

That question again. "I just got hired," I said. "My first day on the job."

"I knew that, silly," she said. She put the pill in her mouth and swallowed. "I knew you weren't one of us. Gestalt Holistic hired you, right?"

"Dr. Sinclair did, yes."

"He and I like to talk about dreams."

"I can't hardly ever remember my dreams."

"Close your eyes."

I closed them.

"You are walking on a road. What's beneath your feet?"

"I don't know. Oh, okay. Loose stones. It's not paved."

"How do your legs feel?"

"Tired."

"You see a house in front of you. What does it look like?"

"It's old. It's two stories tall with wood shingles. The paint's all worn off from the wind."

"What's behind the house?"

"The sea, or at least a big body of water. I see clouds in the sky. Sea gulls." I laughed out loud. "This is some crazy game."

"I invented it. Now go up to the house and open the door."

"My hand is on the doorknob. I'm walking in."

"What do you see?"

The image was brilliantly clear. I knew exactly where I was. And I did not want to be there. I opened my eyes, and Gloria was staring at me now. I was amazed and distraught that she could have done that to me. She had taken me to a place I had worked terribly hard to forget. Three people in a room. Three people I did not want to think about on this, the first day of my new life.

"You don't have to go back there if you don't want to," she said. "Don't worry about it."

I wanted to be angry at her, but she had done nothing. Foolish little game. I smiled the smile of someone who had totally lost his professional demeanour, lost his cool.

"I crown you the Queen of Rorschach."

"And I crown you the mighty Prince of Prozac."

"Feeling better?"

"I'm getting there. Just wish I could do it on my own."

"I'm looking forward to working with you, Gloria."

"Me too," she said. She wiped her nose with a handkerchief and got up, stretched and went over to work beside Scotty and Cornwallis.

I lost the purity of my first-day-at-work mental rush after Gloria inadvertently strolled me down a memory lane I had tried desperately to forget. For the remaining clients of New Dawn, I hid myself behind a clinical poster-happy personality. Doris in her souped-up wheelchair; Steve, his body racked by cerebral palsy; Lynn, a young woman with glasses like Coke bottle bottoms and twin hearing aids; and Bob, who looked to me to be a perfectly ordinary thirty-year-old man from some rural Nova Scotia harbour.

All seemed very pleased to see me. None required more than shallow conversation from me. Before the day was over, I had grown to know and like this tiny, odd community. Walking out into the late afternoon sun, I had put my small mistakes behind me, I had capitalized on the good will of everyone, I had scored a date with Connie. I had made friends and found a mentor in Dr. Henry Sinclair. Driving across the A. Murray McKay Bridge, I congratulated myself heartily.

The strong north wind made lines of waves on Bedford Basin. I was driving over the harbour almost directly above the place where two ships had collided eighty years ago. Two ships bumping together, one loaded with tons of explosives to create a blast that levelled much of a city. A city that recovered. Halifax was a city of wars. Once the basin had been a massive watery parking lot for convoys of ships preparing to cross the Atlantic: World War One, World War Two. Before that, military men had ruled this puny outpost, making it ugly, a man's town of military law and order and hard knocks for everyone.

I was headed home to my Brenton Street apartment, the one that I could now truly afford. But I had a stop to make first. The music store on Cunard Street had a used Yamaha keyboard on sale for $120. Three hundred and fifty programmed sounds. Sampling. One hundred different beats. I bought it on my credit card and got a pair of earphones to go with it.

Six

I had nothing in my apartment at Brenton Street except one old stuffed chair I'd bought used for twenty-five dollars and a bed that came with the place. I had a framed picture of my sister Karen but no table to set it upon, so it sat on the floor by the wall. The kitchen was bare, everything else was bare. I liked it that way for now. Domesticity was not a big thing with me. Nor possessions. Not yet. I intended to do this Zen thing with my new life. Avoid comforts. Live basic. Take chances.

Connie showed up twenty minutes late at Lawrence of Oreganos, but at least she showed up. She'd been drinking and had a sort of glow going for her.

"Alex, you don't really like me, do you?"

"I like you fine. I'm a bit daunted, I guess."

She laughed and lit a cigarette. "I hope this is the smoking section. You did pick the smoking section?"

"Natch," I lied. We were in non-smoking.

"Daunted, eh?"

"You know, daunted, slightly intimidated. You're attractive and all that."

She smiled, holding in the smoke, then suddenly letting it go, like a pot smoker does trying get the most from a hit. "Intimidated? You're sure you're intimidated?"

"Look, go easy on me. I'm the shy type." I was feeling more than a little embarrassed. I wasn't handling this well, and she was toying with me.

"What if I say I'll go to bed with you? Just to get that out of the way, and then we can be friends. Would you still be daunted or intimidated?"

My vision blurred and I scrambled for words. "I guess. I don't know."

"But you'd like to go to bed with me, right?"

"I suppose." An odd truth rose inside me: the surprising fact that I did not want to take this very attractive woman to bed.

"Let's have dinner first," she said. "I'll order, okay? I'm starving."

So I let her order Italian — penne something or other — and soon we were dipping French bread in a little plate of vinegar and olive oil that, when mixed, reminded me of the last time I'd drained the oil from the crankcase of my car.

We drained a bottle of red wine, and just as she was about to order another, Boyfriend B arrived.

"Charles."

"Connie."

"Oh, Charles, this is Alex. New rehab counsellor at New Dawn."

"Alex."

"Charles."

As Charles hovered over us, the Ice Age began. Charles was invited to join us. He and Connie proceeded into a lengthy argument that didn't have anything to do with me. I had been displaced in the conversation, my role now that of audience.

Charles had combed his immaculate dark short hair with some kind of oily stuff similar maybe to our baguette dip. He had a chiselled face like a guy on TV, and he wore wire rimmed glasses. He was probably carrying the results of his bar exam in the inside pocket of his three-piece suit. Those results would have been very high. "Why can't you go to St. Kitts with me?" he asked Connie for a third time.

"I have to go out west," she said, lighting another cigarette. Our waiter came over about then to say that this was a non-smoking section, but Connie pretended not to hear. She had a carefully practised way of looking through a person she chose to ignore, and it worked exceedingly well.

"What do you mean, out west? What's out west?"

I knew that Greg, Boyfriend A, was out west.

"A conference," she lied. "Alex told me about it."

Charles looked prepared to cross-examine me, but he said nothing as he sized me up and deduced I was not competition. "A conference?"

"Rehabilitation and environmental illness," I said. "New diseases and disabilities keep opening up new territory for us. It's a high growth area." Did I sound more like an investment analyst than a rehab counsellor? If so, I was inspired by the company.

"Can we go somewhere?" Charles said, turning away from me and realizing, perhaps for the first time, that Connie was somewhat sloshed.

She was already nodding. "But we have to apologize to Alex first."

"We apologize," Charles said.

Connie raised her hands and reached for her coat. Had she tromped on my ego? Yes. Had she treated me like a piece of Kleenex? Yes. How dare she come on to me like that and then leave just because this asshole showed up?

Strangely enough, I did not feel either anger or hurt. I had drunk half a bottle of wine with Connie (it had been a competition — she had won only narrowly), I'd sopped up some oil and vinegar in a way that was new to me, and now I would not have to sleep with a beautiful but superficial woman that I'd have to face in the morning at work. For now I was a free man.

When two dinners arrived, I ate most of both, left a tip magnanimous enough to bankrupt me until my first pay cheque, and walked out onto Argyle Street a bloated but wiser man. I listened to a street musician play old Neil Young songs, another who imitated Stan Rogers and a third who had Dylan down like a dog bone buried in the back yard. Halifax was a sweet, saintly city that would indeed permit me a life, I admitted to myself.

The feeling of well-being that I had doctored into my soul lasted until nearly three a.m., when I woke up in my bed in a cold sweat. In my dream, Karen was still alive, she was still ten years old, and as the dutiful older brother, I was pushing her on the swing in the back yard. Higher and higher, up into the hard blue sky. Wild blue yonder, we used to call it. My parents were gone to Saint John in the dream and I was left in charge. Karen was having a fine time. I was having a fine time. It was summer. The back yard smelled of rotting kelp because it went right up the edge of the Bay of Fundy. I loved the smell. It was the smell of my childhood. Gulls circled, an osprey dove into the sea. Puffs of cloud stood stock still like monuments in the air.

I pushed Karen on the swing. She sailed up into the sky, but then suddenly she was gone. And then the swing set itself was gone. And as I turned around, the house we had lived in was gone.

And then I woke up screaming.

Self-definition was my designated worry for the day as I drove to work. A simple identity crisis. I am. I am. Who the hell am I? Son of Alexander Senior. Son of Elizabeth. Brother, protector of Karen. Failed protector. I had been a good older brother. And then I stopped being an older brother. Without a sibling you cannot be a brother. High school taught me the paradox of being successful and unhappy as if the two were part of the same full-meal deal. Great at academic anything and abysmal at everything else. University wore me down. Graduate school tore holes into my intellect, did worse things to my self-esteem. I had concluded that the world is full of useless knowledge that, if it is rammed down your throat long enough, will make you gag. "Stay in harness," my advisor kept saying. Why the horse metaphor? I was more like an ox at that point. Large and sluggish of mind, filled with nonsense, hauling a cart of academic dung heavy as the thick brown Irving ice in the Saint John River, carrying it down a rutted road to nowhere.

The Reversing Falls on the Saint John. I was that falls. Tidal water racing backwards, miraculously headed inland, *up* a waterfall. Against the current. Amazing in fact, not at all exciting in reality. New Brunswick, land of anomalies: Magnetic Hill, where your car rolls uphill with the engine off; Reversing Falls, where water surges up the falls instead of down; and the Bay of Fundy itself, with its highest brown turgid tides in the world. Tourists seeking spectacles and finding nothing more than a clock in downtown Moncton denoting the next time the low, flat wall of water would well up and pass through town.

Connie did not show up at work the next day, and I soon learned that this was a fairly common phenomenon. Henry

Sinclair looked more than a little preoccupied, and his only instructions were to keep everyone busy and happy. Rebecca already seemed to pretty much have everything under control in the so-called jewellery training area. Everyone greeted me like an old friend. I thought I should be acting like an authority figure, but no one seemed to allow that.

"I like the days when Connie isn't here," Gloria said to me, and she handed me a present: a single page of paper. Every square inch of the paper had been written on in beautiful but miniature script. The concentric message began in the middle and spiralled outwards. "Poetry," she said. "A nonlinear prose poem, I guess you'd call it. Writing always begins in the womb of a single word and then gets pregnant with language. Once it reaches the margins of the page, it spills out into the world. Birth. It breathes, it lives. That's what writing is. Are you a poet, Alex? Everyone is a poet."

She had already answered for me, but I wanted to say I was not a poet. I did not find amazing beautiful things in the world around me. I was not one of those chosen to do so. I usually found redundancy instead, or at best discipline and order, and at other times meaninglessness and chaos. "I am if you say so."

"I say so. Everyone is a poet. And not just people. Everything is poetry. Wind. Sky. Sea. Dogs running. Elephants eating leaves. Boulders by a beach. It's endless, don't you think?"

"Endless." And suddenly I felt much better. To hell with my travesties and dreams. Staring at Gloria, I saw the hint of radiance for the first time. I also saw the wildness (or craziness, I guess) in her eyes, and that is what I liked best about her. She held my gaze, and I considered how opposite she was to Connie. Connie, for all her sexy nature, played a bland, sophisticated game. Gloria lived in a world of spirits, and although I knew she had her ups and downs, I preferred her authenticity. I tried to decipher the word at the centre of the page, the womb of the poem, and discovered my name spelled fully: Alexander.

"Alex, keep the poem. Can I say one more thing?"

"Sure."

"I think you've always been afraid of being fully alive, but you don't have to stay like that. You can change. You're already changing."

It was the craziness in her talking. Nothing more. I gave her a goofy grin to let her know I thought her remark was funny but I felt as if someone had just slammed a concrete block into my head.

"You got any gum?" Roger asked Gloria, then me. I offered him a mint left in my pocket from the restaurant, and he accepted it with disappointment. Lynn and Doris were cutting copper wire from spools into little circles for making loops. Jules was staring out the window. Steve, Scotty and Jeff were casually filling boxes with computer housings and Styrofoam peanuts. Off in a corner, Cornwallis was sitting at a bench filled with broken radios, TVs and VCRs.

I thanked Gloria again for her poem, tucked it into the pocket of my shirt and went to find out more about Cornwallis Itwaru.

"I'm getting behind on my projects," he announced. "Okay if I go light on the packaging today?"

"Fine by me. You fix these things?"

"One out of five. It's not professional, I know, but I can only fix some of them. That's my average."

"That's not bad. Batting .200."

"In the old days I was batting closer to .400. But it was easier to fix old things. Harder to fix the new stuff."

"Still, you have a skill. That's what this place is all about."

Cornwallis had a pair of the ubiquitous New Dawn needle-nosed pliers in his hand and was studying the innards of a Sansui cassette deck. "Be serious. This place ain't nothing about skills, at least not the way you mean it. This place is about family. Social services figures that out and we're all back on the street somewhere or sitting in pee-stained underwear in our bedrooms watching the soaps on TV. You gotta decide soon, new man, if you are in or out of the family."

Cornwallis had suddenly taken me a step deeper into the workings of New Dawn Workshop. I had been getting this signal already, but now it was coming in more sharply. "Family's one of those words I've had problems with," I admitted.

Cornwallis seemed insulted. He set down the pliers and rubbed his hands as if they hurt. "Guy like me got no family left. This one's gotta do. If it don't, I'm in a big, deep pile of shit. Soon as I saw you walking in through that door I was thinking you'd be good for us. I liked Connie, mind you, nice gal to look at, but you wouldn't want to be sinking on the *Titanic* with the likes of her and hoping she'd remember to throw you a life jacket. And Henry Sinclair has a heart as big as Hudson Bay but he don't have two sticks to rub together when it comes to common sense. So we have this little problem, and some of us are counting on you."

"What do you mean?"

"I mean, look around at these people here. Good people. Lost people, some of 'em. My family, whoever the hell they are. I've been reading the papers. Federal cutbacks, provincial cutbacks, municipal cutbacks. You saw that suit walking through here yesterday. That man retired from the human race a long time ago. He don't care about us. He's looking to cut some budget somewhere and we look pretty expensive to him. He probably thinks the government is wasting its precious money on Henry Sinclair's funny farm. You gotta help us, Mr. Nubody, or I think we gonna sink like that *Titanic*. I can smell the icebergs already. And you can bet your skinny ass it ain't gonna be Ms. Gavin who will be hard up for seating arrangements on the safest boat out of here."

Cornwallis went back to fiddling with something inside the cassette deck after letting out a great sigh. I knew he was telling the truth. Times were as the times were. Just like me to land a job on a sinking ship at the very tail end of the era of social compassion. I hoped he was wrong. But Cornwallis struck me as a wise man with insight even beyond his own many years.

"Maybe it's not that way at all. Just 'cause you're old doesn't mean you're right," I told Cornwallis, then immediately wished I hadn't said it. Where was my professionalism?

Cornwallis laughed. "Touché, my friend. But just because you're young don't make you right, neither."

"I think I know that."

"Tell me something, Alex. You got anything wrong with you? Anything physical?"

"Nothing worth mentioning."

"Good. So let me give you my list. Consider it like my résumé. I got weak kidneys. I got arthritis in my legs so bad that sometimes my brain tells them to work and they fire the news back that they're on strike, and if I try to move them they gonna make me hurt real bad. I got a spot on my lung from smoking for forty years before anybody told me it was unhealthy. I'm old and I'm feeble, but I can live with all that. You want to know what the big problem is?"

"Yes."

"I got this Alzheimer's thing creeping up on me. When it hits, sometimes it's like my grade two teacher standing at the chalk board, and she's just erasing and erasing until there's nothing left on the board. Most days I'm okay, and then one day I wake up and I don't even know who I am." He reached into his pocket and pulled out a little slip of paper. He handed it to me.

"Cornwallis Itwaru."

"Pretty funny name, eh? But it's my own. I carry it there in case I need to look it up. Problem is, I don't usually remember to look there."

"You seem fine to me. You must have learned some excellent coping mechanisms." The professional had spoken.

"Serviceable, not excellent. Ever fake your way through a conversation when you didn't know anything about what was being talked about?"

"Often. In graduate school."

"I've got a PhD myself in how to get by with knowing next to nothing. I got it all worked out 'cause I hate it when it happens and I hate it worse when someone knows I'm losing it. Memory is a fragile piece of machinery, Alex. You can have all the fine ideas and remembrances in the world stuffed in your brain, but if you can't find the keys to the kingdom, you might as well kiss your sorry ass goodbye on the short train ride to handsome hell."

"How often does it happen?"

"Often enough. And gettin' worse. Not better. But don't feel sorry for me, Mr. Nubody. Just take care of my family. This one, I mean. And I figure you need us as much as we need you."

"I guess wisdom does come with age after all." I felt as if I'd just sat down with someone who could peer into my soul. I handed him back the little slip of paper with his name on it. "Unusual last name, if you don't mind my saying so."

"It's a common name if you go lookin' around where my people were from."

"Africa?"

Cornwallis snorted. "All you white people think the same thing. Name like Itwaru gotta come out of the Dark Continent. Well, sure, I've got some kind of roots going back to that place. But then, so do you, if you get right down to it. Africa or some place close enough that it might as well be."

I had a hard time imagining my father believing that his ancestors found their way to Scotland from Africa, but it was a warm thought. "Where then?"

"Jamaica. My people were the Trelawny Maroons. Or so they called us. Shipped there by the Spanish, taken over by the ugly British. British couldn't handle us. We loved our freedom. But they tricked us and put us on the *Dover* and the *Mary* — those were the big ships — and sent us off to what was supposed to be freedom in Nova Scotia. Middle of the bloody eighteenth century. Lost our land in Jamaica. Supposed to get some new land here. Food, clothes. But people in Halifax back then thought we were wild and uncivilized because we had more than one wife and because we buried our dead on top of the ground and piled rocks on the body.

"In the end, we all became cheap labour, that's all, man. Cheap labour and Christians. I don't know which of the two was worse. They didn't call it slavery but it was. And we were cold here. Finally most of my people got on a ship for Sierra Leone. I got family there, I know that, if I was to ever go there. My own ancestors stayed on, and my parents grew up here in Africville. So did I. Didn't have much. You know anything about Africville?"

"Not really. It was in Halifax, right?"

"*Was* is the part that's correct, Mr. Alex. *Was*. Africville had me for a boy and me and Africville got along real good. And then somebody took Africville away from the Itwarus and the other families. I bet you don't know what it's like to lose your home, have it taken away from underneath of you. I bet you don't know nothing about that."

Cornwallis Itwaru stopped talking and he looked hard at me. I thought at first it would be better to say nothing. I saw rage in him. But the rage I saw triggered some deep aching loss within me and I had to dam it. "No. I do know what it's like to lose your home." It sounded hollow and unconvincing.

"Some people think they know, but they don't. Sometimes I can't understand why my family didn't go on over to Sierra Leone with those other Maroons way back when. Sometimes I really can't understand it."

"For a guy who's afraid his memory isn't sharp, you sure seem to have a pretty good handle on history."

He shook his head and scratched at the short greyish stubble on his jaw. "A man can forget his name, but he don't forget history and what history done to his family. That stays with him to the grave."

"A fine and private place."

"What?"

"The grave. I was quoting something stuck in my head from a poem about the grave being a fine and private place."

"Nothing, nothing fine or private about it. When I'm dead they better let me lay down on top of the ground. I want my family from this here New Dawn Workshop to pile rocks on me, just like the Maroons did in the old days. I don't want none of that under-the-ground-in-a-coffin kind of shit that Europeans brought over. Think they'll let me go to my rest that way?"

"I don't think so. I think there are laws."

"Why should laws have anything to do with you when you're dead?"

"They shouldn't."

"When you're dead, you're dead." Cornwallis went back

to fiddling with the cassette player and found a loose connection. Without putting the casing back on, he plugged it in and popped in a tape. Jazz. Sax and piano and a haunting, lilting female vocalist, but I couldn't put a name to the song. "I just upped my batting average," Cornwallis said. "Not bad." Then he reached back into his shirt pocket and pulled out the little slip of paper with his name on it, unfolded it, laughed and put it away.

Seven

History was precisely what I wanted to forget. Cornwallis had reminded me how hard it would be to give up. My move to Halifax had been intended to make a clean break between who I was and who I could be. I had finally, after thirty years of living, succeeded in running away from my family and running away from myself. My old self. The one I had called Alexander the Least. Antithesis of Alexander the Great, King of Macedonia and conqueror of the Persian Empire. Aristotle had schooled the young Macedonian, and when he grew up and went off to wage war upon the world, he had been prudent or foolish enough to take along a team of scholars. Babylon fell, as did Susa and Persepolis. He spread learning as well as destruction; in my own mind the two were invariably linked, so this made perfect sense. Eventually, though, his men refused to conquer India. They simply wanted to go back home before they were too far away to ever return in a lifetime.

Alexander only lived to thirty-three years of age, but he had conquered a huge chunk of the world. History seems to forgive him for murder and brutality and instead graces him with praise for helping to "spread civilization."

History is polluted with other Alexanders in Italy and France and Russia. Men of such great weight that they created hell and havoc and left great depressions on the landscape of history. I rifled the pages of old historical tomes from the stacks of the UNB libraries and could find little good about the legacy of any of them. Some battled for religious authority, others for land, some wanted revenge for past grievances and had armies and money enough to get it. Most were scoundrels who fought whenever necessary. Alexander I, Czar of Russia, had an ally in the Russian winter that destroyed Napoleon's army, but Alexander II lost the Crimean War, a war we in the West sometimes forget about; later he was assassinated by what the historians call "a nihilist."

I myself thought the philosophy of nihilism to be the most workable of any in the twentieth century and felt a certain kinship with a man who believed in nothing at all, especially one who believed in it so fervently. I also felt a kinship with this unnamed nihilist because he had destroyed one of the great Alexanders who was helping to wreak havoc on the world.

And so in name if not in bloodline I descended the staircase of all the Alexanders of history, most recently picking up the crippling duties of survival from my own closest Alexander, my father, Alexander McNab.

If Alexander the Great had spread civilization in a bloody yet scholarly and cultural way, my own father, Alexander Senior, spread a dark infectious philosophy into the lives of my family as he waged a losing war against the rest of the civilized world.

My father sometimes worked on the boats of local fisher-men, seeking hake and flounder and lobster from the waters and the sea floor of the Bay of Fundy. In the summer, he spread rotting seaweed and eelgrass over the hard clay and shale soil of part of our back yard, which would eventually begrudge him a few blue potatoes. I remember helping him pull up the plants and wrestle the potatoes from the decomposed eelgrass and stubborn soil. Sometimes I would pick up round stones and put them into the wheelbarrow, mistaking them for clay-encrusted potatoes. My father always found this very funny, and he laughed at me with great satisfaction.

And so Alexander the Least grew up on the shores of Fundy near Point Lepreau and knew little of history at all, except for the fact that he had descended from Scots Loyalists who had traipsed north during the American Revolution to remain faithful to the King of England, whose armies had conquered their own ancestral Scotland. The Loyalists had been running from revolution, I suppose, and towards taxes, subservience and, to a degree, oppression, but they didn't seem to mind. It was one of those "devil you know" situations, the devil they didn't know being the anarchistic (although not nihil-istic) American revolutionaries who despised taxes on tea and newsprint.

Beyond the forests of Maine, that other Alexander McNab of yore fell behind the retreating armies of Red Coats led by Edward Cornwallis, and he traced the coastline north and east but fell short of finding the promise of the Saint John River Valley, where many would settle and prosper. Instead, Alexander McNab was granted a patch of land at Point Lepreau, two days' wagon ride from the seaport of Saint John. A dreamer or a fool, McNab liked the place for the view, but the farming was dismal. Once summer turned to winter,

47

he realized he had chosen a difficult spot to homestead, but he was too stubborn to change his mind. And hence generations remained equally stubborn and loyal to that patch of land.

Yet, generations later, that property and that coastline begrudged me nothing. I loved the old house, I loved the stones and potatoes that came from the ground, I loved the skeletal rocks of the shoreline over which I clambered in my short pants until my knees and palms bled bright red blood. I loved the sea, the fog, the fishing boats that seemed to float in the air above the water, and the big oil tankers magnified by the damp air to look like monsters upon the sea.

I was one of those children born with wonder and love, and it was not until I was at least six years old that my father began to wage war against my optimism and naïvete. Perhaps I had simply not paid much attention to his words up until then. I had heard the angry, despairing music of his language but had not grasped all of the words or the history. My father could not, I learned, forgive his own father for making several critically bad "business decisions" regarding real estate, fishing and politics.

My grandfather had failed to vote for the right party and lost certain favours regarding roads and short-term contracts that might have put more food on the table. He died before he made it to fifty, presumably of natural causes, but I don't think my father had learned the art of forgiveness by then or at any other time in his life.

My father, too, had made several crucially bad decisions as a young man, but one of his better ones was to marry my mother, Elizabeth Carr. Photographs attest to the fact that both were quite handsome in their youth. My mother never fully lost the beauty afforded her by the genetic generosity of her ancestors, but an impoverished life in a damp, chill house on the Fundy shore stole much of her loveliness by the time I came along.

My father never really trusted boats and for good reason — New Brunswickers on boats drowned with alarming regularity during fishing season. He was a hangashore by nature but apprenticed himself to a neighbour with a weir and certain rights to portions of the sea floor, privileges garnered by political favouritism, according to my father. Privileges, I later learned, that were stolen from local Maliseet Indians who had taught the Loyalists to catch fish with those clever stationary fish nets.

Weir fishing is really not fishing at all. It's almost too good to be true. Since the Fundy tide drops with such magnitude, it's possible to take a horse cart out onto the muddy floor and pound a series of poles into the soggy bottom. String netting or wire around to create a cage with an opening on the landward side. As the high tide retreats, fish swim in and get trapped because most of them can't find the same doorway back out. Soon the water is gone and the fish are left flopping on the mud. All a man has to do is go out there when the saltwater has been pulled off to parts unknown by a benevolent moon, throw the fish in the cart and head for shore well before the sea arrives to reclaim the real estate. Then do it again tomorrow.

But it was the neighbour who made the money on the fish, not my father, who was paid a scant wage for doing most of the work while the neighbour stayed on shore with clean shoes to pal around with the politicians and fisheries officers.

My mother was a singer, although she never performed on stage or even for an audience more significant than myself and the seagulls resting in our back yard. Elizabeth Carr could

49

have been famous, I believe, as an opera singer or a country and western performer, but she was married to Alexander McNab, who thought singing was not "sensible." Although my father was by no means sensible himself, he pontificated against all who "wasted their time" at any activity not aimed at some form of income or "profit." That very faulty reasoning had led my father to dulse, and dulse would become one of my father's grand calamities.

But even before the dulse, rudimentary jobs usurped his days and left a man in no mood to come home to a singing wife.

My sister Karen was an accident, as was I. My father blamed my mother for both, although he must have owned up to some complicity in bringing two unwanted children into the world. I had come through the birth canal as a boy, so at least I could earn my keep once my legs were sturdy enough to support my body. I could help dig potatoes, carry firewood and shovel snow when the heavy white curse of winter descended upon our lives.

Four years after I arrived, my father was reminded that intimacy with a woman would be punished with another mouth to feed when Karen was born. The fog was thick on the shore that day, and you could hear the fog horns warning incoming ships of the dangers of Saint John Harbour. My mother was in pain and my father, I expect, was feeling poorly about the money it would cost for the gas to put in his old car to drive his wife to the hospital in the city. I went along for the ride, and I recall dimly that it took place mostly in silence. My mother squelched her pain as best she could, and when we arrived at the hospital, she was wheeled away in a wheelchair.

My father splurged and bought me a bottle of Sussex cream soda at a nearby store, and we didn't go into the hospital until he figured it was "all clear," which meant that the baby had been born. The whole time we were alone, my father fiddled with a scab on his knuckle and tried to explain things to me that I could not possibly understand. I may not be remembering this truthfully, but I'm sure he kept saying, "Just wait till you grow up and have to go through this. Just wait."

The McNabs, after all, were from the loser clans of the world, a great swath of humanity that outnumbered the winner tribe. A girl in the family was a punishment worse than losing three fingers to a lobster winch. But he would brace for it and bear up as best as he could, as well as his forefathers had suffered through their indignities. He wore his nihilism as a bright badge, although he had no political or ideological label for it.

The baby slept on the way home that day. My father would not allow my mother to stay overnight in the hospital. It was not the medical bill, which would have been covered by the government, but the expense and "time wasted" in driving home, then back again to pick up my mother and her new daughter. Hospital staff scowled when he explained this position boldly to the doctor's face, but my mother had had a normal enough delivery and my father had his way.

Halfway back to Point Lepreau, Elizabeth Carr began to sing to her firstborn daughter, and she let me hold the baby, swaddled as she was in sheet and blankets. What I felt on that day I can only translate from an adult perspective, but I am certain that, when I held Karen in my arms, I discovered this: I had been lonely through most of my short life. I was ecstatic to be holding my baby sister and realizing that she would be living with us from here on. I had never known such a feeling. I had lived an isolated existence, with no friends and few playmates, surrounded by the negativity of my father, insulated by it from the impractical notions of my mother. I had lived in isolation, and now I would never be alone again.

"Your sister is going to need your help," my mother said. A natural bit of news, but perhaps she was referring to something more.

"You're going to have to be responsible for her," my father echoed. "When you're not at chores or helping me, that is."

My father looked at me in the rear view mirror, and I saw something hard and fierce in those eyes. I had seen it before, but it startled me nonetheless. He was not angry at me or at my mother or my sister, I am sure. He was at war with the world, one of many great and lesser Alexanders who could not simply rest as an emperor or a defeated soldier. The enemy could not be found or labelled, but the war must go on.

I looked away from him and down at the baby girl in my arms. Then my mother began to sing again. My father cleared his throat in a loud manner, but that did not stop her. He tilted the rear view mirror up and away and continued to drive but said nothing more. I don't know what my mother sang. I don't think the song had words, just melody. Her voice was soft and sweet and reassuring and carried us back through the forests and past the lakes and on into the Fundy fog until we reached Point Lepreau and our home.

Eight

Sinclair had left a memo for me on my desk. My first official counselling session with a client was to be with Gloria Vincent. I looked forward to it. I already felt as if Gloria and I had some kind of rapport. It wasn't apparent to me exactly what her problem was, however, and I hadn't been able to locate her file, so I decided to simply ask her why she was here at New Dawn.

"When I was born, well, I wasn't ready to be born. I think that was how it started."

"You mean you were premature," I offered.

"Nope. Well, maybe yes. But not the way you think. I was still in the other place. I don't like to give it a name because names get confusing. It was the place, wherever it may be, where you are before you are born."

"'Not in entire forgetfulness do we come.'"

"Precisely. 'Trailing clouds of glory' and all that."

Gloria knew things I didn't expect her to know. Wordsworth, for example. I was beginning to believe she knew much more. I was entranced.

"I was, like, on the other side or whatever, and I didn't *want* to be born. But boom, there I came, sliding down the old birth canal like it was playtime at the neo-natal theme park. They say I simply refused to take my first breath. Or my second or a dozen after that. I didn't like this place." Her arms motioned towards the walls around us.

"Which place?"

"You know, earth."

"You were just born and you were wishing you were some place other than earth?"

53

"Yes," she said with absolute certainty.

"Where? Mars maybe? You were hoping for Mars?"

She could tell I was goofing on her and she didn't like it. She tapped my forehead with a knuckle, gently chiding me for my rudeness. "I wanted to be back *there*. I still do. But I've adjusted."

"Is this the nature of your" — I groped for the polite word — "situation, your condition?"

"Yes. It's all tied in with why I'm different. Why I am considered crazy."

"Do you think you're crazy?"

"Doesn't everybody mistrust their own sanity?"

Whew, that was a bombshell. "I don't know, do they?"

"Don't you?"

"No." I said. I lied. I had my own worries, but I was the counsellor here, right? Keep the professional guard up.

The sun popped beneath a heavy ceiling of dark cloud. The sunlight coming through the window was warm on her face. Her grey-green eyes were full of life. "Jeezus," I said.

"Jesus what?" she asked.

"Jesus, you are one beautiful, crazy woman." I said it out loud and then quickly turned away, realizing I had probably made a really stupid mistake.

Gloria hid her face in her hands. "You found out."

"I guess I shouldn't have said it like that. I didn't notice it at first. Then, wham."

"That's because I've worked very hard at appearing plain all my life," she said with great pride and authority. "Plain and simple. They go together. Like tea and toast. Like pigs and piglets. Like apples inside pie. Like clouds in a sky, like rain on the roof, like stars and stripes, strippers and straps, stamps and envelopes. Whoops. Sorry." She took her hands away from her face. "I do that sometimes."

"Do what?"

"I make connections. I get carried away."

"We call it free association. The Swedes say it's healthy."

"But the Swedes think rolling around in the snow after a sauna is healthy. I wouldn't trust the Swedes."

She was looking me straight in the eye now. My professional rapport was shot to hell. "When we sat down, I was supposed to be having a counselling session with you. We were going to discuss career options."

"Sitting and sewing, doing beadwork, making looped jewellery from wire. Filling cardboard boxes with Styrofoam beads."

"Yes, that sort of thing. How did we get onto this?"

"Because you caught on."

"Eh?"

"You now know I am beautiful. Even though I've tried all my life to keep it hidden. Now you know. But don't tell anyone."

I had lost my cool altogether. "I want to tell everyone," I said. Suddenly, I was totally entranced with Gloria, with her eyes, with her wild, free-association mind, with her stories. A bumper sticker talked to me from the back of my brain: *Risk Everything*!

"Plain and simple has always been preferable to beautiful and smart."

"Why?"

"I can avoid danger."

"What kind of danger?"

"You. The kind of danger that you are." Her voice wavered, but I didn't know if it was because this was a teasing, funny game or if she was revealing something deeper.

"I'm not dangerous."

"I know. But look out there at those clouds. The sun on the underside of them. Later the sun will set and be gone. Yellow.

Red. Magenta. Then poof, dark blue, grey, grey, grey, then black. Night time." She stopped and walked over to the window.

I took a deep breath. I felt disoriented, displaced. I had feelings for Gloria I should not be having.

"Did you know I can read people's minds sometimes?"

"No."

"Then you haven't read my file."

"Not yet."

"Do you believe I'm psychic?"

"I don't know. What am I thinking?"

Gloria walked back and put one index finger to each side of my forehead. I closed my eyes. *Risk Everything.* I must have been smiling.

She pulled her hands away. I opened my eyes.

"That was easy."

"Was it? Then what?"

"You like me." The words came as a surprise. These were the words of a girl, a little girl, a third grader perhaps, who has discovered a classmate with a crush on her.

I laughed. "My god, you're good!" I said, way too loudly. "Can you tell the 649 lottery numbers for Friday?"

"I can but I won't," she said with total self-assurance.

"Gloria, I wish we didn't have this . . . this situation here. I wish I met you in some other place."

"If you saw me on the street, I would appear very plain to you. Simple and plain, plain and ordinary. Remember, I do it very well. It's just that today I had all this energy and I had to do something with it. So I let you see me as I really am. Do you ever feel like that?"

"Like what exactly?"

"Like you have more energy in your mind than your body can keep in?"

"Not often, but I have felt that way."

"I used to feel that way all the time. Exploding with possibilities. But I couldn't figure out what to do with all my thoughts. My feelings. Too many, too often. It scared my parents. It scared my teachers. It scared my friends. Heck, it scared me. So then my parents got me into medication."

"Screw the drugs."

She put a hand to her mouth. "Such language from a professional."

"Sorry. I just meant . . ."

"I know what you meant and I thank you for it."

There were others in the hallway now arguing over who was a better batter, Mantle or Maris. It was probably old territory, like a religious war about to flare up again. Maybe it would be my job to break it up.

"Shh," Gloria said, before I could speak. "Do you want me to give you something?"

"Yes."

"Close your eyes again."

"Closed."

She touched my forehead again, this time in the very centre, very lightly. "Do you see it?"

"Yes," I said, "but I don't know what it is I'm seeing."

"It's your third eye. I just had to remind you it was there."

"Like in Hinduism."

"Like in Gloria-ism."

When I opened my eyes, she was gone, out the door.

Nine

This business of being alive. I was only now, in my thirtieth year of practising for the occupation, only now just beginning to get a handle on it. My father had deeply imprinted the message that I came from a tribe of losers and that it's always better for losers to stay lost. Those who tried to break out of the ranks might find themselves in worse shape. Those who succeeded partially in changing their lives for the better became, according to my father, assholes.

I was risking the latter, but I was haunted by what Gloria had said to me. Afraid of being alive, I desperately wanted to break ranks with my own kind, turn traitor and join the legion of those who *knew* they were alive. I was, after all, embarked upon a new life, I had this crazy, wonderful job, and I would fight to defend every living breathing human soul of my new family at New Dawn.

Later that morning I carried in the Yamaha keyboard from my car and opened the box carefully in front of Rebecca, Jules and most of the others, who were hanging around. I set the keyboard on the table, then plugged it in. I selected a rhythm patch and played a C chord in a synthesized replication of a church organ. I was looking at Jules, but, even though he was watching me, he did not react.

"It's for Jules," I said.

Everyone nodded. They understood.

"Jules?"

No response.

"I'd play something but I don't really know music," I said. "Cornwallis, you know how to play?"

Cornwallis ambled forward and hunched over, picked out a ragged boogie woogie riff, but then shook his head. "That's about all I'm good for. Haven't played piano since they tore down my church. Long time ago."

"Come on, Jules, give 'er a try," I said.

Rebecca touched him on the arm and signed something, but he didn't move.

Gloria came over instead and changed the sound selection to "orchestra." She moved her delicate fingers over the keyboard and the room filled with music. "Just play the black notes and something usually comes out that sounds good. I don't really know much about music, either." But the sound was rich and wonderful. She kept playing, improvising, and we all let the sound wash over us.

After a few minutes Jules did get up and come over to stand behind Gloria. He watched intently, and his eyes darted back and forth as he followed Gloria's fingers. His mind had engaged and he was rapidly processing information, or so I believed. Gloria stopped playing, turned around and smiled, then moved aside and placed the fingers of Jules's left hand on three black notes, then patted them down for him to make his first real musical sounds.

I guess I hoped that Jules would smile, but he did not smile. Smiling was not in his repertoire. At first his fingers were frozen on the keys like that, while a long, languid, Celtic-sounding minor chord resonated around the room. His eyes continued to flit east and west along the keyboard as if he was planning an intricate strategy, but when he finally lifted his fingers he proceeded to strike at keys in quick, random patterns. It seemed as if he was striking them in anger. The sound was discordant, imprecise at first and downright ugly, but as he continued to strike the keys, a thin trickle of a melody began to emerge out of the noise.

Gloria looked at me as soon as she heard it. Jules continued to play fast and furious, but then he began to slow down, and more order took shape out of the chaos. The melody line of "Ode to Joy" rose from the wasteland of raw notes, as if Jules discovered pattern and structure while he was playing. The Yamaha orchestra had come fully into its own, but even as the melody solidified into something clear and vivid, simple, with a pronounced chord structure, Jules began to create variations on the theme, and his fingers ranged far and wide over the notes.

Jules played for at least ten minutes, and when he stopped the quiet in the room was a profound music in itself. His hands remained fixed in the air when the last notes died to silence. We all applauded loudly, and I noticed Henry Sinclair at the door. He studied the room full of people who were supposed to be working, and he looked directly at me. I returned his gaze, but I was not sure I saw approval. Sinclair simply nodded and walked away.

Rebecca then led Jules back to the table where they worked together. She turned to me and mouthed the words, "Thank you, Alex," without sound. Before I had a chance to unplug the keyboard, Roger came over and discovered that by pushing one of the rhythm selections he could produce a funky, thumping dance beat. Something barely more sophisticated than old disco, what the kids were now calling dance music. Roger was very proud of himself and drew another round of applause. Jules had been unable to show any observable pride in having performed a magnificent musical feat, but Roger took great glory in his one-fingered creation of an endless dance loop.

I left the room then, but I could hear Roger's dance beat going for at least forty-five minutes before someone finally pulled the plug. The look on Roger's face lingered in my head, though. That kid look, that big, goofy smile. For all his damaged brain, Roger knew how to be happy. Roger knew how to be alive. And I felt envious. I wanted a piece of the action. That's when I saw Jeff coming down the hall.

"Jeff? You think you can drive?"

"I know I can."

"We'd have to stay in the parking lot."

"Okay."

"Tomorrow at lunch, okay?"

"You're going to have to tell me what to do."

"I will."

"You really think I can do it?"

"Of course."

The rest of the afternoon was ruled by music: Haydn to hip hop and back, with the keyboard hosting Jules, then Roger on the beat loops, Cornwallis finessing his boogie woogie and Gloria discovering ethereal melodic patterns. Everyone else packed and shipped and bent little copper wires into earrings. If anyone had wondered about exactly what my role was in this family, there were no longer any questions. No, I was not the father here. That role was reserved for Henry Sinclair, bivouacked in his office, performing the Herculean management and financing tasks necessary to keep New Dawn alive. Instead, I was the cool older brother, giver of gifts and inventor of fun. Responsible yet reckless. And it was oh, so good to be alive.

At the end of the day, after everyone had left, Sinclair waved me back to the building from the parking lot. I saw trouble in the lines of his face. I was suddenly afraid that I had overstepped my bounds, blown it, taken everything too far, too fast. What had I been thinking about, anyway? Wasn't I here to do a job? Oh, Christ.

"Alex," Sinclair said soberly, "today was one of the good days. I know that. While I can't say I approve of everything you did, I do approve of the spirit in which you did it. But things might not always work out."

"I guess I should have consulted you first."

"Should have."

"Sorry."

"It's okay. Your motives are pure. You're good for them. They like you. They trust you now. But there will be bad days."

"What do you mean?"

"All I mean is, hang onto the good days. William Saroyan said something about the greatest happiness coming from figuring out that you don't necessarily require happiness."

"You think I'm not a happy person?"

"I didn't mean you in particular."

"Mr. Sinclair, if you hired me because I came in looking like a hard luck case and you felt sorry for me, I want to thank you for doing that."

He shook his head, pretending to deny that this was the situation, but I knew that what Connie had told me was true. "You had credentials. I made my decision based on your experience."

"You're a bad liar, Henry, but I thank you again. I had no experience to speak of."

"But you had a good attitude."

"And it's getting better. This is what I was meant to do. Up until now, I've just been wandering in the wilderness."

"Wandering in the wilderness is good for you."

"Not in my wilderness it wasn't."

"But now you're here with us. I like your work. Just don't get carried away."

"Today was golden. Jules. Roger. Jeff. Cornwallis. I've never met people like these before in my life. Especially not in university."

"We hide our saints well."

"But I've discovered your secret hiding place."

Sinclair smiled, took off his glasses, traced his finger along the rims. "Connie phoned in this afternoon to say she's quitting. Moving to Calgary."

"Jesus. Boyfriend A?"

"Greg, I think the name was. In the oil business. Boyfriends B through — what is it? D? — will have to let her go."

"Connie was really helpful in showing me the ropes," I lied. All Connie had really done was tease me into almost making a fool of myself.

"I can't hire someone else."

"Why not?"

"Financial problems. Things aren't looking all that cheerful from where I sit. But don't worry. Been down this road before. Always a surprise. Always a way."

"So I'm on my own. No big deal. I'm a fast learner. Just point me in the right direction."

"I think you already found your direction. Just don't lose the path. See you tomorrow, Alex. Hope it's another good one."

"See ya."

Sinclair walked ever so slowly to his car, a vintage Peugeot. He opened the door, carefully placed his briefcase on the passenger seat, and then got in and hitched his seat belt. He looked like a man with all the weight of the world on his shoulders.

Me, I left my car in the lot and walked down the road through the industrial park until I came to the Bristol Tavern. I opened the doors and walked into a dark, smoke-filled cave with the worst of the worst country truck-driving music on the jukebox and a dozen zombie-eyed warehouse workers squandering their money on video slot machines.

Ten

I drank two beers and stared a baseball game on TV until it finally sank in that I had spent my day in the world of the living and now had stumbled into the land of the walking dead. I left there, sadder but wiser as they say. The contrast had been a healthy one.

It was a warm summer evening. I had nowhere in particular to go. I walked back up the hill to the New Dawn parking lot but couldn't bring myself to get in my car and leave. I felt as if I was standing on sacred ground. Nothing would ever be as good as today.

It was just a paved parking lot in a big, ugly industrial park, but it might as well have been heaven as far as I was concerned. The beer buzz couldn't come close to the glow inside my head. The sky was blue, clear, immense and inviting. I wanted to get closer to it. I studied the flat-roofed two-storey building that housed New Dawn and noticed a rusted metal staircase that led to the second floor and a bolted-on ladder that led from there to the roof.

The view from the top of the building was extraordinary, considering where I was. The sun was a blinding ball of light in the west, but if I shielded my eyes I could look southwest and see the blue waters of Bedford Basin and Halifax Harbour, and beyond that the silhouette of the city of Halifax. And to the south, the sea.

Dollops of creamy clouds lingered above me as I lay flat on my back and stared up into the heavens, feeling happy and peaceful. As I closed my eyes, I felt a slight burning in my chest and an old familiar sensation as if someone was squeezing me. There was just the slightest trace of pain associated with this feeling, and I recognized the annoyance as my old companion from graduate school: stress. All my life, I had felt squeezed in some way or another. Into molds, into other people's routines, into an identity that was not my own. Pressure all around.

Here, alone, on the rooftop, I should have been free of the physical reminder. But I was not totally free of my old identity. I would relax, breathe deeply, and it would go away . . . or I would learn again to ignore it. I opened my eyes and pretended I was ascending, weightless, into the sky. The heat of the roof felt luxurious. The small stones that made my bed seemed comfortable enough. It was a moment of pure self-congratulation and indulgence.

The footsteps on the metal stairway, I knew, were feminine. I would not be alone for long. I sat up and felt myself go slightly dizzy, then I almost blacked out. I was just regaining my bearings when Gloria stepped onto the roof.

"I saw your car and I guessed you might be here," she said.

Gloria was wearing an old-fashioned summer dress, a print of bright flowers, a liquid, flowing garment completely out of step with fashion. Her hair was brown with tints of red in the sunlight and her face was warm and radiant. Her smile was genius and madness and beauty. I was dazzled and dizzy and without vocabulary.

"I live down there," she said, pointing to a cluster of featureless apartments off towards Windmill Road. "Something told me you would be here."

I was still speechless. Tongue glued to the roof of my mouth.

"You wish I was Connie, don't you?"

I shook my head. I wanted to say that I wished we were meeting for the first time, that we were strangers and this was going to be an extraordinary occasion, that I was not her counsellor. Instead, I had a role, I had responsibilities, I could not allow myself to be attracted to her as I was. But what I said instead was, "You're more beautiful than Connie."

She tried to hold my gaze, but beauty and genius yielded to the sway of madness and she looked up at the sky. "It looks empty but it isn't," she said.

"Air, clouds, birds, an ocean of sky."

"When I was a little girl, I read all about angels. Anything I could get my hands on. Not just the church stuff, but books and books have been written about angels. I learned that angels can have very complicated personalities. Of course, they can fly and that's an advantage. That's why I wanted to believe I was an angel and not just a human being. Don't get me wrong, I didn't think I was such a great person or anything. That wasn't it. I wasn't better than anybody. I simply identified with being an angel. Maybe I just wanted to fly."

"We all wanted to fly when we were kids. I wanted to be an osprey and be able to dive into the ocean like they did."

"We had that in common. Alex, what were you doing, just before I came here?"

I suddenly felt a little embarrassed, like maybe she thought she had caught me at something. "Nothing. Nothing at all."

"No, I mean really."

"Honest. Nothing. I was lying on my back staring up into the sky. Relaxing."

She smiled and bobbed her head. "That's not nothing. Nothing is nothing. That was something. And that's why I knew you were here. It was as if I could see up into the sky through your eyes."

I laughed, looked away from her and then said the wrong thing. "You're crazy, you know that?" But as the words spilled out, I lost track of who I was talking to. To her, crazy meant something clinical.

"I know. That's why I'm not normal," she said sullenly.

"No, Gloria. That's not what I meant."

Silence.

I tried to apply bandages to the conversation. "Go on. Tell me about seeing the sky through my eyes."

She sat down beside me and tucked her hands into the folds of her dress in front of her. "You don't believe me."

I had erected a language barrier, a Berlin Wall between us, and I wanted desperately to break it back down. I reached out and touched her hair, smiled at the way the sunlight made it come to life. "Gloria, I never admitted this to anyone, but I'm crazy, too. They don't have a word for it yet, I'm that far off the deep end. I bet I'm crazier than you are. I just pretend I'm sane to keep my cover."

As she looked at me, her eyes were steady and bright. The dark side of Gloria had given way to the sun again. "Don't joke, Alex. You carry a lot of sadness but you're not crazy. Actually, I don't think anyone is crazy. Some of us just don't

67

fit in as easily as others. Most days I think the world is an awful, insane place and I'm the only one who can see it for what it is. On those days, I wish I was an angel. I wish I could fly above all the problems or enter into the lives of others and create miracles."

"Big miracles, like eradicating hunger, destroying all military weapons?"

"No, I would settle for small miracles."

"Like what? Doing away with tooth decay?"

"No, silly. Angels work on specific miracles, not big, general, abstract ones. Sometimes I believe I'm already capable of small miracles."

"So give me an example."

She looked off towards Halifax now and let her long hair fall down in front of her face as if she needed to hide behind its magnificent curtain. "Like you," she said in a hushed voice. "I think I brought you here."

I laughed. I thought she was teasing me. "Oh, yeah. That's why I was down there in the bar and I heard this voice in my head. 'Go back to work and go up on the roof.' That must have been you."

She spoke again but in a voice quieter still. "Not that. I mean I brought you to us. To New Dawn. I did that."

I didn't laugh this time. I gently parted Gloria's hair and looked at her face. She had become a child. Like a fool, I had hurt her feelings and she was afraid of me now.

I knew then that I did not know the first thing about being a professional. I would never be able to keep my emotional distance. Gloria had ceased forever being a client; she had tugged at my heart. The ache I felt for her was not altogether unlike the physical pressure in my chest created by stress, but it was something much more profound. Ever since my two disastrous affairs in university, I had protected myself. My attraction to Connie had been physical and trivial compared to this. Against my will, I was falling in love with an emotionally unstable young woman. And I would not pull myself back to professionalism. All my life I had let others dictate the rules I should play by. But I had left all that behind me in New Brunswick.

"Gloria, I believe you did bring me here. I really do. Something led me to this job, to New Dawn. There is a reason I am here. Do you believe that I believe you?"

I could tell by her eyes that she did not. I leaned forward, cupped her cheeks with my hands and kissed her. She melted into me. I had not meant to up the emotional stakes so quickly, but already it had happened. It was my first time kissing an angel, and her wings did not get in the way.

I may not have fully believed Gloria to be some kind of a psychic communicator or an earthly angel, but I was certain she was a fully qualified healer. She had a gentle power that I had never encountered before. We lay down on our backs and stared up into the skies, our only contact our hands, which were cemented together. I closed my eyes in the warm evening and became one with her in some soft, powerful way that transcended sex. In fact, I felt no great sexual craving towards her at all. It was a chaste, respectful attraction that, for the moment, seemed pure and uncomplicated.

As the sun set, we spoke of many things that were the bits and pieces of our lives. I walked her home, back down through the ugliness of the industrial park, past the Bristol Tavern, across the railway tracks, past the gas stations and the Tim Horton's. Gloria was the most beautiful, most alive woman I had ever met. When I said goodbye to her at the door to her apartment, I was amazed at how difficult it was to leave her. Why was I so afraid of walking away? How had I let myself fall so head-over-heels in love with her? I wanted to stay there with her but knew I needed some distance from this new emotional tide. I think I was afraid more for me than for her.

We kissed again. It was only the second time. Standing there by the evening growl of traffic, the noisy trucks and clamouring cars, I embraced her fully and again felt my being melt into her. The sky would not be a large enough geography to contain what I was feeling. A "small miracle" she had called this, but it was much more than that.

I drifted back up through Burnside to find my car still sitting in the lot at New Dawn. It was finally dark, but I could not believe it was still the same day on which I had gotten out of bed. Looking at the keys which I retrieved from my pocket, I cursed Henry Sinclair for having given me my own pass key to the front door and to all the rooms in the building. Yet I did not want to return to the isolation booth of my Brenton Street apartment. I thought of just driving around all night, but I couldn't leave without first going inside.

My office felt alien and lifeless to me. Sinclair had given me permission to look at any of the clients' files, but I had preferred to get to know them first. Now I felt driven to find out as much as I could about Gloria.

I walked to Sinclair's office and opened the door. I felt like a spy, a thief, a criminal with the worst of intentions, but I could not make myself leave. I opened the filing cabinet and found Gloria's file. I switched on the green-shaded lawyer's lamp on Henry Sinclair's desk and set the folder down in the pool of light. I wanted to know why she was here with the other marginalized souls of New Dawn, reasons beyond her simplified explanation.

I had known already that she had been labelled a schizophrenic. Although I was not truly schooled as a psychologist, I knew that to be a generic term, a catch-all phrase. I was less familiar with the more precise and somewhat outdated term for her illness: hebephrenia. Sinclair's notes suggested that someone with this condition was prone to withdrawal from reality, foolish behaviour, delusions, hallucinations and self-neglect. His clinical language both surprised and angered me. I simply refused to accept that Gloria could be as badly off as this.

The good news was that she had responded well to medication, and as long as she took the pharmaceuticals as prescribed she led a fairly normal life, although Social Services had still deemed she could not handle a normal workplace or be fully responsible for her own financial welfare. Hence the sheltered workshop and subsidized housing. A one-page report signed by Connie said little more than that Gloria was sometimes "non-sociable" but that she had "good dexterity skills." To Connie, Gloria was just another client.

But there was another more technical report in the file, a copy of a case file by Dr. Todd Fraser of the Abbie Lane Clinic. The report was at least four years old, but it revealed the darkest of truths, one that I was not in the least prepared for. According to Dr. Fraser, while Gloria was a patient of his at the Abbie Lane, she had become involved with another mental patient. They had some kind of affair and then the boyfriend left the hospital and presumably broke off the relationship. Devastated, Gloria had tried to kill herself. He was not specific about her method, although it sounded like something horrible and physical, not a mere overdose of drugs. Recovery, Dr. Fraser said, was successful, and, after three months of suicide counselling, Gloria had been released from hospital.

Eleven

By the time I was ten and Karen was six we were strong friends as well as brother and sister. In the winter, my mother would dress us up in layers of clothing, and we went out on cold, raw days to slide on our sleds down the hill onto the frozen marsh. Together, on one old wooden sled with ice-polished metal runners, we flew down the hill over and over and raced out onto the slippery expanse of the snow-covered marsh. Time diminished to nothing. A morning slipped to noon, a hot lunch of some home-made soup or stew, and then more afternoon excitement.

My father would be working somewhere in the woods, hauling logs for pulp. He'd arrive home later, a dark, sullen cloud that stole the sun from the sky. He did not like the work or the men he worked with. The world was always conspiring against him, against us. My mother had been brainwashed by the old man's negativity and so was I, whenever he was around. I had, however, created an elaborate network of shields (or so I imagine in retrospect) to protect Karen from his bleak outlook.

Karen's presence granted me the need to re-invent the world as it could have been, not as it really was. When my father was not around, I made up elaborate, fantastic stories, ridiculous, perhaps, but Karen loved them. Her favourite ones featured the Lords and Ladies of Lepreau and the King of the Bay of Fundy.

The Lords and Ladies of Lepreau lived in a big castle deep in the forest, and they had nonstop parties with loud Acadian music accompanied by all kinds of exotic seafood on silver plates. They rode around on silver steeds in secret fields not far from here, and none of them ever had to work or worry about anything. This was their life. They had no worries, needed no money, had not even heard of K.C. Irving or Premier Richard B. Hatfield. The forest dwellers were fine and happy people oblivious to everything but their own happiness. They had no children and they lived forever, these Lords and Ladies of Lepreau. They were, of course, invisible to all adults, but children could see them if they peered deep into the forest. Or sometimes the reflections of the Lords and Ladies could be seen in the clouds.

Fine and fluffy, whimsical, fleeting and frivolous were the Lords and Ladies of Lepreau. They were also my good friends because I had concocted them, and creatures of my own imagination appealed to me much more than real people.

The Lords and Ladies of Lepreau enjoyed winter as much as Karen and I. They rode in sleighs with bells behind those silver steeds and they skated on ponds of diamond ice. When frozen rain gave way to winter sun and daggers of brilliant ice decked the spruce trees, I told Karen that the Lords and Ladies had begun their party late the evening before. There had been fiddle music and accordions, and they had danced through the forest right up to where the party had spilled over into our back yard. All of the servants had been kept busy redecorating everywhere, hanging jewellery and delicate dustings of snow upon the trees.

The King of the Bay of Fundy was another matter. He lived beneath the sea, of course, farther from here, somewhere near Grand Manan Island. He was fabulously wealthy but kept all the wealth to himself. He trusted no human but cavorted with whales and porpoises, whom he allowed to pass from the Atlantic into this Fundy kingdom and his protection. The tides obeyed his command, and he controlled some gargantuan floodgate that allowed the spill of the greater sea into the

Fundy arm. The King of Fundy insisted, however, that the water be returned each day, and he enforced this decree with whatever it took.

An amazingly powerful being, the King of Fundy was a moody loner at heart. He would never have a wife or children, and he was doomed to live forever in the cold and dark of his own making. His dreams stirred the waters of the Bay of Fundy. Good dreams might result in calm spring mornings with a piercing blue sea, dolphins diving into the air, gulls singing the only song they know, fish swimming in schools, racing like lightning in the cold, clean underwater rivers. But the dark, brooding dreams brought storms, raging seas, dead fishermen, the shrieks of widowed women and the wreckage that washed ashore.

The saddest part of my story was the fact that the King knew of the Lords and Ladies of Lepreau. He could never make contact with them for, if he did, they would be infected with his broodiness and his dreams. However, the Lords and Ladies could not exist without the King of Fundy. If the King were to stop issuing the tides, the rains would stop and the forests would die of drought. The coastline would become a desert. Unlike the forest elite, the King had no servants to help him with his private affairs or with the massive responsibilities of the tides and the policing of the bay. The King was well aware that he was expected to live forever and carry out the endless obligation of his monarchy.

The Lords and Ladies of Lepreau knew not to get too close to the shoreline of the Bay of Fundy, and the closest they ever came was when they danced among the crystalline spruce jewellery in our frozen back yard.

On stormy, blasting winter nights, Karen swore to me she could hear the King of Fundy roaring in his dark, lonely dreams, and I would have to sing her a song in a low voice to put her back to sleep. For I was Karen's brother and her protector. Even though I had conjured him into being, we both feared the mythical king, but more often we felt sorry for him. I wondered aloud if there was not some way to free him of his duties, but I knew that his responsibility and his lonely suffering was somehow tethered to the casual freedom and pleasure of the Lords and Ladies of Lepreau, and, if the King abandoned his job and his underwater castle and allowed himself to roam the floors of the world's seas, then our coast would change to a desert and the Lords and Ladies would disappear. All of our lives would change in unimaginable ways.

Many nights the sea roared and hammered waves against the short cliff that was the edge of our property and the limit of the lands of the Lords and Ladies. I rocked Karen to sleep in my arms and sang a song with no words.

Often in the summer we scanned the southerly horizon for a glimpse of the head of the King of Fundy. I had told Karen that the King could not stop himself from sometimes breathing the air and feeling the warmth of sunlight, but no more than twice in any year did he raise his massive head, with hair of kelp and skin pocked with scallops and barnacles, to gaze upon the world above. I was amazed but not shocked on the day in mid-July of my tenth summer, when Karen and I had been left alone at home while our mother and father had gone on a rare shopping trip to Saint John. We saw the crown and brow of the King of Fundy for the first time.

We were collecting shells and shiny stones along the shore-line when we heard thunder and, looking due south, saw what must have been a thunderhead — a massive, dark-textured cloud rising like a nuclear mushroom from the sea. Karen sucked in her breath and I think I stopped breathing altogether.

The wind had suddenly ceased, which almost never happened in the middle of the day, and all the gulls had stopped squawking. A second shuddering boom echoed in the air.

The head of the King of Fundy was strikingly clear now: tangled hair, jagged crown, furrowed brow, grim sunken cheeks and granite jaw. "He's blind," Karen said, for there were only dark sockets where his eyes should have been. "He doesn't have any eyes. I never thought he'd be blind."

"But he's trying to see us," I said.

"Should we hide?"

"No," I told her. "Just be very, very still."

So we stood frozen, Karen fearing that if we moved he would sense us, and he would know that the Lords and Ladies of Lepreau had been in our seaside yard and that they were not far off, just down the sledding hill and beyond the marsh. We knew he resented the forest people, and we worried that someday he might try to harm them or, perhaps, those of us who admired them.

When you are young, you see things that cannot possibly be real and you know that, but you are a believer nonetheless. As I was that day. I remained standing on the shore with Karen hugging me for protection, neither one of us moving, until the sky above went dark with frightful clouds and lightning seared into the bay. A curtain of torrential rain advanced toward us from the distance, as if the King had discovered us and sent dark forces to attack.

We watched the curtain of rain advancing rapidly, pounding the peaceful surface of Fundy with bullets of water. When the rain was nearly upon us, I took Karen's hand and dragged her up the escarpment to the grass. We ran blindly to the house as heavy dollops of cold summer rain splashed down on us, raindrops larger than I had thought possible.

Before we reached the house, the rain had turned to hail, pellets of ice the size of golf balls. I picked up Karen now and raced with all my strength for the back door. Incredibly, the door was locked. In my panic I had not remembered. My father had convinced my mother that we should be locked out of the house until they came back that day. The reason: Karen had been getting into the sugar, spooning it from the sugar bowl and eating it on the sly. It had been my job to police her, but I had not done my job very well. So now the house was locked. There was no porch to shield us from the falling ice. We stood at the locked door, wet and scared, with the King of Fundy wreaking his vengeance upon us.

I picked Karen up again and, as she screamed, I ran for the safety of the woodshed, kicked open the door and stumbled inside. I set Karen down and then sprawled on the old wood plank flooring. Karen was crying and I was trying to calm her, but it was hard enough to calm myself. The ice pounded on the roof for another solid minute, then suddenly ceased. The sun came out, the ice turned to rain, and then the rain stopped.

We remained in the woodshed shivering for at least fifteen minutes before I ventured back outside. Ice covered everything, but it was melting already. The summer yard had been turned into winter, and it reminded me of the winter parties of the Lords and Ladies. Yet what I saw before me looked more like a wreckage of ice. If you ignored the returning warmth, it was as if this was the debris of a winter festival that had gone awry. The party had been pounced upon and beautiful things shattered and crushed. The spruce trees drooped with the weight of the hailstones. Branches had been broken off by the storm.

Karen picked up some of the ice, now turning to slush. We were both wet and cold and thankful that the sun brought heat back into the world. Off to the south there was no sign of the thunderhead, no visage of the King, only calm sea and blue sky.

By the time our parents came home, the ice had completely melted and the yard was nearly dry. My mother said she was sorry for having locked us out of the house. I could tell she felt guilty. But my father said that we deserved it. Neither believed a word we said about the ice storm, for there was not a shred of evidence left, and we said nothing, of course, about the surfacing of the blind king.

Later they would admit that there must have been "a little summer hail" after they heard from the neighbour that his greenhouse had some busted panes. And, although Karen's sickness that followed may or may not have been the result of being cold and wet on a strange summer afternoon, the storm preceded the first of many trips to the Saint John hospital. In my mind, I cannot let go of the connection between the vision of the blind King of Fundy and what was about to happen to my little sister.

Twelve

Connie was back in her office when I arrived at New Dawn. She was cleaning out her stuff. "Hi, Alex. Sorry about the other night."

"No problem. Henry told me you're Alberta-bound."

"Not sure I'm doing the right thing. Or at the right time.

But at least I can leave here with a clear conscience now that you're working. Thanks for that."

"No problem again. The clients will miss you, though."

"Will they really?"

"Roger is madly in love with you. I know he will."

"Boys will be boys. I'll leave him a couple of extra packs of Juicy Fruit. It'll tide him over until he finds a new flame." I couldn't determine if her humour was good-natured or intentionally cruel. I think it was just the way Connie was, a witch with good intentions in the body of a *Playboy* centrefold. For some bizarre reason I still kind of liked her. I wanted to ask for advice about my Gloria problem — was I doing a truly stupid thing by allowing myself to be attracted to her? But I knew Connie wasn't to be trusted.

"I'm getting married, you know. Will you send me a present?"

"You're getting married?"

"It might only be a temporary situation. We'll have to see."

"Whatever happened to the 'till death do us part' thing?"

"I figure that it's just one of those opportunities too good to pass up. But if Greg turns out to be an asshole, I'll move on."

"You really think it's that easy?"

"It is for some of us."

"Just like moving on from here, leaving New Dawn behind."

"I'll miss this place. I'm not without a heart, ya know."

I stood in silence as she picked up a collection of photographs from the drawer and put them into her purse. "I was good for this place. And I never got paid what I was worth. But like I said, I have no regrets."

"We'll all miss you," I said with as much sarcasm as I could muster.

"You're mad because I didn't go to bed with you?"

"No."

"You don't know if I was kidding or serious when I said it."

She had me. She had played all the games and played them well for years now. I was out of my depth.

"It's not important," I said.

"I was serious. Like Sinclair, I think I felt sorry for you. Wanted to give you something nice."

"Something nice? This is your view of making love with a person?"

"Just let it go. Can we part as friends?"

I tried to see things through her eyes. My father's dualism crept up in the back of my brian, however. Winners and losers. Winner take all. The users and the used. We had a fine specimen of each in the room right now.

"Can I still get a quick one right here on the desk? You and me right now with the door closed?"

She smiled, liked the brazen absurdity of my words, then checked her watch. "Sorry. Got a plane to catch. Calgary awaits. Take a rain check, maybe?"

"But you'll be married."

"Shouldn't be a problem."

She made me very angry, but she put her arms around me and gave me a hug, and it at least seemed genuine. I hugged her tightly, breathed in her perfume and thought of Gloria in my arms. Maybe there is something about embracing a woman that gives you the sensation that she is every woman. It may not be possible to truly love more than one at a time, but it's somehow conceivable to love them all at once. The woman, whoever she is in your arms, is your lover, your wife, your mother, your sister, your grandmother. She is she and you always embrace womanhood. It always feels right.

"I'm not going to do the little speech in front of the goon squad." She reached in her purse, came out with a half-consumed pack of Trident gum. "This'll have to keep Roger until I can mail him a couple of packs. Tell them all I'll miss them very much but that marital bliss was too much of a temptation."

"I will. Take care of yourself."

Now all the games were behind us. She sighed, turned back as she was halfway out of the office. "Alex, I promised myself not to tell you this. But I will anyway. New Dawn is bankrupt. Sinclair's been keeping it going with money out of his own pocket. I haven't even cashed my last three cheques. Funding is drying up. He's hanging on by the skin of his teeth. All of these workshops are. It's not why I'm leaving, really, so don't think that. I figured you were better off not knowing how bad it was, but now I think you need to know."

"I won't let them close New Dawn."

"Henry will like that spirit."

"I can't let them close New Dawn."

"I know," she said, and she left, closing the door behind her.

I sulked in my office for the rest of the morning, filling out forms on clients as if I was supposed to do, having no fun at all. By eleven-thirty, though, I decided I was through with wallowing for one day. It was lunch time and I was prepared to take my leap of faith. Any direction would be fine.

"Turn!" I screamed to Jeff, who was about to drive my Dodge Shadow straight into a seventy-five-ton pile of scrap iron.

Jeff turned right instead of left. I hadn't provided all the information a blind driver needed. We were now racing at thirty miles per hour straight towards a rocky embankment. Mahon's Office Supply warehouse was at the bottom of the drop-off. We would land on the flat roof, crash right on through into an elysium of paper products, office furniture and computer software.

"Just stop the car!" I screamed at the teenage driver.

"The brake is the one in the middle, yes?"

"Yes."

That's when we both gave the shoulder harness a good testing. We would have made excellent crash test dummies. My faithful red Shadow skidded on the asphalt, one front wheel slipped off onto the loose stones, and we came to a halt.

It had been Jeff's first time driving a car that wasn't immobile, jacked up on blocks in his front yard. And it was a pretty big deal to him that I had so much confidence in his ability. Jeff had been blind since birth. Blind with a capital B. "Not just legally blind," he would remind me. "Blind blind."

Jeff was smiling now, straight at the windshield, as he settled back against the seat and rubbed the sore spot on his shoulder where the harness had kept him from catapulting through the glass. "Are we doing all right?" he asked enthusiastically.

I peered ahead to the empty air, saw the precise spot where we might have landed on the warehouse roof. "Jeff, man, we're doing A-one. You've got this thing wired."

"I always wanted to drive."

"You're like Mario Andretti."

"Is that good?"

"Hey, we're alive, right?"

"Right."

"Think you can find reverse?"

"On the H, it's, like, in the middle and way over to the right."

"Close. It's way over to the left and then down." If he had shifted into fifth gear the car might have stalled, or it might have rolled just far enough forward to send us into an end-over-end drop face-first toward dustpans and destiny.

"Five speed. Cool. I keep forgetting."

"You're doing great."

With very precise directions, I let Jeff have the honour of driving us back to the front doors of New Dawn Workshop. They were all there standing at the front door, waving and cheering as we approached, tacking back and forth like a sailboat across a lake. "You hear that?" Jeff asked me.

"They love you. They can tell you're a natural at this."

"I knew I could do it. I just knew."

"Now turn left. Easy. Push in the clutch and gently depress the brake."

"The middle one, right? Just kidding."

A gentle stop. Jeff turned off the ignition and handed me the keys. "Thanks, Alex. You saved my life." He opened the door and stepped out, then looked up straight into the sun. Betty, the secretary from New Dawn, was whistling and clapping. Rebecca was grinning like a cat. Cornwallis slapped Rodney on the back. Roger held up a two-finger V-for-victory sign that Jeff would not see.

I was waiting for the adrenalin to drain out of my heart so it could slow its pace. I took a little notebook out of the glove compartment: "June 24, 1997. Rush is everything. There is no life without risk. Believe in the impossible." I closed the notebook, tucked the pencil behind my ear and opened the door. Jeff had been swallowed up by his friends, his family. My family.

There was sunshine for our famous arrival. It was a blue day in the industrial park, a blue ribbon lunch hour. Jeff and I had broken a few laws, abolished the limitations set upon him by his own dear parents and defied the critics. This would be my messianic mission, my creed.

83

After lunch, I spoke with everyone in the workroom. I made sure each client was busy at some task or other. Thanks to the lunch hour performance, everyone was in a good mood. Rebecca led Jules to the keyboard, and he played some Debussy that he had learned from listening to a CD. There was music, there was soldering, packing, taping and shipping, and there were a couple of people just sitting in wheelchairs by the window watching the trucks roll by outside. I gave Roger the Trident, gave Scotty-Rodney and Cornwallis a thumbs-up. Then I made the announcement: Connie was gone but everything was going to continue as normal. I'd take over all her duties.

"Guess she's just moving on," was what Cornwallis had to say, the only one to make the obvious observation.

"I'm not gonna be as easy on the slackers as she was," I said loud enough for everyone to hear. I was testing them to see if they trusted me, if they'd think I was straight with the line.

"We'll go on strike," Jeff shouted out. But he was smiling.

"Yeah," Scotty added. "We'll demand thirty cents an hour instead of a measly quarter."

"On the surface I may look like a wimp, but deep down I'm a hardass."

"We'll see," Rebecca said. And with that Jules, whose fingers had been hovering in the air, playing the notes without touching the keys, began to play audible music again. "Moonlight Sonata," if I recognized it correctly. And I knew it would be another good day at New Dawn. Gloria, however, had not come to work. In one way I felt relieved, for I had not yet figured out a way to meld my personal relationship with her and my professional one. I didn't even know if such a union was possible. On another level, I was worried about her. I knew she was absent about one day out of every five. I knew it had to do with mood swings and medication and all that. But now I carried the weight of knowing what she had once tried to do to herself. Now I carried the fear that I would lead her into dark territory where she had already travelled and that I could be responsible for hurting her.

Doris and Steve were studying me. I was, after all, just standing there looking out the window. Thinking about Gloria. Doris and Steve were an odd alliance — two very different individuals relegated to wheelchairs. Rolling metal chairs seemed reason enough for a close bond. Steve was shaking badly, and Doris was holding his hand. When I caught them studying me, they turned away. Doris pointed to a robin that had landed on the telephone wire outside. I walked over to them and squatted so I would be at eye level.

"Don't worry. Everything will be fine around here. I promise you that."

Steve's head shook as if to say no, no, no. But it was the incessant dance of his physical illness, not his mind and certainly not his spirit. "We knew you was good for this place as soon as you walked in through the door," Doris said. "To hell with the Connie Gavins of the world. To hell with 'em." There was real venom in her voice. Perhaps she was the only one who could come out and say what many of them felt: they felt abandoned. Connie had not even said goodbye. After that, I realized I couldn't do the little false speech I had promised Connie I would make. I would not let her off the hook. The used would not make amends for the users.

Then Doris put her arm around Steve, and Jules changed the keyboard sound to something emulating a harpsichord. Was it Beethoven, Bach, Debussy or some odd mesh of the three overlapping?

I swallowed hard and tried to conjure up something important and intelligent to say to all of them, not about Connie but about us. I wanted to inspire each of them with a message of hope. I wanted to teach, but I didn't know what it was I had to offer. I had no technical skill, none of the psychological insight that should have been essential for someone in my position. I felt embarrassed to be so ill-prepared to lead this ragged workforce on into the next century, or even into next week. There had to be more than packing and shipping, more than soldering copper ringlets, more than all this busywork for these important people to fill their lives with.

Doris hugged Steve hard. He was shaking very badly now and he had begun to cry. I had not seen that before. Wheelchair clanked against wheelchair. There was love between them, something that defied easy categories of boyfriend-girlfriend or mother-son. So many levels of love could be explored, and I realized I was a novice. So many faces to it, such complexity. Pity could be part of the map of love — pity evolving into compassion — and there was nothing wrong with that, nothing at all.

Pride, I realized, is a hindrance to receiving compassion, to receiving help, and we all need help of some sort. Compassion and love are close cousins. Good intentions were the only weapons in this army. In a very short time New Dawn had changed me in some vital way. Years had gone by, and I had blundered on without so much as changing my brand of toothpaste. Now I was up to my eyeballs in — how would Gloria put it? — "learning to be alive."

I went around the room once again, saying something positive and something kind about the task that each person was performing. Just before I left the room, Cornwallis grabbed my sleeve. For a second, I almost thought he was going to tell me to cut the crap and stop trying to be a goody-two-shoes. Instead, he pointed at my faded and wrinkled denim shirt and said, "Alex, I like that shirt. Where'd you get that shirt?"

"Frenchy's," I said.

"Good thing you got there before I did. That's a nice shirt. You got a good sense of style, my man." He let go of my sleeve as I thanked him. I had to have a talk with Henry Sinclair. I knew that Connie had told me the truth: New Dawn was in big trouble. All anyone had to do was read the papers to know we were still in the throes of a backlash against compassion and kindness. Conservatives, liberals, reformers and a dozen other breeds of political cliques had conspired to make the country leaner, meaner, and financially greener (for the rich), and to hell with social safety nets. There were already big gaping holes in those nets, and every day people fell through. Henry Sinclair, I surmised, was a likeable conjuror trying to hold together some invisible, diminishing force field that kept New Dawn in existence.

Thirteen

Industrial parks have no souls. Certainly Burnside Industrial Park lacks one. Once upon a time, however, in an era before bulldozers carved, I am sure this hillscape did possess a soul. In those long-gone days, these bushy hills and this lichen-bearing bedrock had beauty. Down through the pestering ages, this benign wilderness area has had its bedrock scraped twice by glaciers that shoved all the soil, all the life, off into the sea. They left it there in a frozen mess to thaw and eventually do some good — creating the Grand Banks, a fecund place for fish and every other living thing that sustained itself in the rich sediments.

In the thin, acidic soil left at Burnside, the stunted spruce had grown, along with the wind-sculpted pines whose branches, like long-elbowed arms, reached out away from the sea winds. From the window of my small, lacklustre office at New Dawn, I could still see the tops of the few pine trees not yet mowed down for factories on John Savage Drive. Unless some diverted Greenpeacer or Sierra Club altruist came to chain himself to those trees, I expected that they too would fall.

There were streams here too, small ponds and even trout. The Mi'kmaq had never settled here. They found more comfort elsewhere, but in summer they did walk and canoe here to fish, hunt and commune with the gods of sun, wind and sky who favoured this high ground.

The land still had a soul as long as trees still stood and rabbits still chewed on pigeon berries. It remained intact right through the ravages of the Halifax Explosion in 1917 and the ammunition magazine explosion of World War Two. Even when fires wasted the land, plants and animals returned. Eventually, though, the big machines came to break the rock and level the hills. They gouged and gored; men planted sticks of dynamite and blew the rocks sky high. The rabbits fled or got mashed by the indifferent tires of earth movers, the hawks and eagles flew off, the fish died. Ponds and lakes disappeared, filled in with rock and the chunked-up concrete of torn-down buildings and the asphalt jags from torn-up city streets. Hundred-year-old black spruce trees that had stubbornly grown to the height of human adolescents fell and were plowed under.

And so the soul was surgically removed from this place, and men and women came to work here in buildings made from I-beams of steel, sheathed by outer walls of aluminum and inner walls of gypsum board. It became a practical place, devoid of architecture and natural beauty. The only warmth in this land of the lost would be a Tim Horton's, with good coffee and bloated, tasty donuts.

For all of the bad intentions of Burnside, I did not hate it, for it was home to my new family. I would have much preferred the scape and scope of the primeval Burnside, but like other employees before me in this industrial park, I learned to adapt to my surroundings and even look forward to my daily arrival. I marvelled at all the flat roofs sealed over with a solidified gum of tar and stones. Where does all the water go when it falls from the sky? I wondered. The flat roof made perfect sense to the industrial designer — he could avoid the extra lumber or steel for a pitched roof. We worked in such a building.

My office, twelve feet by twelve feet with a grey steel army-surplus desk, was lit by fluorescent lights. It was a place to fill out reports and forms. It was also a place to be alone. And I loathed being alone.

Sometimes Roger or Jeff or Rebecca, Cornwallis or Gloria would come for a counselling session and we talked. I always felt much better then. I had no real training for the job of counselling, but somehow, after any given session, both counsellor and client would feel better. We would talk about chewing gum, revved-up bored-out engine blocks, baseball scores, hockey players or the meaning of emptiness, but I would file a similar report for each: "The client appears to have a very positive attitude towards his/her work and is exhibiting good developmental patterns of performance. Continued adherence to the prescribed program of training is indicated, and viability for placement in the outside workforce is predicted if this pattern of progress continues."

I had variations of this prognosis but what I said *to* each of them was this:

It's all gonna be okay. You're doing just great.

I had no desire to send them out into the real world beyond New Dawn, to work among the yoyos and yahoos of Burnside. My "clients" were happy here. Hell, I was happy here. We were truly sheltered from the outside world beneath our flat pebble-and-tar roof. Beneath us was nothing but solid, bulldozed bedrock. Henry Sinclair was our guardian angel. Maybe some of us wished we would never have to leave. If we had to go home at night, we were, for the most part, relieved to return in the morning and find that, seven blocks uphill from the noise and snarled traffic of Windmill Road, was our safe haven: New Dawn Workshop.

When you are a failure at nearly everything in life and you suddenly find something you are good at, you want it to last forever. As if the history of Burnside was teaching me that all the scraping and carving of rock, the geological formation, the glacial bruising, the bulldozing occurred to provide this incongruously ugly and perfect place for me and my friends to spend our days. New Dawn had been in existence for only twelve years, the product of a time when government largesse had extended to citizens who would never fit perfectly into mainstream society.

I knew there was a pretty thin line between them and myself. Certainly all of the clients here (sometimes considered to be employees, since they all received a small wage) had at least one special skill that gave them an advantage over me. I was all too aware of my own bulky emotional baggage but could do nothing less than carry it all around with me: in my car from New Brunswick, on my shoulders every day, in my troubled dreams at night. And I was well aware that I had no special skill to offset my handicap. It was a very thin line, I might argue, between my being a counsellor and my being a client here at New Dawn.

Ever since I had taken this job, I was as happy as I had ever been in my life, no matter how shaky the financial foundations of New Dawn might be.

"We have only twelve clients," Sinclair said, sitting in my office, staring up at the fluorescent lights. "Federal funding has been cut to the bone and we're in some sort of interim period. We've been there before. Once we had fifty people working here. Many of them are out in the workforce now. Employable."

Later I would learn that this was more myth than fact. Stories would trickle back. Three of the former trainees had taken up more or less permanent residence in the Nova Scotia Mental Hospital. One ended up in jail. Several had retreated to a life at home, under the care of aging parents. A few had snagged jobs in packaging plants in Burnside, only to be the first laid off when the economy went slack.

"Small steps forward. That's all we work for here. And we succeed." Sinclair had a way of stroking the unshaved hairs on the flabby part of his neck, a gently professorial motion that seemed to assure him that all would be well . . . if he just said so. "People have dreams, Alex. They're willing to fulfil those dreams if we're willing to give them belief in themselves and a handful of viable skills."

Belief and skills. That was Henry Sinclair. That was his solution. Safe and simple. An age-old formula that he touted to industry and government. He didn't need a PhD to have dreamed that up. Sinclair admitted that he was once a die-

91

hard Boy Scout patrol leader. "Nothing I learned in graduate school comes close to what I learned in the woods as a Boy Scout. Like I say, a couple of good skills, two good ones to rub together, and throw in a good attitude. Simple. Sweet. Don't tell anyone I put it to you this way."

He saw that I looked puzzled.

He rubbed his throat some more, smiled, checked his watch. "What I mean is this. If everybody knew it was that simple, we wouldn't be able to get one red cent for this place. So we tart it up a little."

"Behaviour modification. Work therapy. Employability."

Sinclair nodded. "When it comes to funding, words are everything. Big ones. Nobody in this society will pay you for good deeds or good work. What the government wants to see is a big fat report. I don't think they ever read past the first ten pages, but it's gotta be there, buddy boy. Keeps us floating."

I really had no idea what it was that my boss had come to tell me on this fine morning. Pep talk time, I guess. Honest. Levelling. I liked the man immensely. If he asked me to jump from a bridge I would comply. I knew that the New Dawn clients felt the same way.

Henry Sinclair had worked a similar charm on important people; he had pictures on his office wall to prove it. Shaking hands with Pierre Elliott Trudeau in the last days of Trudeau's prime ministership. Jean Chretien was in the background, smiling his slightly mad smile. New Dawn had been a final gesture in the great long heave of human compassion that liberalism had mustered before being dismantled by the Mulroney mandate. Sinclair had sailed New Dawn through the stormy seas of Tory power, somehow always keeping his ship afloat by last-minute forays into the dark and secretive coves of corporate sponsorship and the narrow, rock-strewn channels of social welfare spending.

Henry Sinclair shared the same name as Prince Henry Sinclair, who supposedly sailed to Nova Scotia from the Orkney Islands in 1398. Prince Henry, it is said, carried with him nothing less than the Holy Grail, the cup from which Jesus Christ drank at the Last Supper. Prince Henry and his men intended to found a New Jerusalem in what is now Nova Scotia to avoid persecution of the Templar sect. Nobody knows what became of him, although some researchers say he built several castle-like fortresses. The burial site of the Holy Grail itself is suggested to be either the so-called money-pit at Oak Island, a hill top near Truro, or an undisturbed grassy mound in a pasture about a twenty-minute drive from Burnside.

My Henry Sinclair believed this story to be rubbish, but, he admitted, among certain prominent Nova Scotians who also happen to be of the secret society of Masons, "Just my name opens a few doors."

I would likely not be willing to trade my one modern Henry Sinclair for ten of the long-dead explorer, although I added that ancient Sinclair mariner to my list of people to emulate. In my attempt to banish the timid young man I once was, I had started a list of the brazen, the bold and the nobly foolish on the wall of my bedroom. Evil Knievel, Albert Einstein, Marilyn Bell, Alexander Graham Bell, Joan of Arc, John Lennon, Benjamin Franklin, Joseph Howe, Neil Young and . . . and Henry Sinclair times two. "Risk Everything," I wrote beneath the list. Thumb-tacked to the wall was a single Tarot card: the Fool. I tried to convince myself that I was on a journey to amalgamate what was left of the old Alex into a new man, like Adam, like the first man, one with an open heart — pure, brazen, naive and unknowledgeable, willing to try anything new, willing to re-invent the world, or invent it. If necessary, willing to make something happen. I craved explosive, epiphanic moments. Each day, every day.

The man in this world most unlike Henry Sinclair, PhD, was, without a blink of a doubt, my own dear and damned father. It was he who dedicated a significant portion of his life to training his only begotten son to be anything but a fool, to be worldly-wise, aware of his own meagre worth and worthy of his family's hard heritage.

"Two kinds of men in the world," my father had said. "Winners and losers. Just remember which side of the fence you're on and you might make it through life in one piece."

On a Fundy beach, on a crisp, clear summer morning, this was intended to be a prophetic statement of fact. Sunlight sparkled in the tiny waves lapping at the pebbles on the shoreline. It was the rarest of father-son encounters. Someone had buggered up the canning machinery at the herring packing plant. My old man was off work. We had already been driven off our land by a factory that would create steam from nuclear fission. We lived in the belly of Saint John, but today my father had taken me on a pilgrimage to the beaches of his youth.

"I see fellers who try to make more of themselves than what they are. You either end up an arsehole or you get kicked in the arse. Me, I want neither. And I don't want it for my son. Men like you and me, boy oh boy, we've found our ways to cope. I'm just telling you this to save a whole lot of grief."

A fishing boat was passing by, a swarm of seagulls trailing in the breeze. I could see the fishermen cutting heads off the fish and tossing them to the gulls, who would fight and claw at each other, sometimes fight so viciously that the food would drop to the sea and a third, less-pugilistic bird would scoop it up and fly shoreward to eat in peace and quiet. My father noticed that I had caught the Kodak moment. "Let that be a lesson for you, Alex."

I always wished that I had known my father before he had become the third gull who waited for the scraps to fall from the more aggressive members of his gender. I had seen photographs of him as a boy, and he had a cocky, self-assured look in his eyes. He was a kid I would like to have known.

We walked for a good five miles that day along an empty shoreline. I skipped stones into the water. He told me I was doing it all wrong, but each time he tried to show me how to do it better, the rock caught an edge and sank deep and quick. "Bastards," my old man would say. Although I didn't know who or what he was referring to, he seemed to know who to blame for everything. But he chuckled once or twice. At an odd bit of boyhood memory, only half-articulated, or a ragged little scrap of a tune. One or the other.

"Things in those days, Jesus," he'd begin. "Back then along the shore . . ." and he'd trail off. "Didn't take much for fun back then . . ."

"Tell me what it was like." We both saw the fog bank now. You had to look far into the Fundy distance, but it was there. The sun would be gone by noon. It was a rare father-son morning, alone on the shores of his boyhood, but already natural limitations loomed. A limited tenure on the happiness of a father-and-son losing team.

"What was it like, you ask." Again he shook his head as if there were no words in his vocabulary. "What's the point in dredgin' it up?"

"No point at all, I guess," I said, my voice filled with disappointment. My father was stingy even with the scraps of his life. Fish heads and guts, ready to be tossed to the wind for some good or ill. Then held back.

"It was different, Alex, I know that. Things had a nice clear edge to 'em. You'd wake up in the morning and you'd know who the devil you were and what you wanted to do that day, that's what."

"This was in the old house back at Lepreau?"

He screwed up his face, stopped, sucked in the salty, musky air. The smell of seaweed filled our nostrils; the wind had come on shore, and the fog had caught the express train shoreward. My father, Alex Senior, rolled a tiny, thin cigarette with a single hand, his other hand dangling loose at his side. "That old place. That was something. It's gone now, you know that. Tored down. Bunch of pipes and ugly buildings and junk there now. Everything turns to shit if you give it enough time."

"I know it's gone, Dad."

"But there were plenty of good times when I was growing up. Nobody gave a hoot about money. We had it all. A kid could walk down to the shoreline and find a piece of sun-dried dulse and stick it in his mouth, chew on it until lunch. That's all he needed. You go home and there's your mother with the same damn chowder from a big pot she's been feeding you from for lunch and supper for a month maybe, and it still tastes like the best thing you ever had in your whole frigging life. She'd toss you a ripped-off piece of hard bread and that's all anybody needed."

"I wish the old house was still standing," I said, regret filling my head.

"Don't work that way. Can't stop some things. Just gotta move out of their way to save your arse from being run over." He sucked in the dregs of his hand-rolled cigarette. I watched it burn and disappear until there was nothing left on his lips but a piece of glowing tobacco. Then he spit it into the wind, but there was nothing left really but dead ash. He'd sucked that little smoke until there wasn't a nick of nicotine or shred of tobacco left in her.

My father started poking through some seaweed up on the shelf of slate along the high tide mark. He picked it apart and showed me tiny dead silver fish with eyes all bugged out. He smiled some kind of knowing smile, but I didn't ask him what it meant. He picked away until he found a dry piece of purple seaweed that I knew to be dulse. He broke off a piece, wiped the sand from it, gave half to me, and chewed on half himself. He closed his eyes.

I chewed, but it smelled and tasted bad. When I took it out of my mouth I noticed that there was some black stuff on it, but I didn't say anything. It was oil from one of the leaky Irving tankers.

I knew that up around the next little headland we'd be close to where my father's old home was, where he had been born and where I had been born. The fog had now stalled less than a mile offshore. A fog horn blew in the distance. The low throttling of a couple of lobster boats could be heard. If we rounded the headland, we'd see the stacks of the nuclear power plant. My old man had taken me back before, driving there by way of the highway, just to lament the loss of his family homestead and the loss of a way of life. "No point in going further," he said. "Better to turn back here and get on back aways before the tide comes in and we have to hightail it through the trees. What do you say, Alex?"

I nodded. "Think we'll see anything on the walk back?"

"Not likely. Seen all there is to see on this stretch. No surprises here. The fun's all behind us now."

Fourteen

I did not call Gloria that evening as I wrestled with my moral dilemma. I tried hard to pretend that everything was just fine. Gloria was okay. New Dawn was not about to go belly-up. I was going to be an award-winning rehab counsellor. I sat up late into the night reading a book of stories by Alistair MacLeod, and then I fell asleep.

The next morning, Henry Sinclair had a desk full of spreadsheets in front of him when I walked in. I think our conversation had already begun on some level before either one of us spoke. I had two things on my mind: Gloria and New Dawn. I had abandoned concern for myself, perhaps for the first time in a long, long while. Long ago in my childhood, Karen had taught me, by her very existence, how to be selfless. I had punished myself and been punished by the world for that mistake. And I had learned, as my father would have had it, to protect myself, to keep up my guard, to look out for number one. In so doing, I had sacrificed compassion and hope.

Sinclair, for the first time in my presence, could not contain his despair. "I don't know how to deal with numbers," he confessed. "I know people. I know how to help people, not juggle numbers."

"Can't you hire someone to help?"

"Wish I could. I think you know that the wolves are at the door."

"I guess I figured that out."

"Don't tell any of the clients."

"Lips are sealed. What can I do to help?"

"Oh, not much. Maybe get the Liberals out of federal and provincial government. Can't replace them with the Tories, though, they're much worse. I don't even trust the NDP after what they did in Ontario, so you'd have to invent a new political party overnight, one that believes in the value of health care and social service, one that might tax corporations a bit more and close a few loopholes for the rich. So get rid of Chretien and his bunker of old buddies and find a new minister of finance. Then work your way down. Find a new premier and reverse all the cutbacks. Do that for me, would you, Alex, and do it by tomorrow."

"Consider it done."

"You're a good kid. Naïve, not a care in the world. I need that right now."

"Seriously, what can I do?"

Two hands, palm up, waiting for miracles, waiting for brilliant answers. "Put a good face on it, I guess. You seem to be doing that so far, but that's because you didn't know just how bad it is."

"How bad is it?"

"Want a quick history lesson? Here goes. Mulroney cuts back transfer payments to the provinces, the provinces follow suit and start cutting back on hospitals, welfare, social programs, training programs like ours for people who need the protection of a sheltered workshop. You realize that some of those people out there might be better off in Mexico 'cause at least they'd have a crack at employment?"

"Somehow I can't see Jules and Roger fitting in on the night shift at the Ford plant in Chihuahua."

"Well, you know what I'm getting at. Look, I used to have staff. Once upon a time. Connie was the last to go. I had a secretary, an assistant, people to do the government bullshit.

All gone now. Just me and the bank and the suits from the province who come snooping."

"You've got me. I love this place."

"You're a bloody fool, Alex, and I thank God you stumbled in through the door when you did. But there must be something better you could do with your life than go down with this sinking ship."

"I've hard that metaphor once already, but I guess if I'd been on the *Titanic* my bones would still be down there on the ocean floor. Can we think about a rescue operation?"

"Salvage operation is more like it. Maybe some new hi-tech idea. That's what the suits like to hear about. Some internet crap, selling junk to Third World countries. Hell, I don't know. It's not what we need, but we might get some funding if we can convince those assholes that we're very, very hi-tech. There's still money out there for machines but not for people. That's the essence of the problem. Maybe something with phones and computers."

"What about phone sex?"

"Right."

"I've heard that it's a trainable skill. Three dollars a minute. Doris, Rebecca, they'd be perfect. Cornwallis can make his voice go high. Lynn maybe would go for it."

"Jesus, Alex. At least you haven't lost your sense of humour yet. I have. I know what you're saying, too. People are willing to pay big money for something as worthless as scripted dirty talk over the phone, but they don't want to see their taxes going to help the down and out."

"I don't see those people in there as down and out."

"That's only because the doors to this place are still open. It's only a matter of weeks — days, maybe."

Henry began crumpling up the computer printouts. "New

Dawn is part of the old economy. We don't stand a chance."

He picked up a copy of the *Daily News* and tossed it to me. The picture on the front page was of Charles D. Lawrence, federal finance minister — a short, thickish man with an immaculate haircut. He was glad-handing his way through a crowd in Victoria, BC. "He just made the final cut that will ensure our demise. Mulroney whittled away the bulk of it. Not much left for the Liberals to do but carve away and then pull out of our kind of social programs altogether. That's what Lawrence announced in Ottawa. Now he's on a cross-country tour, doing luncheons with businessmen who are patting him on the back. That's what's become of Canada."

"You could have told me this when you hired me."

"So I didn't tell the truth, the whole truth and nothing but the truth, so help me God. You're pissed at me?"

"No."

"You're wondering about your pay cheque. Guess you heard that I bounced a couple on Connie. Felt bad."

"It's okay. Don't pay me anything. I'll hang in for a while, borrow some money from my family to pay the rent. Something will work out."

"These are desperate times. I'm not writing off phone sex. I'm not writing off anything. All the rules of the game have changed. Jesus, there are no rules any more. Did I tell you that if New Dawn goes down I lose my house?"

"Are you worried?"

"My wife is."

"I got a one-bedroom place on Brenton Street. You two can sleep on the floor."

"And the dog and the two kids?"

"It'll be a little crowded."

"Alex. You give me one good day at a time."

"I love that cliché."

Henry stared at the glass covered graduate degree hanging on the wall. "You think William James, Sigmund Freud, R.D. Laing or Carl Jung are much good to me in this predicament?"

"Try Boethius."

"I know. The Wheel of Fortune. If you're on the bottom of the wheel, everything's rotten, you have nowhere to go but up, so you should be optimistic."

"And if you're on the top of the wheel, which we are not, you should be pessimistic 'cause there's no place to go but down."

"Keep in mind that ancient Romans didn't like Boethius any better than we do. He wasn't exactly rewarded with extravagant royalties for his *Consolation of Philosophy*. He was executed for treason."

"Imagine how that must have put a smile on his face. With something that bad happening, he had to assume he was flat out on the bottom of the cartwheel."

"I'll try to remember that. Alex, you're the oddest person I've met in a long while, and I'm glad I hired you even if I didn't have two pennies to rub together to pay you for your work here."

"Connie says you hired me because you felt sorry for me."

"That may be true. You looked like you needed some good news. I can't lie to you about that, but I also hired you because I was feeling sorry for me. I needed all the allies I could get. And you looked like part of my clan."

"Which clan is that?"

"Leonard Cohen had a term for it. Guess it's a cliché, too, by now: beautiful losers."

"I'm flattered."

"I want you to give Jeff another driving lesson. I think he needs more practice."

"You knew about that?"

"It was a ballsy thing to do. The kid deserved it."

I had wanted to talk to Henry about my Gloria dilemma, but I knew the time was not right. I had cheered him up a little, perhaps, but I couldn't burden him with my lack of professional standards. I knew that I was not taking advantage of Gloria. What I felt for her was genuine. I went back to my office and opened Gloria's file again. My intention was just to find her phone number and give her a call, but there was a yellow Post-it note with a message left for me on the file. Connie must have written it just before she left: "Be careful" was all it said.

I read through the file one more time, but the psychiatric report revealed nothing. However, as I closed it, I discovered a second folder in the pile I had brought to my office to study. It included a collection of handwritten poems by Gloria. I picked one at random and read:

> the shield of night
> alone, random winds from four corners
> barking dogs, the envious stars
> polar leanings in the minutes before dawn
> love like ice, brittle and cold but shining in the sun
> count the hours of happiness in the veins of the leaf
> count the days of sleep in the clouds tonight
> comb the hair of the wind and arrange the tools
> to decide
> where and when

It resonated with the sensibility of this young woman I had fallen for. It was not unlike my own college poetry — pages and pages of it, all burned ceremonially while camping alone on an island in the Saint John River during flood season.

I wanted to pretend that Gloria was not the complex, suicidal schizophrenic that her doctors believed her to be. I refused to read any more of the poems, closed the files and put them back in the filing cabinet.

I dialled her number and she answered.

"Hi, Gloria. I was worried about you."

"Alex? I'm okay. I felt awful yesterday. Today is not so bad. It's because I keep thinking about you."

I wanted to tell her that I had read her file, that I knew about the suicide attempt, that I was scared I was leading her into dangerous emotional ground. Hell, I was leading myself into dangerous emotional ground. The phone was not the means to get into it. "Can I see you today?"

"Not today," she said. "I'm okay, really. I just need to get reacquainted with the level I'm at."

"What do you mean?"

"It's like a whole new level, the way I felt being with you. We got there too quickly. I need to get adjusted."

"Are you sure I'm not creating, um, some kind of new problem for you?"

"You read my file?"

"Yes. Was that wrong?"

"No. I want you to know everything about me."

"But now I'm worried."

"I'm stronger now. It's not like back then. I was young."

"I've been there. Not as far, but I think I came close."

"What did you do?"

"I ran away. Did you ever run away?"

"No. I never did. Why did you?"

"Couldn't handle it."

"Will you run away now?"

"I'm older," I echoed. "Stronger."

"Where is it we are now?"

"What do you mean?"

"You and me. I need to figure out where, what level. I need some reference point. What do we have going?"

I wanted to say I loved her, but I think she had already put up a caution sign. I would go slow, observe the speed limit signs. "I think it's beyond just a professional relationship."

"That's good."

"I think it's a good thing for both of us."

"I like the sound of that."

"I think we just have to see where it goes from here."

"I'm not too worried about uncertainty any more."

"I believe you. Gloria?"

"What?"

I noticed that my hands were sweating. The phone was wet in my hand. I felt like a thirteen-year-old kid with a crush on a girl for the first time. I had a truly stupid question that had to come out. "Gloria, do you think we're going to be okay?"

"Yeah, Alex. I think everything is going to be all right."

Fifteen

It was a time of both love and anger in my life. I was in love with Gloria and I was enraged at the forces that wanted to bring an end to the sheltered world of New Dawn Workshop. Love and anger — not such a bad cocktail as long as they did not mix. And in my case at least, the polarity created a healthy focus on what was right and wrong with my private world.

When she returned to New Dawn, Gloria appeared more "normal" than before. Only when we were alone did she wax eloquent about the dreamy, esoteric world of her imagination. I meant to own up to Henry Sinclair that I was in love with one of our clients, but the words could never find their way out of my mouth. Henry, I was hoping, understood human nature far better than financial management, and he would not accuse me of irresponsibility or of a breach of some professional code.

I bought lawn furniture from K Mart and anchored it securely on the roof of New Dawn so it would not blow away. This is where Gloria and I spent our early evenings after work. She read her poetry to me, some of it light and whimsical, some dark and brooding. I said it was all wonderful and it was good for her to be exploring the full range of her feelings with words. Would it all be a book some day? No, she said, a writer only needs one person for an audience, and I was that audience.

I learned to love summer in an industrial park and had no need of beaches, resorts, mountain air or pine-scented forests. The tar smell of the roof and the sun setting over Bedford Basin was world enough, and time was both ally and enemy.

Gloria and I were free to create our own strange but secure place of sanctuary and exile. I loved everything about her. While I was reticent about my past, she was as open as the evening sky.

"My parents were kind to me, and I was spoiled. I simply did not want to grow up. I loved simple things and rebelled against teachers and all the obligations of growing up. I was unfair to everyone around me in that regard. I was irresponsible, but I didn't understand why I couldn't live on my own terms.

"When my parents started taking me to the shrinks, the news was that part of me — part of my personality, that is — was stuck at a developmental age of eight to ten. That was the part of me I liked the most, and they wanted to take it away from me."

I studied her long, radiant hair, her eyelashes, her cheeks and the delicate earring that dangled like a small metallic waterfall, and I asked, "How old are you now?"

"Twelve or thirteen."

"When I was twelve, I was the sorriest little boy on the face of the earth. I was cheated out of everything that might have been fun for a kid at that age."

"Why?"

"I don't know," I lied. "I guess I just did it to myself." I did not want to speak any further because a canyon of guilt opened up in my chest. I heaved the boulder of anger down into that canyon but it fell long and far, never hit bottom and did not plug the dull ache.

"So maybe we're both working on recovery of lost childhood. Maybe that's what brings us together."

"Right. Our emotional age, as they'd say in psychology class, is around thirteen. Both of us. Is that right?"

"Might be. Nothing wrong with that."

"Nothing. But it sounds like a dangerous game. I'm thirty years old, you're what? Twenty-five?"

"Twenty-four. Does it matter?"

"No. Very few things make sense to me. You and me, we make sense."

She became serious just then. "But there's something about us that you don't trust. You've seen my records, I know you have. You know about my time at the clinic, at the Abbie Lane."

I wondered when it would finally come out in the open. It was one of the things I feared most about Gloria. What if I was setting her up for something horrible? I didn't understand enough about her problem or her. All I knew was that I loved her.

"I broke a single pane of glass and used the jagged edge to cut deep into my wrists. I wanted physical pain. I wanted to die. It was the first time in my life I had been in love, and I had fallen in love with the wrong person."

"You don't have to talk about it if you don't want to."

"Everything about my little world had been shattered. Everything. He lied to me. I believed him. Of course, he had problems, too. That was why he was there. He had been abused as a kid. You can imagine the whole grotesque story. I thought I could help. I wanted to be a healer — like you."

"I'm not sure I'm exactly a healer."

"You are. We all are if we want to be. But I wasn't strong enough for that. I loved him and I was not at all prepared for the avalanche of emotions. I was buried by it. When he hurt me — no, not physically, just the kind of hurt any girl feels when she's dumped — when he hurt me like that, my fragile set of beliefs shattered and I wanted to die."

"But you didn't."

"Look it up. Read up on the recovery time: two years. By

then I was dependent on a finely tuned concoction of pharmaceuticals to keep me in one piece."

"And now?"

"Now I have you. And I'm better than I've ever been. I think I could give up the Prozac and the other stuff."

"Don't. I'm not sure I want you normal. I think I like you just the way you are." What I really meant was that I was afraid of messing with anything medical or psychological. I was scared to death that I was going to hurt this fragile woman. I was scared to death that I had made a big mistake in leading her into this relationship we were falling into.

"We're not going to be able to hang onto all this, are we?"

"Why not?"

"New Dawn, this summer, this rooftop. You and me. It can't stay like this."

It was a statement about our love but also about politics and economics and so much more. We hadn't made love. I was amazed at how certain we both were that we should hold off as long as we could. I did not sleep over at her apartment and I never invited her to Brenton Street. It was all a matter of caution. Caution and caring. When I had left New Brunswick, my code was to break all the rules I could find, tear down my personal barriers, re-invent myself and the world around me, and, above all, take chances. I would take those chances on anything, but I would not risk hurting Gloria.

"Part of my therapy," she said, "was to begin to take the world more seriously. So I listened to the news, I read papers. I never did that until last year. They taught me that I was part of *this* world and needed to know what was going on. So now I know too much. Too much about suffering nearby and far away. I also know that New Dawn is not going to survive."

"That's not true. Henry will keep it going, no matter what." Like Gloria, I favoured illusions.

"No. The big decisions have already been made. The prime minister on down. New Dawn is a thing of the past. Just ask Chuck Lawrence."

I looked around at the evening light, the gulls flying overhead. I felt a warm summer breeze dance across my chest. How the hell did Chuck Lawrence, federal minister of finance, find his way here into our very private place?

"The Chuck Lawrences are everywhere," Gloria said. "He's coming to Halifax next week. You haven't been reading the papers."

I had been reading the papers. It had been a long while since a public figure had garnered so much of my wrath. Chuck Lawrence boasted to business luncheon guests that he had wrestled the debt down and slashed federal transfer payments. A labour union organizer turned corporate lawyer, he had ascended the ranks of politics as a pseudo man-of-the-people and still spoke to crowds with his shirt sleeves rolled high enough to reveal a tattoo on his lower arm.

"My psychiatrist said it's good to act out aggression in a positive, constructive way."

"Should we go downstairs and get the minister of finance on the phone and give him a piece of our minds? Or if he's not in we could send a fax." I honestly thought she was joking. It seemed so unlike Gloria to care about anything like politics.

"No. I think we should go protest when Lawrence comes to town."

"Like in the sixties?"

"Like in the nineties. Like now."

"What's the point? You know it's a losing battle."

"What's wrong with fighting a losing battle?"

"I don't know. It just seems pretty futile. There's a lot of stuff you can't change." It was my father talking. Suddenly

I had a flashback. Protestors at Lepreau. Young men and women from Saint John and Fredericton, protesting at the work site of the power plant. "What a waste of time," my father had said. "Nothing anybody can do about it now. It's a losing battle." "Stupid buggers," he called them. He wouldn't even walk down the road to join them for one hour, wouldn't take even a symbolic stand against the government and the power company that would take away our land and our home.

"Maybe there is no point. Maybe there is only us and New Dawn, but what we have here is worth saving. My grandfather was from Cape Breton. He lived not far from Glace Bay, worked in the coal mines, but had a wonderful little farm house on the edge of a cliff that was being eaten away by the sea at a terrific rate. Every time I went there, the sea was a couple of feet closer to his back door. Everybody else nearby had retreated inland but my grandfather wouldn't. "You gotta make the best out of what you have to work with," he'd say.

"After digging cold black rock all week long, he'd spend his weekends building a stone breakwater beneath his cliff. He lugged rocks down in an old wooden wheelbarrow, and sometimes a weekend's work would simply wash away in the next storm. He knew it was a losing battle, but he didn't seem to care. It drove my grandmother nuts, but it was what he did, and he did it for over ten years. Eventually, the cliff was right up to the steps of the back porch, but they still lived there. When a hurricane hit Glace Bay, he and my grandmother were asleep upstairs as the house began to shake and tilt. My grandmother had to drag him outside, where they stood by the road in their pyjamas and watched as their home tumbled over the edge and into the Cabot Strait."

"That's terrible."

"Funny thing, he had no regrets. He felt he had fought the

good fight and was perfectly happy about all the years he had lived in the house he loved. He died of black lung when he was little more than fifty-three. I visited him only once in the hospital and he never complained about how he was feeling. I remember him telling me about how much he used to enjoy building what he called his "seawall," and how he had been a lucky guy to have matched wits with the sea, even if he lost. "It was good outdoor work. Clean and hard. Lots of fresh salt air."

Sixteen

Jeff learned to drive that summer better than many drivers I encountered on the roads of Halifax and Dartmouth. By wearing a Walkman and listening to an entire library of classical music, Jules memorized the great works of Beethoven, Brahms, Tchaikovsky, Rachmaninoff, and Rimsky-Korsakov. I also organized wheelchair races between Doris and Steve in the hallway, and these challenges gave them great satisfaction and entertained all of us.

I convinced Computerland to donate all their out-of-date, nearly-junk computers to New Dawn, and, with the help of a correspondence course, Scotty and Cornwallis started to learn the inner secrets of CPUs, hard drives, serial ports, modems and random access memory. Scotty found a simple loose wire in one of the old Compaqs, fixed it, and we agreed that it should go to Gloria. I found her a typing instruction program and urged her to write on the computer so she could spend her days at New Dawn being creative. Instead, she volunteered to do as much secretarial work for Henry Sinclair as was possible.

For reasons none of us could fathom, however, Roger had become severely depressed and was sent for treatment to the Nova Scotia Hospital, where he received what they now called "electroconvulsive therapy" and a new prescription to keep his spirits up. He returned looking somehow more mature than before, but his childish good nature seemed to have given way to an attitude of morose but benign resignation. Even a double pack of Doublemint didn't induce much enthusiasm. Rebecca coaxed him back to working on the packing and shipping projects. Every once in a while Roger would stop working and just look at his hands, disbelieving perhaps that he had grown up into a man but remembered hardly any of it.

Gloria still had bad days, and while she did not rebuff my attempts to comfort her on those days, she much preferred to be left alone. My intense feelings for her had taught me to go slowly. I respected her fragility and would let our relationship develop at its own pace.

My father's rage against an unfair world had been within me all the years of my life, but planted deep beneath the surface and covered over with many layers of my own troubled personality. I could hate in the abstract but not in the particular. Certainly I had no enemies at New Dawn. But there remained those larger forces beyond this safe haven that wanted to close us down, and at night, in my restless, turbulent dreams, I was seething with anger, frustrated and enraged beyond reason. I wanted nothing short of an all-out war with whoever was responsible.

Each morning as I made myself instant coffee, slurped my corn flakes and listened to Don Connolly on *Information Morning*, I reassured myself that I was ill-equipped to alter the direction of North American politics. One lone befuddled rehab counsellor railing against the near-religious dogma of fiscal responsibility would do no good at all. Nonetheless, I was mad at them all: prime minister, premier, every minister and every member of the federal and provincial caucuses that would soon swing the axe blade down on programs like New Dawn. The talk was all about "mainstreaming" instead of creating special-needs "ghettos." But it was all bunk and bullshit.

I was in Wal-Mart, looking to buy a new tape for Jules, when I walked past a bank of television sets during news hour and saw Chuck Lawrence, smiling, sleeves rolled, walking up the steps of Parliament. Chuck Lawrence was multiplied by twelve in front of me, and maybe Chuck Lawrence times twelve was enough to stabilize the image of a foe in my head. Beloved by Bay Street, dazzled with praise for slashing the deficit, here was the federal minister who had hacked and hewn at social institutions. Federal transfer payments to the have-not provinces had shrivelled, and it was only a matter of weeks or months before New Dawn and other threads of the social safety net would be unravelled.

I found a tape of the Prague Symphony Orchestra doing Beethoven's Sixth, paid for it and left.

Henry Sinclair was not at all opposed to my joining the protestors when Chuck Lawrence came to town. Henry himself felt that he could not be seen in the midst of such a protest, since he was in last-ditch negotiations with provincial bureaucrats to save some remnant of New Dawn, once the work at the chopping block was finished. "Take the day off," he said. And then the surprise: "Take some of our people with you. It would be good for them."

"You're sure?"

"Absolutely. They need to see they're not alone. They need to feel they have a voice, too."

"But it's a losing battle."

"What isn't? I wouldn't take Roger. He needs more time to recover. But take whoever else you want."

On a warm, drizzly July morning, Jeff, Gloria, Cornwallis and Rebecca walked across the New Dawn parking lot to my car. "I'm driving," Jeff said with his boyish enthusiasm, and I almost wanted to give in and let him do it.

We had protest signs in the trunk that we had made in the shop. We felt excited and charged up for our confrontation with Chuck Lawrence. We would let him know that he was hurting people. Our voices might fall on deaf ears, our signs might go unread, but we would be there face to face with the man trying to tear apart our family.

"This makes me feel like Africville all over," Cornwallis said.

"I feel good about this," Rebecca said.

"Please let me drive," Jeff pleaded.

Gloria was radiant in the seat beside me. Everyone in the car knew about our relationship. Everyone at New Dawn approved. "You're really enjoying this," Gloria said to me. She saw the smile on my face.

"Yeah. I didn't know I'd feel this way. I feel good about this."

"I thought you said it was a losing battle. A no-win situation."

"Maybe. Maybe not. It doesn't matter. I like hating Chuck Lawrence."

"Hmm," she said, "Doesn't sound . . . healthy."

"I know. But it feels good. I used to be angry at myself an awful lot. I didn't like that. This is different."

"Anger can be a good thing if it's channelled into something constructive," Cornwallis said.

"How do you know?" I asked playfully.

"I got me a college degree in being angry."

"Funny, you don't show it."

"Just 'cause I'm old."

Chuck Lawrence was meeting the Board of Trade for a luncheon at the Lord Nelson Hotel. I parked near the Public Gardens. We unloaded the placards from the trunk and walked through the gardens towards the hotel. I had felt ambivalent about Gloria's presence. I kept wondering if it was good for her to be part of this event. The Public Gardens were in full bloom with flowers and children. Geese and ducks paddled the muddy waters of the ponds, and pigeons parted on the sidewalk as we walked through. Much like New Dawn itself, the Public Gardens seemed a protected place, a sanctuary of beauty and life. A high, black wrought-iron fence enclosed the park, and the gates remained locked all winter. Only in the warmer months was the public allowed here, only when the trees were green and the climate-sensitive flowers properly transplanted from the greenhouses into the well-fertilized soil. A low, soft mist hung over the place, making it other-worldly, a dreamer's paradise. I found myself losing touch with my anger.

"This place smells great," Jeff said.

"I feel like we're on a school field trip or something," Gloria added.

But in a minute we were back out on Spring Garden Road, passing through the giant Victorian swing gates and back into

116

city traffic. I checked my watch: eleven-thirty. "Come on," I said. Rebecca led Jeff across the street, and we found ourselves amidst other placard-carrying protesters, waiting for the minister of finance to arrive. New Dawn had formidable allies among single mothers on welfare, hospital workers, social workers. Several hundred people were jammed along the sidewalks, some chanting, some chatting. We joined the throng crammed around the driveway to the front entrance of the hotel. Police were on hand to try and keep us back. Some protesters yelled slogans. Some shouted at the cops.

I tried to keep an eye on my own troops, but we were jostled one way and then another. I held onto Gloria's hand, however, and tried to ensure that we would be near the front of the crowd. I wanted a good look at Chuck Lawrence in the flesh. I wanted him to see my sign, to see my face.

The Halifax police were handling things poorly. The protestors had spilled over into the short driveway so that cars could not pull up. It was too late to make us move back out of the way. Lawrence's limo turned the corner and the driver stopped. Along with two other men, Lawrence got out of the car, smiled and waved as if we were a crowd of admirers, and then, before the police were able to clear a path for him to the door of the hotel, he waded into the crowd.

Some of the protestors were polite, but I was not among them. Maybe if he hadn't smiled I would have been okay. Instead, I let go of Gloria's hand, and I began shouting at him. For the first time in my life, I let the rage I had inherited from my father surface in full force. I pushed forward until I was within inches of the man, and then I shouted as loud as I could. My placard was logical and articulate, but my words were the opposite. I must have been screaming near his ear: "You god-damned son of a bitch!" The words felt like honey in my throat. The anger in my head mingled

117

with some sort of joy equivalent to an exploding pressure cooker. I think I was about to yell something else, something equally eloquent. I was still holding my placard up high as I saw two policemen approaching me out of the corner of my eye, but I was caught completely off guard when Chuck Lawrence stopped dead in his tracks and stared at me. Perhaps the well-heeled politician had been very successful at ignoring protestors *en masse*, but he had a hard time ignoring my contorted face and my words trumpeted into his ear. Because he did something just then that shocked not only me but the rest of Canada, who would catch the incident on the six o'clock news.

Maybe, for a split second, he was no longer the minister of finance of Canada but just another kid called a bad name out on the playground at noon. For he looked me directly in the eye, pulled back his arm and let go with a punch that caught me square in the jaw. I fell backwards into the arms of several welfare mothers, who tried to catch me but failed. Lawrence, however, must have been dying to vent his frustration against naysayers like me for many long miles across this wide, free-thinking nation, because he pounced on me, pushed me to the ground and got his hands around my neck. But he did not squeeze.

My head hit the concrete sidewalk, and I felt stunned. My eyes couldn't quite focus, but his face was in front of me. I was breathing his breath, I saw his rage. I saw something in his face that I recognized as my own. I did not fight back. I was in shock as I waited for his hands to squeeze my throat, but already he had started to cool. The welfare mothers were screaming at him now, and the police were all over us. I caught one final message in Lawrence's eyes: he knew that he had just made a significant mistake. He started to stand up. Two policemen helped him.

"The bastard attacked me," Lawrence said to them, but the news footage would prove him wrong and make the situation far more embarrassing for him.

One cop turned me over and pushed my arm up into my back. I heard Gloria shout my name. I heard Cornwallis screaming at the police to leave me alone. And then Charles Lawrence must have been ushered away into the Lord Nelson, and the police were staring down the hostile mob.

By then I was feeling pleasantly numb except for the pain in my jaw and a sore spot on the back of my head. Truth was, I had never been hit with a fist like that before. Strangely enough, I felt some pity for Lawrence. I knew that this would not play well in the media. As the policemen lifted me onto my feet and led me away to a van, I caught Gloria's eye and smiled to reassure her I was okay. She had that detached look on her face, and I saw Cornwallis standing with his arm around her. I saw Rebecca and Jeff as well. I tried to wave, but my arms were restrained.

All the hate had washed out of me, and I suddenly felt tired.

"Where are we going?" I foolishly asked the cop who was driving the van.

He just laughed. "Tell me you've never been arrested before."

"Never," I said. "What happens next?"

"You'll see," was all he said.

Seventeen

My father told me that if I didn't play it by the rules I'd end up in jail one day, and I guess the old bastard was right after all. His belief was that anyone from our clan of lower-class coast-dwellers who became uppity in any way would be cut right back down by the powers that be. I never knew what "the powers that be" meant, but now I was getting a pretty clear picture. My neck was a little sore from where the powers had grabbed hold. My jaw felt stiff, and the back of my head had a goose egg on it. I had acquired all this bodily memorabilia from my brief discussion with the minister of finance, and it came as a bit of a shock to my system.

Actually, I had never known any politician to be so direct. Hell, I didn't think they paid any attention at all to what folks had to say. But Lawrence proved me wrong on that count.

I had lost track of Gloria, Jeff, Rebecca and Cornwallis, but I had faith that they could find their way home. I would like to have been able to tell Gloria that everything was fine as far as I was concerned. I didn't want her to worry. I was hoping that she had been faithful to the medication that day, for she still had days when she'd dare to live her life unencumbered by helpful drugs. Some of those were grand creative days, other times she began to slip into the abyss. Usually I was there to help her pull herself back out, but today I would be occupied with other worries.

So once again I admitted that my father's rules of living proved true. Only difference was that now, at thirty years of age, I finally didn't give a good god damn what my father's rules were all about.

I ended up at the city police headquarters on Gottingen Street, where I was fingerprinted and photographed. I can't say people were nasty to me or anything. The one cop who had led me into the building told me I was in mighty deep shit because of "the federal nature of my crime."

"But it was the federal nature that hit me. I didn't touch him."

"I guess it'll all come out in the wash."

"My mother used to say that."

"I'm sure she was a fine woman," he said as he led me into a room with a table, two chairs and no windows.

I was left alone very briefly and wondered if someone could spy on me through a peephole. It was all very cinematic. And I was, to be truthful, extraordinarily pleased with myself. I could not begin to comprehend how deep the shit was that I had fallen into, but for some damn reason I didn't mind the smell. I gave it the Gloria test. How am I feeling? *Fine.* Are you feeling fully alive? *Yes, most certainly. I have just been attacked by the Prime Minister's right hand man for standing up for the rights of people in need. I have rarely felt this great.* Physical damage was good for me.

I admit I did detect that recurring, slightly annoying pressure in my chest again. I took a deep breath and closed my eyes. That's when a man in a suit walked in. "Bob Atkinson here," he said.

"Alex McNab."

"We know. Alex, do you know how serious this is?"

"Shouldn't I have a lawyer or something?"

"You can if you like. The officer read you your rights already, though."

"I guess I wasn't listening. Skip the lawyer for now. I know that's not smart of me, but I'm anxious to see what happens next, so I'd rather not have to wait on a lawyer."

"Fine. Can we establish why you were there today when the minister arrived?"

"I was there because I wanted to let Chuck Lawrence know that his cutbacks were hurting the people I work with."

"And your job?"

"Counsellor for special needs people."

"I see. And that's why you attacked the minster of finance?"

"No. I shouted an unkind remark at the man. But I didn't even touch him. I'm not that type."

"What type are you?"

"You'd like to establish a psychological profile of me?"

"Something like that."

Maybe I had watched too much television. Why was I enjoying this? Wasn't I in serious trouble?

"You don't have a previous criminal record."

"Do I have one now?"

He laughed.

"Is there any sort of organization you belong to? Do you have, like, a doctrine or something?"

I felt obliged to say something important. "I give money to the Council of Canadians."

He nodded knowingly as if I had just said I had studied Lenin and Marx and trained with the FLQ or Che Guevara.

"Doctrine, hmm," I continued. "I believe in the sanctity of life, the right of every citizen to live above the poverty line, to live with some degree of dignity in our society. I also think people should be nice to each other." I almost started to giggle. A voice in the back of my brian that sounded like my mother told me to just shut up, but I was having too much fun. Maybe there had been brain damage when the minister of finance knocked me down on the sidewalk.

A phone rang in a room nearby and the door opened. A nod. My interrogator left. I closed my eyes again and worked on refining my doctrine, but when Bob Atkinson came back in something had changed. "Look, I'm going to take you to a cell for a while. We've got to gather some more information on this."

"I'd like to make a phone call."

"You'll have another chance for that. For now, just relax. Go with Officer Cranmore here."

"Sure."

And so I was led to a not-terrible jail cell. There were bars and there was a lock and a key. Just like the real thing. I even had a cellmate. He had long, raven-black hair, a pudgy, boyish body and a broad friendly smile. I guessed he was either Mi'kmaq or Maliseet.

"Jeez, I was in need of someone to talk to," he said. "Whadja do?"

"I was assaulted by the minister of finance. You?"

"Oh, hey. I was there. I guess I didn't see you, though. I got arrested before Charles Lawrence even got there."

"What for?"

"I'm an artist, eh? So I had done up a really nice large poster. On the poster was a very fine illustration of a penis and on the head of the penis was an excellent caricature of Mr. Lawrence's face. No words or nothing else. I wanted Mr. Lawrence to see my work of art, but a policeman asked me to leave. I told him I was an artist and that I deserved freedom of expression, but the man disagreed on that point."

"Whatever happened to freedom of speech, anyway?"

"I hope they didn't ruin my painting."

"I'd like to see it. By the way, I'm Alex."

"Hi, Alex. I'm Tony Christmas. Like the holiday. You know much about art?"

"Not much. But I really like the Salvador Dali painting in the Beaverbrook Art Gallery in Fredericton."

"Salvador Dali was one very rough trader. Slick and insane. A good combination in the world of art. My painting of Mr. Lawrence as genitalia was done in egg tempera. Just like what Michelangelo used on the Sistine Chapel."

"Lawrence should have been impressed."

"It's very sad he didn't get to see it. To be honest, I was trying to hurt his feelings. I've got a half-sister who's living on the street because of the dude's cutbacks."

"I take it you're not a fan of cutting the deficit."

"He cut in all the wrong places. You must not be in the man's fan club either."

"I was refused membership, but he and I did have this intimate encounter."

"Did he really beat on you? That's what I heard someone say."

"That's the way I remember it. But now I seem to be in this Franz Kafka novel. What happens next?"

"Dunno. I'm not too worried. I'm very good at waiting. My grandfather told me that waiting patiently was one of the great skills. My grandfather was a chief for a little while but got booted out. He didn't seem to mind because his philosophy was that you never do anything in life that's a failure. You're always winning. The big trick is figuring out just what game you're actually playing."

"Good one."

"Like today, right?"

"Yeah, this is okay. Where you from?"

"Chapel Island, Cape Breton. You?"

"New Brunswick. Lepreau area."

"Uh oh, here comes buddy."

Buddy was Bob Atkinson and another suit he introduced as Jerome Castonguay. "He's from the PMO," Officer Bob said.

"Mr. McNab, we need to talk."

"Fine by me. Guess I gotta go, Tony. It was good to meet you. Hope you get your painting returned."

"Nice to meet you, man. Hang onto your dreams."

It was a nice thought.

We returned to the windowless room. Somehow, I wasn't afraid that I was about to be tortured for a confession. Bob and Jerome both looked pretty awkward, as if somebody in the room had just let a silent but deadly fart and they wanted to pretend there was no stink.

"What?" I finally asked.

Bob nodded towards the TV and VCR as it was rolled into the room. Castonguay took a deep breath. "Alex, we have this little problem here."

"Of a federal nature, right?"

"Let's just say it's of a very delicate nature."

"Do you really work with the prime minister?"

"I do. Want to watch the screen?"

"This like free video rentals for the inmates?"

"Please. Wanna just watch?"

It was a film clip from a noon-hour news broadcast on ATV. I saw Lawrence's car come into the camera frame, I saw him get out, and the camera jiggled a bit as the cameraman tried to keep up with him. Then I saw me. I did have a fist raised in the air, but so did many other people around me. I was shouting, but I didn't sound much louder than anybody else, and you couldn't make out a word of what I was saying. I was kind of leaning towards the minister when *wham*, a sucker punch to the jaw and full frontal assault. I was down on the ground with Chuck Lawrence all over me, his hands grasping for my throat. There was hate on his face, on mine only shock and surprise. And then the police moved in, Lawrence was lifted off, and someone put a hand over the camera lens.

"Just to be square with you, Alex, I'll say that this has already run on the air."

"So everyone in Halifax has seen this by now?"

"Everyone in the whole freaking country has seen it."

"And so you have a problem."

"We have a problem."

"*We* do?"

"We're dropping all charges against you."

"Gee, thanks." I rubbed the sore part of my neck, then traced a finger over the raw part of my jaw.

"He overreacted. The Honourable Charles Lawrence would like to apologize."

"Really?"

"He's been under a lot of pressure. He overreacted."

"Can I leave now?"

"You can, but like I said, we need your help."

"My father taught me never to forgive someone who takes a swipe at you when you're not prepared."

"Forgiveness is a very high calling."

"What do you want me to do?"

"The minister is waiting for you out front. So are a few TV cameras. He wants to apologize. He means it. He feels terrible."

"He feels terrible that his career is about to go down the toilet."

"He might yet become prime minister. It wouldn't hurt to be able to get to know the prime minister on a first-name basis."

"He wants me to be his friend?" I was relieved that the Kafka novel had been left behind. Woody Allen might have written this script because it was too much fun for it to be Kafka.

"He wants to shake your hand."

"He won't pull another sneaky punch?" I was fooling around and that worried them. Two loose cannons here: me and the good finance minister. I saw sweat on the lower neck of Jerome Castonguay. I was in a favourable negotiating position here and not quite ready to let it go.

"Will you let my cellmate go?"

"The guy with the pornographic poster?"

"It was art. Egg tempera. He'd like it back."

"It was a painting of a big dick."

"It was an honest representation," I said, mimicking Tony's phrasing.

"He'll be out of here by one o'clock. No bail, no charges, nothing."

"Good. Let's go meet the brawler."

"Will you promise to be civil?"

"As long as he doesn't use a left jab again."

"You'll have police protection," Atkinson said, and I suddenly realized that he was more amused by all this than he had let on.

Outside on the steps of police headquarters, the sun had broken through the mist. ATV was there, as were CBC, MITV and a crowd of about a hundred protestors who had found their way over from the hotel.

The crowd was kept back as Chuck Lawrence emerged from his car and walked briskly up the steps with the TV cameras on his trail. I was still trying to get my eyes adjusted to the bright, early-afternoon light as the minister of finance shook my hand and apologized. Words tumbled out of his mouth, and he was looking more at the cameras than at me. I knew that if it had not been for the video footage, this would not have come to pass. Castonguay's people would have lied through their teeth and none of this would be necessary. But here I was shaking hands with the man who wanted to be the next PM, and as he rambled on I realized he was talking about me. He introduced me as a social worker — inaccurate but not offensive — and as a "concerned citizen." He put an arm around my shoulder, which I found a bit too much for the situation. And then he proceeded to put a positive spin on the whole thing: "In these most difficult and troubling times, the most important thing is that we all work together for change and get past our petty differences . . ."

A man slams you to the concrete and he calls it a petty difference? He talked fast and, it seemed, sincerely and blamed his own working-class upbringing for his "social faux pas." His speech was long-winded and weird. Yet, by the way he phrased the story, it sounded as if we were both victims of the media, he and I, but truly heroes of the people. I knew I wasn't supposed to talk in this situation — it had been choreographed, scripted and staged to make Lawrence look better than he really was — but I would not let him get away with it.

"I'd like to say something, if I could," I interrupted, leaning close enough to the CBC camera so that I could not be ignored.

Lawrence held his hands up to get the crowd to quiet down, as if this had all been his idea. "Give the man a bit of breathing room and let him speak," he said, a nervous smile dancing across his face.

"Hey, all I want to say is, I think it's really great that Chuck Lawrence can admit to the error of his ways today, and I hope he'll see that cutting back on funding to the provinces, cutting back on social programs in particular, hurts a lot of people just as bad — or even a lot worse — than a punch in the jaw from a politician. I'm wondering if he might consider reversing some of those cutbacks so people around here who don't have good jobs or an easy life can live with dignity."

With those words I felt my first thrill of the power of public rhetoric. When I heard people cheering from the street, I realized I had made my point. Even though I wasn't shrewd enough to avoid letting Lawrence co-opt the situation after that, my words would be heard in living rooms across Canada. They were barely out of my mouth when Lawrence jerked my right arm up as if in mutual triumph and shouted, "Here's to human dignity!" The people in the crowd were still cheering, and it almost appeared as if they were cheering for him. They weren't. Then, before the cheers could fade to boos, Lawrence let go of my hand and was led by an assistant down the steps and into the waiting car. I noticed that the morning's limo had been replaced by a lowly pale-blue rental sedan.

Jerome Castonguay led me back into police headquarters as the TV crew retreated.

Inside I said, "I'm free to go, right?"

"Free as a bird. I think that went quite well, don't you?"

"Not bad. I'm new at this, you know."

"I've been advised that we should have a doctor look at you. I've got an appointment with the on-call doctor, the same one used when the prime minister or a head of state is in town. Shall we?"

"No, thanks," I said. "I'm okay. Don't worry, I won't sue. It's not my style." I didn't like hospitals or doctor visits. I was sure I was fine, and most of my experiences with the medical profession had been negative. Overall, it had been a very fine day for this soldier of the social cause. I didn't want to have it marred by hearing something from a doctor that I didn't want to hear.

Eighteen

1977. The year they retired the King of the Bay of Fundy. Or maybe he was overthrown. Maybe he gave up. He could have just grown tired. The tides would still go in and out, but Karen and I would not be there to see them. It was the year we moved into Saint John, heartland of the Loyalist losers. My father's people. Once we were settled into the upstairs of an old frame house near the centre of the city, I refused to believe that the harbour several blocks away could possibly have anything to do with the bay. It smelled of sewage, and the air above carried the stench of the oil refinery and the pulp mill — sulphurous gases like you'd breathe in hell, my father said. And there were diesel fumes from ship engines and truck engines.

There is nothing good to be said about the year 1977, except perhaps that I learned in a Saint John city school (a dreaded place inhabited by brutal kids who picked on me nonstop) that astronomers had discovered evidence of water outside our galaxy. According my science teacher, Mr. Vaughan Greenspoon, this was excellent evidence that there was indeed life in outer space. It was a bit of trivia, I suppose, as far as the world news of that year went, but I had this sad notion that it was somehow tied to the fact that I half-believed the King of Fundy had moved on somewhere else. I was going on eleven and sceptical of some childish things, never a full believer in my own myths. But my sister was, and so I wanted to remain a believer as well. The Lords and Ladies of Lepreau would not dance for us again. The King of Fundy would not smite us with his weather, nor would we ever see him again.

So why exactly was it that in 1977, for the first time ever, scientists had discovered water in space? Maybe it hadn't been there before, that's why. Maybe, just maybe, the water detected beyond the rim of our galaxy was from the tides of Fundy. The lonely king had settled for the solace of deep space and carried some volume of the sea with him.

But I'm getting ahead of my story. The story of 1977. Early in the year, in the depths of a hard winter, men from the province came to our Lepreau home to inform us that something wonderful was about to happen in our community. The Maritimes' first nuclear power plant, a six-hundred-megawatt CANDU nuclear reactor, would be built less than a mile down the road.

The tall, thin man, I recall, stood in the doorway, for my father would not invite him into the house. He had an odd way of pronouncing words. My mother and father would argue later as to whether it was a speech defect or a foreign accent. I don't think I ever saw his face, just his silhouette. He called nuclear power "the most significant source of energy known to man." My mother finally asked him to sit down for a cup of tea as my father chewed on the flesh inside his own cheek.

He was a friendly man with good intentions, I believe, but how could he not realize the death knell he was sounding for

131

my childhood? The word "megawatt" came up again and again like some powerful incantation. "Safety" was also uttered repeatedly.

The bottom line was this: some families in the area were being offered a "more than reasonable" price for their property so that construction could begin as soon as possible.

"You're asking us to give up our home?" My mother was shaking.

"We're offering you a goodly amount, more than the market would bear."

"How much?" my father asked. All his life he had been dreaming of a windfall. We were living in the very house he had grown up in. He had never been a fan of his own childhood, and I don't recall that he ever had a nice thing to say about his own now-dead parents.

The man wrote down a figure on a full sheet of yellow foolscap and passed it to my father, who studied it as if he was reading a menu at a fancy restaurant. "You're offering this for an acre and a half of mostly scrub spruce?" My father had spent too much time working pulp in the woods and estimated the value of our woodland, insignificant as it was, for what it could yield to K.C. Irving's pulp mill. He was prepared, I could tell, to let the place go for whatever was offered, and I wanted to scream. But Karen was there and I didn't want to scare her.

"We're not selling," my mother said. "We don't give a rat's ass about no nucular energy." I clearly remember how she mispronounced that word. It was not a common word at dinner table discussions in our home.

"I know that these things take time to consider," the man said. "I'll give you some time. I'll be speaking with your neighbours, too. Oh, here's a brochure about nuclear energy.

You might have heard some bad things in the news, but nuclear power is the safest, cleanest power. Did you know that the sun gives us its warmth through nuclear fusion?"

"I didn't know that," my father said. "Guess I learned something new."

"So I'll come back in a couple of days and we can talk."

He was nearly out the door when my father got up. "Wait," he said. "We accept your offer."

A hush fell over the room. The man simply nodded and left without saying another word. When the door closed, I watched my mother slap my father hard on the face. Not once, but twice. It is to my father's credit that he did not respond with anger. Alexander McNab Senior was a cold man and the victim of many things, including his own pessimism, but he was not violent. "Only the lowest of the low, the worst bloody losers on the planet, hit their family," he had said once over the dinner table. And he never did strike any of us, despite his insistence that we *were* the lowest of the low on the planet.

My father touched both his cheeks and rubbed his hands up and down so we could hear the sandpaper sound of his whiskers. Suddenly he had become so much more human. The look in his eyes told me he was doing what he had to do, not what he wanted to do. Yet he said, "I deserved that. Nobody wants to give up their home. But I was worried maybe he'd go down the road there to Bill Waylon's, and Bill'd be willing to sell for even less than what was offered to us. He's been dying to get out of here for years. Then we would have missed an opportunity, eh? They'd go and build their infernal machine in Bill's backyard instead of ours. Then where'd we be? Elizabeth, you know as well as me that we don't ever get an easy break. This is one right here. Or

133

it could be. We move to Saint John. I get a job at the mill or the refinery. Better money all around, and what he's offering is . . . jeez, woman, it's double what this place is worth."

My mother just hid her face in her hands and cried. Karen followed suit, and since my father couldn't stand to look at women or girls in tears, he stared at me. My face was like a rock, just like his: stubborn, defeated, angry, bitter.

What my father couldn't comprehend was that the province was buying up *all* the land around here. A nuclear reactor took up a lot of space, and it was better to move everyone away as a precaution. The people of Lepreau up to that time didn't know much about enriched uranium, coolant problems, faulty fuel rods, heavy water leaks, radioactive steam releases. Words like plutonium, core breach and meltdown simply weren't in the vocabulary of the fishing families and forest workers who eked out a living along these impoverished shores.

Amazingly, the province discovered legal problems over the ownership of our land. Since my father had not paid his taxes for nearly twelve years, he no longer had legitimate title to the land at all. They said it was a miracle that it hadn't been bought up in a tax sale by now. So my father had to hire a Saint John lawyer at great expense, and he had to borrow money to pay the back taxes and the accrued interest. My mother begged him not to sell the house. It wasn't much, she argued, but she loved it. It was her life. "I know it sounds foolish," she pleaded, "but there's something about this kitchen. The sound of the oil stove, a cup of tea at the kitchen table on a cold winter morning. I love this place. I would feel lost if I didn't have this one small, safe place in the world."

Karen began to cry when my mother said that, and I hugged her to me and stroked her hair. I realized then how my father had tried to train all of us to be unemotional. We were supposed to be tough and inexpressive. Any sign of human emotion was a weakness — in man or woman, boy or girl. In ancient Greece my father might have won praise for his stoicism, but for us it was a lifelong curse.

My mother had been a good mother to us as little children, but she had been browbeaten and brainwashed by the old man to "know her place" in the world. She had learned to be a silent woman and a submissive one for the most part. And she had surmised that "her place" was not so bad after all. "Her place," ultimately, was the simple geography of that kitchen: a stained porcelain sink, an Enterprise oil and wood cookstove, a hardwood table and some metal kitchen chairs with torn vinyl seats. An Irving Oil calendar appeared fresh each December and hung on a nail near the old Inglis refrigerator that had been hand-painted several times to cover up the rust. The floor was ancient linoleum, grey with speckles of red and blue, ugly as someone's thrown-away corduroy pants. But the cupboards were stocked with food: cans of Habitant pea soup, 'Lantic molasses, bags of sugar, gingersnap cookies that the mice would get into in the spring, and an enormous supply of loose King Cole tea leaves in a polished tin — as if my mom was expecting a shortage someday and she was prepared for the calamity.

I confess I never understood my mother, but I think that tea was her one and only vice, if you could call it that. She drank at least seven cups of tea a day, more if she entertained the rare visiting neighbour. We all need *something* to sustain ourselves, I suspect. Some get by with booze or cigarettes or romance novels; maybe it could be sex or love or money or

TV soaps or who knows what? For my mother, tea got her through the day. It doesn't sound like much, does it? But it was what she had and what she made do with. What sustained my father I will never know, unless it was some unhealthy curiosity about what bad luck would come next.

"They're gonna tear down the house anyway," my father told her. "Maybe we can take the bloody kitchen with us."

It was illogical, but I think it was all my mother needed to hear. Alexander Senior had offered at least some small consolation. If not the kitchen, then at least everything in it would go with us to Saint John. There, my mother would try, with great gusto but ultimate failure, to reconstruct her private geography in the city. Maybe all she needed was a small kitchen and a big tin of loose tea. But once a person's sanctuary is dismembered, it can never be reconstructed. Wood and stone and linoleum conspire in magnificent ways in the centre of even the most unhappy families to create order and meaning in the chaos of life. Once the force field collapses, it can never be repaired.

And so the power of the atom that once levelled Hiroshima and sent the citizens of Nagasaki screaming and burning or slowly dying of radiation sickness was the very same power that laid waste to my childhood. Without the grand drama of a nuclear explosion, the atom quietly but with deadly force drove us from the Lords and Ladies of Lepreau and sent the King of Fundy scudding off into space.

There was no freezing rain that winter to glaze the branches in the yard and almost no snow. The ice on our little pond was always too bumpy for easy skating, and yet the driveway was dangerously slippery and smooth. A work site was established down the road, and chain link fences went up. The power plant itself would not be situated in our backyard or very close at all to where our old oil stove sang its clumsy old-fashioned song of heat, but our land would soon be absorbed into the overall compound where heavy water would be stored and spent fuel rods would wait out eternity until they were no longer dangerous. The land would ultimately belong to New Brunswick Power, but the deal was not signed yet, and my father was grim over the fact that, day by day, lawyers were siphoning off money that was rightfully his in order to clear the title to the property.

When the first convoy of protestors arrived that spring, my father ordered us all to ignore them. "Nothing but troublemakers," he insisted. He loathed the Volkswagen van loads of college students from Fredericton and the church wives from Rothesay. "Dangerous people who don't care about nothing but trying to stop progress," he said, referring to the English teachers and organic farmers, folk singers and long-haired idealists who descended upon Point Lepreau to express their dismay over fissionable plutonium and non-renewable energy.

My father went off to work in the woods with his pulp crew, and my mother insisted that we go nowhere near the demonstrations, but Karen and I walked the trails through the woods anyway. We went to the construction site and watched in fascination as these strangers climbed out of their cars and trucks and vans and gathered together with protest signs. We watched them chant and march as if partaking in some ancient, primitive ritual. We saw them laugh and then get angry and shout at construction workers. We saw one bounce his picket sign off the hood of a truck, and then a man in a hard hat got out of the truck and pounded the demonstrator with his fists until other protestors pulled him off.

The protesters set up a little camp farther down the road and slept in tents or in their vans, and, after school each day, Karen and I would secretly study them. On the day the TV cameras arrived, I could not hold Karen back any longer. She was a bright and curious seven-year-old girl who had led an extremely sheltered life. I had not trusted these outsiders at first. It was as if we had been invaded by aliens. But it was becoming clear to me that these outsiders were also our allies, even though they didn't even know who we were. It took Karen to break the ice.

It was an afternoon when the first breath of spring had snaked through the trees, when the first pungent, moist scent of a warming earth found its way to our nostrils. We had seen the first flower of the year, the one called spring beauty, show its brave little head in our backyard, and a lone crocus was about to burst into bloom as well. We followed the deer path through the trees beyond our house and found the demonstrators drinking tea boiled over a small fire of twigs.

"Who are you guys?" a friendly, hippie-looking woman asked Karen, not me.

"We live near here," I said. "But we're moving."

All at once we had an audience. A man who introduced himself as a Unitarian minister said, "You're the reason we're here."

"We are?" Karen asked. She was smiling. She liked these people, although I felt more cautious and defensive.

"They have no right to take away your home and build something that will poison the land and the sea."

"Easy," someone else told the guy. "These are just kids."

"Sorry."

"It's okay," I said. "I know a little about what's gonna

happen here. I feel bad. We all feel bad, but there's nothing anyone can do about it."

A long-haired guy who reminded me of pictures I'd seen of Jesus sat down in the dirt at Karen's feet and looked up at both of us. "No, man. That's why we're here. We believe in the power of people to change things. Don't matter how big. If it's wrong, we're gonna be there and tell it like it is."

I thought this character looked a little frantic around the eyes, a little insane maybe, but Karen reached out and touched his long hair and then giggled.

Everyone laughed. "You kids want a bottle of pop?" somebody offered.

We both nodded and someone handed us each a bottle of Sussex cream soda that tasted like summer. The Unitarian minister offered us some cookies, and after a bit the whole scene felt like a party. As local children who were about to be kicked out of our homes by a nuclear power plant, we were both heroes and martyrs to this crowd.

"We're going to stop this thing from happening," the long-haired guy told me. "We're gonna make them listen."

Since I had been born into a family that believed it was powerless against the larger forces of the world, this guy sounded like a character in a TV show. Here was an exciting and excitable crowd, and once they had offered us a second bottle of pop and another round of pecan cookies, they picked up their placards again and began to walk back and forth in front of the gate.

An RCMP cruiser pulled up, but the Mountie did not get out. He stared at the crowd from behind his closed window and reported back to home base over his radio. Karen wanted us to walk around with the demonstrators, but I said no. I was her protector, and I had seen the fighting here before. The men working inside the fence looked fearsome, although none shouted a word at the protestors. Still, I didn't

139

trust the scene. And even though I admired our new friends, I assumed that each of them was a little bit mad. Everyone knew you couldn't fight the government. It was impossible to change the way things were.

The next day was Saturday: no school. Karen woke me shortly after my father left at five-thirty to spend another weekend day hauling logs out of the New Brunswick woods. My mother had made him breakfast and gone back to bed. "I want to go to the nuclear bomb," Karen said. I opened one eye and saw her face inches away from mine, her eyes wide and alert.

I tried to explain. "It's not a bomb. They're building a nuclear power plant. To make electricity."

"But can we go there? I want to talk to those people."

I wanted to sleep, but I knew my sister wasn't going to go away. "Yeah, okay. Just stay close to me, right?"

"Right."

And so we both got dressed, and we followed the deer track through the misty early-morning woods to the work site. The protestors were already up, and they had the entrance blocked with a Volkswagen van parked sideways. The long-haired guy was just getting out of it, and he punched the air. Everybody cheered.

Then they did a very strange thing. They all gathered together in front of the van and sat down in the muddy roadway leading into the construction site. Some spread old blankets, others just sat in the mud. They began to sing a song I had never heard before, but it sent a chill down my back. When Karen saw an old woman open up a bag of cookies, she tugged me forward. The old woman spread her blanket out further and we sat down beside her.

She held out the bag. "Help yourselves."

And we did. "You kids will have to leave if trouble starts," she said.

Trouble seemed like the furthest thing in the world from this early morning picnic. Everyone seemed so happy and peaceful. "Where'd you all come from?" I asked her.

"Oh, all over. Saint John, Fredericton, Halifax. Some folks here from Montreal and Toronto. They've done this before. Me, I'm new at it. I've always wanted to be at a sit-in."

"What do you do at a sit-in?" Karen asked.

"Sit, I guess. We're trying to make a point."

"Oh," Karen said as I rolled my eyes and frowned a cynical frown I had learned from my father.

Nothing much happened for over an hour. And then a couple of trucks pulled up with construction workers.

"You whiners gonna let us through or what?" one guy with a big bushy beard shouted.

"Sorry, dude," the long-haired Jesus man said. "Not today. Today we're not moving."

The big beard shook his head and left his truck to go talk to the men in the trucks that were stopped behind him. Karen was paying no attention to them but had smoothed the blanket out on the ground. She was holding the hand of the old woman now and smiling up into the sky.

A couple of the workers hammered hard on their truck horns and it frightened me. "Come on, Karen. We have to go."

"No," she said. "I'm staying with my friends."

The old lady smiled but then told her, "Your brother is right. You have to go now. Someone might get hurt."

"Then you need to come with us," Karen said. "I don't want you to get hurt."

She patted Karen's hand and smiled so intensely that her face was an epiphany of wrinkles. "I can take care of myself. So shoo. Go."

I had to drag Karen out of there and off into the woods. A couple of people waved to us. Some gave us a thumbs-up, and the Unitarian minister shouted, "Thanks for coming."

Once we were within the shelter of the dense spruce trees, I relented. I figured it would be okay to stay here, hidden in the trees, and watch what would happened next. At first, none of the workmen tried to move the demonstrators but just shouted angry and obscene insults at them. I tried to cover Karen's ears but she keep pushing me away. When two RCMP cars arrived, four Mounties walked up to the long-haired guy and the Unitarian minister and said they had to leave or they'd be arrested. A CBC camera crew arrived just about then, and everyone began to shout out, "Hell, no, we won't go," even the Unitarian minister. I was holding tightly onto Karen's hand, afraid she might run out to the old lady, who looked upset and uncertain. I was breathing heavily and repeating the slogan I had just heard, repeating it in a whisper as the valiant but foolhardy protestors remained seated in the mud before workers, the Mounties and the TV crew.

When the long-haired guy stood up and shook his fist in the face of one of the RCMP men, however, they grabbed him by the wrists and pushed him down onto the hood of a truck. His hands were handcuffed behind his back as he shouted curses we had never heard at home even in my father's angriest moments.

As another young man walked cautiously towards the Mounties, begging them to go easy on his friend and not to hurt him, one of the workmen in a hard hat tackled the young man, pushed him to the ground and then started beating him. Karen closed her eyes and turned her head away. "They're hurting him," she said. "I'm scared."

I held her more tightly. "Shh, just be quiet or they'll see us."

Two more Mountie cars arrived, and we watched our new

friends try to remain calm as, one by one, they were lifted from where they sat, handcuffed, then led roughly away. Another young man lashed out at a police officer, and I saw the Mountie swing his stick, I heard the crack of wood like the sound of a bat hitting a baseball. The demonstrator was knocked over the head with a night stick a second time and then dragged away.

The workmen just laughed. A police van had arrived, and protesters were being loaded into it. Everyone was shouting now. I held Karen tightly. "They're going to find us," she said. "They're going to take us away, too."

"They won't, I promise. I won't let them." I would protect her somehow. I would make us invisible, or, if I had to, I would run. I would carry her far into the woods where we could not be found. But I was afraid she was about to scream, and if she did, maybe they really would come for us, too. So I gently cupped my hand over her mouth. "Please, Karen, don't make a sound."

It was clear that our protesting friends were not fighters. Some struggled and others went limp as they were dragged away. Some continued to chant, others to sing. Placards were tossed off into the woods. Soon there was no one left sitting in the muddy road. Before the Mounties could stop them, a couple of workmen walked up to the VW van, took it out of gear and then pushed it off into the deep ditch, where it sank into the thick, reddish mud.

I felt Karen's tears on my hands, but I would not let her cry out loud until the police vehicles drove off and the workmen drove through the chain link gates and onto the work site, where someday soon science would unleash the forces within the heart of the atom and fuel a diminished and sorrowful future.

Nineteen

The Saint John streets of my childhood were littered with dead pigeons. I don't know why so many pigeons got run over by trucks and cars, but their corpses were a constant reminder that we had moved into a hostile and treacherous environment. Whenever I took Karen anywhere in that city, I held onto her little hand and made sure we crossed the streets only when it was perfectly safe. I vowed we would not go to our deaths like these incautious birds.

On one of our first forays out into the streets, I remember seeing giant white piles of salt at the edge of the harbour — salt shipped in by barge and stockpiled for use on highways in the winter, I would later learn. Karen asked me if this was the salt "they put in the ocean to make it salty."

"No," I told her. "The sea has its own salt."

"Made by the King of Fundy?"

"Yes," I said, even thought we both knew the King of Fundy was gone.

Once I sneaked up to that white mountain and discovered to my amazement that the salt was all in rock crystal form. Each chunk was magnificent in the sunlight, the way it reflected spears of brilliance, so I collected two pocketfuls and carried them home. My sister and I studied the salt crystals in the sunlight coming through the windows, and then we ate the salt like candy until our throats were dry and raw with thirst.

I went back a second time to collect more salt, but a man working in the highways yard saw me and ran towards me, a shovel in his hand. I raced away as fast as I could, and it wasn't until the following winter, after a massive snow and ice storm, that I saw the pigeons landing in the middle of the streets and eating the small salt rocks sprayed there by the highways trucks. It was only then that I began to believe just how dangerous salt could be.

I never truly ever felt at home in the city of Saint John. Nor did my mother. She never renegotiated a kitchen to her liking. Our chairs and table seemed too big for the tiny new kitchen. It was a dark place, and none of us ever trusted the safety of the gas stove. We all missed the smell of stove oil and burning spruce kindling. Whenever I drank a Sussex soda there or ate gingersnap cookies, I remembered the protestors of Lepreau, and I know Karen did as well.

"I think the protesters were the ones who used to live in the forest," she said to me one day when we were alone overdoing the gingersnaps. Since we had moved to Saint John, I didn't talk about those mythical lords and ladies any more. It all felt a little too ridiculous. A city hardens a boy that way, once he is turfed out of his rural home and the comfortable geography of his imagination is disrupted. I was as displaced as my mother was in her own home.

Home and school were never places where I felt comfortable and so I searched for sanctuary, entering stores, exploring empty warehouses, walking into the train station or poking my nose into churches, hoping to find a place where I felt safe and comfortable. Finally one day, as I ventured down a street that was new to me, I discovered safe haven at last in the public library. I guess I looked wide-eyed or lost or something pitiable enough to bring one of the librarians out from behind her desk. She was a young woman with a round, kind face, and she wanted to know if she could "introduce" me to the library. "Yes, of course," I said. "Please."

She told me that her name was Miss Robichaud and that her uncle was once premier of the province. I don't know why she felt she needed to tell me this.

"Really?" I said, blinking and trying to lift my eyebrows like adults did when they hear important news.

She showed me books, maps, encyclopedias, a collection of records, glass cases of old, rare books, and then more new books and magazines than I thought possible. "Here's today's paper, if you'd like to read it," she said, handing me a copy of the *Telegraph Journal*. "We save every paper from the past year as well, in case you've missed anything you'd like to catch up on."

I guess I looked pretty puzzled.

"We have all kinds of reading material. You know, comics, just about anything." Miss Robichaud was trying very hard to connect with me, and I was sure she didn't have any kids of her own. I don't think she quite knew how to make conversation with anyone my age. But I appreciated her efforts. And I liked her. I liked the library. I liked everything about it: the smell of the books, the lights that hung from the ceiling, the old men sleeping in the leather chairs and the big clock on the wall.

Miss Robichaud was still holding today's newspaper, offering it to me. "What's your sign?" she asked me, turning to the back pages of the paper.

"What do you mean?"

"What's your birthday?"

"March 18," I said. Why would she want to know my birthday?

"Ah. Pisces. I should have guessed." She traced her finger down a column in the paper. "Here it is. Pisces. 'You have put all your fears and worries behind you. Your skies are much less cloudy. Expect great profit to come from your positive efforts today. Ignore all naysayers.' Wow. That sounds like a pretty good horoscope. Here, check it out for yourself. Gotta go."

So I sat on a smooth old leather chair and read my horo-scope for the first time in my life, and I had a new name for what I was. I was a Pisces. And someone who did not even know me had predicted these wonderful things for me today. So I read all the other predictions for the different signs and sadly discovered they were all equally positive. I figured out that Karen must be a Sagittarius, and I tried to memorize her horoscope as well: "You are like sunshine on still waters, yet there is a great depth beneath this surface. Expect news that will make you re-evaluate many things about yourself. Rely on trusted friends. Pisces plays an important role in your life today." That was me, of course. And I began to lose my suspicion of the foolish, good-natured wisdom of astrology.

Just to make the prediction come true, I stopped at a store on my way home and bought Karen some jewellery. It cost me less than fifty cents, but it was like diamonds and pearls to her. Oddly enough, I did not see one dead pigeon on the streets of Saint John on the day I discovered the library.

When I returned to the library the next afternoon, Karen was with me, and this time I had a purpose. Ever since we had met the protestors of Lepreau and watched them get arrested, we had wanted to know more about them. My parents never knew we had been there, and my father would have punished us had he known, limited our freedom in the woods and along the shores. But he was too tired most nights from working in the bush and too busy worrying about how to come out on top in the sale of our home to concern him-self much with his kids.

I found the round-faced librarian, Miss Robichaud, and showed her a piece of paper with a date on it: April 12. "Can I read the paper for April 12 of this year?"

She was surprised and pleased. "No problem. Give me a minute."

Karen and I sat down next to a man who had his head flat on the table. He was asleep and snoring, and Karen was thoroughly amused by the sight. I spread out the paper, slightly yellowed and smelling of must, and studied the front page. Sure enough, here was a picture of the protesters at Lepreau. After studying the photograph, I read the news story over and over several times until I was certain about the names. I took out a pencil and unfolded a piece of lined notebook paper. Karen watched as I wrote the names carefully in my best handwriting: Joe Wood was the long-haired guy who looked a little like Jesus. Muriel Dorworth was the old woman who had given us the cookies. Ben Milligan was the Unitarian minister. There were other names as well, but these were the three who were to become legends of our childhood.

"Joe Wood. Muriel Dorworth. Ben Milligan," I instructed Karen, as I pointed them out in the fuzzy newsprint image of a band of protestors sitting in the mud. "They tried to stop the power plant," I explained. "They would have saved our home and we wouldn't have had to move."

Karen traced her fingers across the newspaper, smudging the ink. Her index finger came to rest on a dark spot on the corner of the photo. *The forest*. Spruce trees. "Us," she said.

"Yeah. We were there. The forest protected us."

"No. You protected us," she said.

I laughed. Many things had been unpleasant in my life, but Karen had been a gift. Maybe some kids don't appreciate a little sister, but I did. I was glad she was with me here in my sanctuary of books and newsprint and old snoring men. It was here that she would be introduced to the writers of the world. Soon she would outstrip me in her reading. For me, books and magazines provided some refuge from bullies and belligerent teachers. But books became Karen's life. They arrived for her in time to refurbish the empty chambers of her imagination, now that we had lost the salty mythology of the Fundy shore. Books would make the going a little bit easier whether I was around when she needed me or not.

Saint John gave us little to savour in those childhood days but I do remember the taste of road salt crystals dissolving on my tongue even after all those years. And I remember the feeling of home in the public library. The cherubic librarian who had led me to newsprint horoscopes had also led me to a touchstone of our own personal history on the day that Lepreau arrived in the media across Canada and even down into Maine. Miss Robichaud and the archived copy of the *Telegraph Journal* she had found for me had given us three names that would be woven into our lives. The hippie, the old woman and the minister had taught us it was worthwhile to believe in a cause, to protest with dignity and kindness, to protect something of value against the tide of progress, and to fight the good fight even if it is a losing battle.

"Joe Wood Muriel Dorworth Ben Milligan," Karen repeated after me to the pigeons bobbing their heads as they strutted around on the front steps of the public library.

"Joe Wood Muriel Dorworth Ben Milligan," I repeated silently to myself as I walked out of police headquarters. The TV crews were gone, but a couple of newspaper reporters asked me what it felt like to be assaulted by the minister of finance. They wanted to know if I was part of some organization, and I tried to be polite, but I realized they were starting to ask me the same things that my interrogators had.

"Look, it was a mistake. He apologized."

"Aren't you angry?"

"I'm angry at the cutbacks to spending on schools, hospitals, health care, special needs."

149

"Are you going to press charges against Chuck Lawrence?"

"No."

"Why not?"

"Why should I?"

"You're going to let it go at that?"

"He said he's sorry. I forgive him for it, really. What I don't forgive him for is hurting other people with what he's done in Ottawa. No one should forgive him for that, no matter what anyone says about the bloody deficit."

But I could tell that the two reporters weren't interested as much in that battle as they were in the scuffle between me and the big shot MP.

"Can you tell us a little more about yourself?"

I saw Cornwallis, Jeff, Rebecca and Gloria coming my way just then.

"Sorry, I gotta go."

I ran towards my friends, and I could see that Gloria had been crying. She put her arms around me and hugged so hard that I couldn't breathe. I turned to see the reporters coming towards us. "C'mon, let's get out of here."

Gloria held onto my hand and wiped tears from her eyes. Rebecca was leading Jeff. Cornwallis asked me, "You feeling okay, Mr. Counsellor?"

"I'm okay."

"Nobody never taught you to defend yourself?"

"I learned everything I needed to know from a bunch of pacifists a long time ago."

"Pacifists always get smacked around. That's my understanding of it."

"I heard him coming at you," Jeff said. "I could sense something about to happen even before it did. I only wish I could have warned you."

"Jeff is very sensitive that way. He really can tell these things," Rebecca said.

"Why did he pick you?" Gloria wanted to know. "Everybody was shouting at him."

I rubbed the spot on my jaw where his fist had connected. "I don't know, Gloria. But I'm glad he did, in a way."

"You like getting hurt? You're crazier than I am."

"No, it's not that. It's just that it all happened so fast. I wasn't scared, and I didn't really get injured, and I think it just might make Lawrence feel a little less cocky about what he's doing."

"Don't fool yourself, Alex. The man's got as much compassion as the concrete in this sidewalk."

"I don't know why, but I still feel good about the whole thing. I see this as a positive event. I really do."

"Gloria," Rebecca said, "you think we should take him to that shrink you see? Maybe he got something scrambled in his brain."

Cornwallis added, "Yeah, they say that when you hit your head like that, your brain crashes like a big meatball into the back of your skull and gets bruised."

"I'm okay," I said. "Really."

"Alex is okay, I can tell," Jeff said.

"How the hell do you know if he's okay?" Cornwallis snapped. "Can't you see his face is all tore up?"

"It is not," Jeff said. "I may be blind, but I know what's going on around me."

"Don't be cruel, Cornwallis," Gloria chided.

I could see that something about the whole incident had stirred up Cornwallis, made him feel angry. Reminders of Africville or other injustices he had seen in his life, maybe.

"Jeff, I've got a surprise for you, son. I've always led you to believe I was a Black man, but I just been messing with your head all this time. I'm actually Italian."

"Sicilian, right?" Jeff came back at him.

"That's right. My mother made my father quit the Mafia when I was just three, though."

"Anybody hungry?" I asked. "Now all I can think about is pizza."

"My people make good food," Cornwallis said.

"Give it up, Cornwallis," Jeff taunted.

"Then you lead us to the food, smartass."

"Fine," Jeff said. And I swear he lifted his head, sniffed the air and pointed southeast. "Corner of Blowers and Grafton is that way. Best pizza in town. Just don't cross the street until the light changes."

We were standing at the foot of the Citadel now, where Brunswick intersects Prince Street. The traffic was heavy and the light was red. "We'd get there quicker if I was driving," Jeff said.

As we stood there on the corner, I was thinking again about New Brunswick, about Lepreau, about Karen, about the lost life of a boy growing up on the Fundy shore. I wanted to tell the story of the demonstrators to my friends, and I wanted to share something I was feeling with Gloria. I had frightened her with what had happened today, and part of me worried again that I was in some way going to shake her mental stability. But now I was beginning to believe that she was much tougher than I had given her credit for. Maybe we all were. And when the light changed and Jeff led the way out across the street in front of the stopped traffic, I pulled Gloria back and kissed her hard on the mouth. She seemed surprised but delighted and she put her arms around me and pulled herself to me.

When Rebecca, Cornwallis and Jeff were on the other side

of Brunswick, the light changed again and they looked back. Cornwallis and Rebecca looked puzzled. A river of cars and trucks passed between us. They would patiently wait for us on the other side, and by the time the light had changed again there was a taste in my mouth. Kissing Gloria had tasted amazingly like Sussex cream soda.

Twenty

I owed Henry Sinclair some kind of an explanation, but I didn't feel like talking about what happened today any more. As I began driving back to the workshop, Cornwallis said he thought I was born to lead a revolution. Jeff wondered out loud if New Dawn might get some additional funding now and be able to stay open, but Rebecca shushed him. There seemed to be an unwritten code at New Dawn that clients didn't talk about the financial problems. We'd all been holding on to the illusion that everything was going to be okay.

In the parking lot at New Dawn, Gloria sat staring straight at the windshield after everyone else had left. I leaned across to kiss her but she pulled back. "Alex, that was all a bit much for me. I'm okay now, I'm pretty sure. Don't worry about me, but back there when I thought something really bad had happened to you, I felt this horrible panic. I felt like I was going to explode."

"God, I'm sorry, Gloria. I didn't mean to do anything to hurt you."

She shook her head. "Alex. You didn't do anything to hurt

me. I'm just still adjusting. Rebecca, Jeff, Cornwallis — they kept their cool. They helped me through it. I don't want to scare you off, though, Alex. You're the best thing that ever happened to me. But what if I discover that this is just a job for you? What if I'm some kind of extracurricular activity?"

I rubbed my eyes and gripped the steering wheel, wondering if I had made a magnificent blunder by getting involved with someone as fragile as Gloria. My old instincts were telling me I had already done some harm and it was time to undertake damage control, make some repairs. Get out while the getting was good to avoid screwing up worse. But I would not follow my old instincts. "Gloria, I love you. I don't know how I let it happen, because I swore I would *not* fall in love again for a long, long time, but you happened. I kept trying to stop myself but I couldn't."

Gloria's eyes looked red as she turned to me. I thought she was going to burst into tears, but she started to smile. She took a deep breath. "I'm sorry Alex. I'm okay now. Hearing you say that changes everything. I guess I just needed reassurance. So, if tomorrow, New Dawn folded — ?"

"I'd still be there." I wouldn't tell her that I was already working for zip, that New Dawn was already virtually bankrupt. Still, we all had hope that something would keep the place going. "Gloria, all my life I've been trying to find someone like you. And I've been trying to find a place where I felt at home. This is it. I intend to hang onto it all. I'm not going to let anyone take it away."

"But maybe your feelings for me are really pity, not love. Have you considered that?"

Even with a distraught face, Gloria was beautiful to me. Actually, I had considered that, but I was sure I felt more. "Gloria, it's not pity. Look, you're talking to a guy who knows pity. Most of my life I've been feeling sorry for myself. I've stopped feeling sorry for myself now and it feels good. A man knocks me down and tries to bust me up and I still don't feel any pity for myself. I feel great. Gloria, you and me — I'll take it at any pace you like. I don't care. I got all the time in the world. You hang in there for me and I'll hang in there for you. We can have a nice long build-up to a healthy relationship, maybe get married when we're ninety. I've got time. Just be there for me."

Gloria let out a long sigh. "I'll be there, Alex. You just have to forgive me if I say anything stupid, or if I have a bad day sometimes. I woke up this morning at about two o'clock and I heard voices — not really voices, you know, just people talking in my dreams. They were telling me to get away from you. They said something bad was going to happen. I wasn't going to tell you this, but I've got to be totally honest with you."

"Hey, who doesn't have dreams with people talking that kind of bullshit? In my dreams I'm still thirteen years old. My father is yelling at me to get out of bed and get ready for school, only I get out of bed and fall on the floor 'cause I don't have any legs. When he hears me fall he comes in and says something stupid like, 'Now look at you. I told you this would happen. It's your own bloody fault!' He slams the door and leaves. I'm on the floor with no legs, trying to roll around to find my pants. You want nutso dreams, how about that?"

"I guess you're right. Listen, someday you're going to have to tell me about your family."

"Someday I will. For the most part, however, I'm trying to forget them. That's why my father arrives yelling and screaming at me in my dreams, I guess. He probably thinks I've got it too easy."

"Alex, I'm okay now. Thanks for being so certain. I think

I'll walk home. I want a nice quiet evening to myself, just settle down. I'll see you tomorrow, okay?"

"I'll drive you."

"No. I want to walk. I'll see you in the morning."

"Bye." I kissed her lightly on the cheek.

I decided I'd better go in and try to explain the whole situation to Sinclair, but he met me at the door. "Cornwallis gave me the full picture." I couldn't tell if he was mad at me or what.

"And?"

"And, if it was me, I would have punched the guy's lights out. I would have made him bleed."

"I'm a pacifist," I said.

"You're also currently a hot property in the news world, my friend. My afternoon has been spent acting as your press secretary."

"Sorry, Henry. I was being held by the police."

"I know. And I saw the TV coverage with that dickweed Lawrence trying to weasel out of the situation."

"Is this gonna be good or bad for New Dawn?"

"I don't know yet. Guess it could go either way. But as far as I'm concerned, we're pretty close to the line anyway. Only thing keeping us here is an absentee landlord who hasn't booted us out yet."

"Maybe the media stuff will do us some good. But don't give me any credit. I never meant for any of this to happen. I was an innocent bystander."

"That's what we all think until we find we're in the midst of some crisis. Then you realize that there are no innocent bystanders. We're all players. If this was a poker game, I'd say you were the wild card."

"Hey, thanks. I like that."

"Buy you a beer?"

"No, thanks. I want to get out into the country and go for a hike. I don't want to be anywhere the media can find me tonight. I just need some space."

"Good man. I know the feeling. See you tomorrow?"

"You bet."

Underneath the driver's seat I'd been carrying around a couple of topographical maps I'd bought at the government bookstore on Hollis Street. I pulled one out and studied a section of the Eastern Shore until I zeroed in on some cliffs I'd noticed at the edge of Parker's Lake, maybe thirty miles east of Burnside. Parker's Lake was one of those long, narrow bodies of water, grooves in the land left by the retreat of the last glaciers. It had once been an arm of the sea, but now it was attached to it by a thin inlet barely wide enough for a small boat. When the big invasion of polar ice retreated, the land was left strewn with boulders and dollops of red mud known as drumlins. My guess is that Parker's Lake had been buried under a massive wall of ice that scraped through the valley and carved away at the land, leaving a high wall of barren rock on its eastern side. At its steepest point, this wall of rock even had a name on the map: Devil's Loft.

I drove east, away from the Dartmouth and Cole Harbour suburbs and on toward the great expanse of spruce forest on the Eastern Shore. When I came to the turn-off near Parker's Lake I drove north —inland — on a muddy, rutted, granite-strewn roadway until I came to the end, then hiked further north on a trail along the east side of the lake until the trail gave out. Before me giant chunks of rock lay jumbled like kids' building blocks on a floor. Rocks had been toppling off the cliffs for eons, I supposed, and they rested in crazy abandon, some the size of televisions or toasters, others as big as my Dodge Shadow, still others as large as houses. Each was adorned with orange and grey lichen. Some were locked into place, others wobbled as I stepped upon them. Along the edge of the lake, I hopped from stone to stone, stopping sometimes to marvel at the pattern of the psychedelic-bright lichen that grew on the dull grey granite surface. The water below the rocks looked dark and sinister but clear and clean as well. I leaned over, cupped my hand and drank healing gulps, but when I sat upright again, I felt the familiar pain in my chest.

Stress. That's what I always chalked it up to. Or maybe some aftermath from the bully MP. I splashed water on my face and rested my back against a giant boulder, a mammoth, near-perfect cube of a rock. Braced like that, I closed my eyes and felt my breathing go short. A slight twinge of something again in my chest, not pain this time, just a funny sort of vibration. And then I began to sweat.

All my life I had experienced funny little twinges of pain in the chest, or this same aggravating fluttery feeling. Once, when I had been a junior in high school, I had passed out in a math class for no apparent reason. The doctor had called that stress as well and suggested further testing, but my father insisted it wasn't necessary. I could not have agreed more heartily with him. My experiences with doctors and hospitals had left me with the conviction they were both part of an evil conspiracy of pain and suffering.

So I closed my eyes, rested, drifted. I was on the second floor of the Saint John Library, safe haven. Karen was with me. We were sitting on a floor that was a mesh metal grating. We could see the people reading at tables below us. We were looking at a book about the natural history of the Maritimes: pictures of whales, cliffs of basalt along the Fundy shore, and page after page of seabirds and fishes. On one page we came across a picture of porpoises swimming in a pod in the Bay of Fundy. Beneath the picture, the caption read, "Just off the coast of Point Lepreau, New Brunswick." And then Karen turned the page quickly, pretending she had not noticed. Later, she said she was afraid it would remind me of home and make me feel bad. Karen said she hated to see me sad, and it was her job to make sure nothing ever upset me.

Twenty-one

Being alone can be exquisite, as long as you're alone by your own volition. I experienced my worst loneliness during the time I was a teenager. The years fourteen through eighteen. Years of alienation. I survived those years, and that alone is a miracle, but there are scars. Saint John cannot be forgiven for the loneliness I felt, nor can my family. The world at large was a hostile place and I woke up nights in primal fear of it. Nothing was safe, nothing could be trusted. My father was more enemy than confederate. My mother, I believe, wanted to soothe my pain, but she could not rise above her own misery.

My imagination was both friend and foe, but more often than not it was my only refuge. Alone in my room at night, I lived in a fully remembered past, a past embellished with beauty. Those conjured sunny days on the shores of Fundy were long and delightful. The forest, the sea and the sky were full of happy surprises on those endless summer afternoons.

From the Saint John Library I had begun to borrow science fiction books, and I became a huge fan of stories about travelling faster than the speed of light and any others that involved time travel. My own life, I began to believe, could exist on many alternate time lines. I could travel back to any point in my past and take a different arc to my present, to the future that might have been had things gone otherwise. In my alternate lives, I was never alone.

Today, however, enchanted by the rocks beneath me, I savoured the quality of being alone by choice. To my back was the high cliff called Devil's Loft, and it was my desire to climb to the top and then just sit there and stare down the setting sun. No newspaper interviewers would find me here, no TV cameras would chart my progress up the rock face. Since arriving in Halifax, my life had been a roller-coaster ride of change. This evening I would pause, breathe the spruce and pine scented air deeply, "collect my thoughts" as my mother used to say. Thoughts, apparently, could scatter, race away, sometimes get lost like loose chickens, straying too far from their roost. Now I would take my time to call together all those wild birds and make sense of my re-invented life.

I stepped from boulder to boulder in the wonderful rubble that seemed like the fallen blocks of some ruined pyramid. Each stone appeared to have been carved square with fastidious precision, and I loved the lichen and the tufts of moss that looked like small, furry green animals. I could hear the birds singing from the trees and from the sky, and when I looked up, I saw the outstretched, motionless wings of an osprey. It stirred a powerful feeling deep down inside me, something reminiscent of the first elevating fiddle riff in a beautiful yet sad Cape Breton lament.

When I came flush against a granite wall, I angled my way up a crease in the stone, hands gripping the rugged face of this rock that had once battled the invading ice and held firm, stubborn as only stone can be against those monumental forces. Gnarled pine and spruce trees, stunted into bonsai, grew out of small islands of soil here and there. Hardwood saplings grew here as well, and vine-like roots crawled across stone to find sustenance in minuscule pockets of earth. I quickly learned which ones I could trust for handholds and which ones I could not.

I saw the peak high above me, but I could not ascend directly up the steep wall. I had left my topographical maps behind, but I was sure that by cautious exploration I would find a safe route to the summit.

I struck on several dead ends where the footing was too precarious. Then I savoured the grace of turning back at the limit of a bad decision and allowing caution to temper my plans. Once when I trusted a living root it snapped free in my hand, and I hugged tight against the stone face, leaning with all my weight into it to avoid catapulting back and outward and falling through the sky into the canopy of trees below.

A chasm halfway up insisted I backtrack nearly halfway down the slope before beginning to rise again. I took my time about it, descending into the cool afternoon forest where squirrels chattered and ravens announced my intrusion. Lady slippers bloomed on the lush forest floor in cerebral purple and white, and I found myself speaking to them as my sister had done when we'd come across these exotic beauties in the forest of Lepreau.

When I began to climb a new path, my breath was ragged,

and I felt the return of that cloying twinge in my chest. I snaked a gulley toward the summit, bracing my legs on either side. I believed that my hike to the summit of the Devil's Loft was a cautious one, just shy of true danger, but each step, each decision felt like some sort of test. How far does one push himself beyond his realm of common knowledge and comfort before he is in danger?

My move to Nova Scotia was intended to be adventure, the adventure I had missed out on all my life. I had been harbouring a ridiculous list in my head. I would learn to ride a motorcycle, surf, hang glide, ski, jump from airplanes with parachutes. I would meet many women and lure them to my bed. I would erase every sheepish cell in my body and replace them with cells fine-tuned to vigour and daring. I would take chances and break out of my shell. I would live.

But my job at New Dawn and my introduction to Gloria had taught me that such things are frivolous, immature and of little consequence. As I tested the fortitude of a small, woody bush as a handhold to get me up onto a sun-drenched ledge, I realized that the commitment I had made to New Dawn, to the people of New Dawn, was far more daring. For once in my life I had made a bold, positive decision. I was the only counsellor for a sheltered workshop about to go belly up. My pay had diminished from the start from minimum wage to nothing at all and yet I felt as if I had been promoted to the highest rank. Someday soon I would have to figure out how to keep myself and pay back the money I owed my mother. It would be difficult to explain to her why I was working for nothing. But "nothing" is a frivolous word. Henry Sinclair and my clients at New Dawn had paid me in capital of inestimable value.

The ledge was flat and warm, and three small lizards allowed me space to breathe and rest. I lay my cheek to the smooth, polished granite and felt the sun's heat stored there, felt the rock allowing me to drift as I closed my eyes, felt small dizzy circles behind my eyelids, and then detected the shadow of a large bird soaring over me. When I opened my eyes, however, I saw neither hawk nor osprey. Maybe it had just been a cloud.

I had no water with me and I was thirsty. In my pocket was one lone piece of Trident chewing gum, my Roger stash. I opted instead for a small round pebble, placed it on my tongue like a sacrament and sucked on it until it seemed to release water into my parched mouth. The stone tasted sweetly of summer, a compression of every summer that I had lived as a child in the country. In the city, I had given up on sucking stones after the lessons of road salt.

I almost laughed out loud to think that somewhere right now, TV viewers were watching repeat footage of my being struck down by the minster of finance. As I sat up, I felt the side of my face, warm but also imprinted with creases from the rock. It felt like a three-dimensional road map, and it occurred to me that if I had a mirror, I could have seen the highways into my own future. I studied the sky and the remaining wall of rock above me, pocked and irregular, steep but not impossible to climb.

Footholds and hand grips allowed me a slow but certain ascent. I would trust no plant or root, only rock, and each time I gripped stone with my fingertips I tested twice before hefting my weight upward. My rule was now of threes: since I had given up on finding any totally safe and easy way around the front face of the summit, I would insure that at least three of my four appendages had solid grip before moving up. This policy failed me only once as I neared the final plateau, when I lost both feet to crumbling stone that had appeared solid. I was down to two clawed hands for purchase on the Devil's Loft, but my fingers held firm while my feet danced in the air long enough to remind me of my mortality.

At the top, I stood up slowly and embraced the blue sky above me. No Everest, this climb, yet I was several hundred feet above the flashing beauty of the lake below. I had enough altitude to mark my spirit for a lifetime, and I could not believe I had never before in my life done a thing as great and as simple. What else was there that was waiting to be done? Simple adventures that I had been too timid to undertake? Not the plane jumping or jet skiing, but the smaller, gladder challenges that any man or woman is capable of undertaking.

I could see only as far as the next ridge on the other side of Parker's Lake, but the valley and water beneath me was a clean, orderly place, a fitting place for imaginary kingdoms. My breathing was erratic and hesitant now, and my heart thumped in my ears like a ragged drumbeat. My eyes shifted frames unaccountably, and a wave of dizziness swept across the expanse inside my head, but these were not unfamiliar reminders of my own frailty. I was never what you'd call a healthy person, but my father had taught me that complaining of physical infirmities served no purpose at all.

I had to widen my stance to keep my footing, and finally I gave in to the will of gravity and sat down, lest I wobble and topple over the edge. I closed my eyes to steady my interior landscape, and when I opened them again I saw the world was still there, as beautiful as before. More than ever, I felt Karen sitting beside me. If I did not move, I was certain I could see her out of the corner of my eye. And I dare not move or she would disappear. I wanted the world to freeze in the present. I wanted the sun to stop sinking towards the top of the western ridge and be still in the sky.

I had come to this: my perfect hiatus in the middle of two

lives — the Alex I once was and the Alex I was becoming. And I gave thanks to the empty heavens that Karen was here to attend my moment. I swaddled the pain of her memory with the beauty that surrounded me so I could forge that aching love into something other than horror. I would not give up my current happiness, for it had been too long arriving. Karen was not asking me to re-enter that old kingdom. I breathed deeply, but it seemed my lungs could not extract enough oxygen from the air. It was not the altitude. This was Nova Scotia, not some Rocky Mountain precipice. But something was happening to me, and I could not tell if it was physical, psychological or transcendental. I was here, but I was not here.

My eyes were closed and the sun was directly before me. I felt that shadow pass over me again, but I did not try to look up. The insides of my eyelids were a warm blush of red. A slight zephyr pushed up the mountain face, and I smelled pine and warm earth and the essential odours of life in the natural world. I felt as if a weight were lifting from the top of my head and wondered if I was about to have some kind of out-of-body experience. I reached my hand out to the side, involuntarily perhaps, still half-believing Karen was there. I imagined my hand had become a bird, and it began to fly off, away from my body. It took great effort to bring it back.

And then such pressure built up inside my chest that I had trouble breathing at all. Something was squeezing me, some invisible force, and I could not decide if I should be afraid or merely curious. I did not believe in devils, but angels remained a possibility. As the pressure grew I felt myself moving and wanted to open my eyes. Was I rising or falling? Ascending to the heavens, or falling from the cliffs to the rocks below, where my corpse would rot and nourish next season's lady slippers?

If I could only have found the strength to raise my eyelids then, I might have wrestled myself back into this world, but instead I knew that something was terribly wrong. Something physical. The dark shadow appeared again from behind my eyelids and this time it hovered; it did not merely sail on by. My fingers and toes grew numb, and the numbness swept up through my body like a dark incoming evening tide. The world of light was all around me, but I was no longer part of it. Every event of the day, every event of my life suddenly seemed ever so distant.

It was not the first time in my life that I had passed out from exercise, but this was different. On that early evening in Nova Scotia in June, I had before me a precipice, but my body had stationed itself on a large flat slab of rock that was well planted in the bedrock of the planet. As I slipped sideways before the setting sun, I did not have far to fall from my sitting position. My body was met by a well-prepared bed of dry grey moss left over from rainier seasons. I fell into darkness and the world went on without me.

When I awoke it was night — still and clear — and as my eyes opened I did not move until I had negotiated with arms and legs to prove to myself that I was still truly alive. I flexed the fingers of my right hand. I touched my face. I curled my toes within my running shoes. I reached out to touch the still-warm rock beneath me. I was lying on my side, and I did not get up for several long, uncertain seconds. Cautiously, I first rolled onto my back and looked up into the night sky. I shivered, not so much from the evening chill but from the fact that I was uncertain just then if I was looking up or down. Reason came back from retirement to assure me I was looking up, and I could not deny the beauty of the night, despite my confusion.

I was alive, I knew that. I was not dead. The slight pain in my chest seemed inconsequential. I felt the full flood of air rushing into and out of my lungs. I lay still and allowed myself to be dazzled by the stars that seemed to reach out to me with penetrating power. The Milky Way was a simmering bridge above me. Satellites traced their courses like miniature glowing fireflies across the heavens. Orion gave me the reassurance that I must still be here on earth. Where I sat was a place of stunning night, but above me was a canopy of space where the stars had bullied darkness away. I felt bravely insignificant as I tried to piece together my identity and my plight.

I remembered the climb, I remembered some small physical discomfort and the fact that I had passed out here on the ledge, far above Parker's Lake. I remembered the joy of being alone, but now it had fermented into a powerful longing to be part of the busy human world again. I wanted very much to go back down the mountain and find my bed in my Breton Street apartment. But I knew that if I was foolish enough to attempt a trek back down the rock face and through the steep sloping forest below, I might kill myself.

I sat up and reached out in all directions but felt nothing. Finally the sound of the wind and its caress upon my face convinced me which way lay danger. I crawled away from the cliff edge on all fours and came across a single large boulder the size of an elephant that would be my companion here on this mountain top. The light breeze was cool to me now, and I scurried around to the lee side and tucked in low. I was very hungry and studied the menu of chewing gum with my fingers, finally admitting it was the best I could do. I loosened the paper and let the gum touch my tongue. I was amazed at how different something can taste in the dark.

Part of me wanted to leave here very badly. Surely there must be another way down this mountain other than the way I came up. But what if I passed out a second time? Or what if I simply slipped? The adage "discretion is the better part of valour" came into my head, and I remembered it was one of Mrs. Robichaud's sayings. I thanked her silently for those words of wisdom, chewed my gum and ran my hand across the elephantine boulder, my twenty-five-million-year-old companion.

I could have had less friendly roommates, but even at that, it was a long, chilly night beneath those blazing stars. There was no moon, for which I should be thankful, because I might have been tempted to trek down the mountain and died in the process. I would not permit myself to take full account of the news my body had delivered to me, for now I felt reasonably well, and I convinced myself that this was another in my recent series of adventures. Alone on a mountaintop in Nova Scotia on a fine, clear summer night. No blackflies, no mosquitoes. Just me and my rock and a hundred million winking stars.

Twenty-two

I want to tell you that when I drove to work the next morning, the world was a bright, cheerful place, that it was the first day of the rest of my life. But it wasn't.

Although the day was warm for Nova Scotia, dark, brooding clouds and a damp breeze were blowing in from the south. A North Atlantic storm was brewing at sea, fuelled by tropical warmth and the eternal promise of summer that was the Gulf Stream, a promise that veered east just south of Sable Island and robbed this place of a truly warm oceanic spirit.

I had slept fitfully, for how else does one sleep on bare rock? My bones hurt, and my head hurt from the politician's assault. I felt that both the natural world and the political one had treated me badly, but, in truth, the rocks of Devil's Loft had been reasonably kind to me. I am sure there are many worse motels than the one I had just slept in. No wild creatures had troubled my sleep and in the morning I was awakened by ravens sitting on the branches of scrubby, wind-sculpted trees. The view from my rocky loft was muted by the grey light but impressive enough to allow me to stop feeling sorry for myself. Nonetheless, I felt both haunted and hunted.

Whatever was physically wrong with me, it had to be something minor. Any doctor could have suggested that it was the result of a fairly traumatic day. After all, hadn't I been attacked, then arrested, interrogated, thrown to the media wolves, and then gone hiking and pushed myself somewhat beyond my abilities?

Yes. All of the above. Now, having slept the night outdoors, I felt a little rough around the edges. That was all. I was as hungry as the ravens around me. Hungrier. Hunger meant I was healthy and alive. Somewhere down there in the human world, coffee was brewing at a Tim Horton's. There were eggs being fried and bagels and croissants. I looked around me for some fresh berries, but the best I could find was a low bush of green blueberries. They were sour and hard. It was time for man to descend.

I scouted the ridge until I found a fairly gentle path: there had been an easier route to the summit after all, and it was well littered with cigarette butts, pop cans and potato chip bags. There were only a couple of tricky narrow ledges along the way where I had to squeeze in against the rock face and trust some trailing tree roots for handholds. It was a longer hike in distance but infinitely easier, and I felt a mild disappointment that the summit was so attainable by anyone who knew the path. At the bottom of the hill I crossed again over the jumble of massive cube boulders and, in my haste, nearly tripped and fell down between two rocks the size of school buses. My car was where I left it, and I found myself driving at breakneck speed down the pot-holed gravel road that led back to civilization. The craving for coffee and food was almost obsessive. It was only seven-thirty.

By the time I arrived at New Dawn it was nine-thirty. I had gone home to Brenton Street, showered, shaved, emptied my refrigerator and was still only half an hour late for work.

Everyone in the work room gave me a round of applause and hoots as I walked in. "Show them the bruises," Jeff said.

"No damage at all," I replied. "You know how the media likes to exaggerate."

"I would have punched his lights out," Roger said. This from a cop who once served as a security escort for Brian Mulroney through the streets of Montreal on St. Jean Baptiste Day.

Cornwallis gave me a thumbs-up and Rebecca touched my

hand as I passed her. "If I'd a known there'd be fisticuffs, I would have come for sure," Scotty said. "I don't get no fun of that sort at all any more."

Jules was out of my vision, but I heard the first few bars of Beethoven's Sixth played in an electronic mimicry of wind chimes.

I said hi to Doris and Steve and held each of their hands. Steve's tremors were powerful, and I wondered what it would be like to live in such constant warfare with one's own body. I adjusted his glasses and told him it was good to be back. Doris lit up like a candle on a dark night and adjusted her hearing aids until they let out a long shrill squeal that seemed to fit satisfactorily into Beethoven's melody.

Gloria was writing in a notebook, off in a corner of the room by herself near the bookshelves, the small idiosyncratic "library" that included Abraham Lincoln's biography, a selection of Leo Buscaglia books, poetry by Dylan Thomas, Alden Nowlan and Irving Layton, and field guides to birds, mushrooms and sea shells, as well as a complete set of the *Encyclopedia of Religion*. She had watched me enter the room but had continued to write in her notebook as I greeted everyone.

"Maybe I shouldn't interrupt," I said by way of hello.

She looked up at me, her eyes dancing. "No, it's all right. I'm writing a poem about you. You are the poem."

I realized then that Gloria was more important than a thousand other things in my life. And yet I was puzzled by the look on her face. Something akin to madness, but it was most certainly joy.

"I discovered this place I want to take you," I said. "You'll love it. It's like another world. I slept last night on top of this look-off. It was incredible." My enthusiasm was partially a lie. I wanted this version to mask what had happened to me.

What happened on that mountain top had scared me to the bottom-most depths of my being, but I had vowed never again to allow fear to rule my life.

"Great. I want to go there with you. Look, I want you to read this."

She handed me her notebook. On the page was what looked to be a fairly simple poem in her ornate handwriting:

On up he climbed
the grain of rock to his touch
like the fingerprints of earth
the path a test of stone and beauty,
a gamble of sky and gravity.
The water below, the sky approving above
each breath a gift of growing into
and above the limits of what we know.

"When did you write this?"

"Just now, before you came in the room. It's not quite right, but it's close."

"It's very close, but how did you know?"

"I know things. It's not like being psychic, really. I don't read minds, but I have images, and when I sit down to write a poem, the images are the poem. In this case, you were the poem. I saw through your eyes. I think I saw this yesterday, but I didn't connect the images until I saw your car pull up outside. It's both scary and wonderful."

"I'll settle for the wonderful part. Gloria, you keep surprising me. You are unlike any person I've ever known. I can't figure you out."

"What's there to figure?"

"You're right. I was taught by my parents to put everything into categories, to make sense of everything. I think everything I learned in university was the same. And it was all wrong. You defy categories and labels."

"And that's bad?"

"No. Not at all. I think you're just way ahead of me. While the rest of us use langauge to put everything into some stupid sort of order, you use language to open everything back up."

"Language and experience can be the same thing."

"See, there you go again. Light years ahead of where I am. I don't understand why you're not, like, some famous poet or philosopher or something."

"You've looked in my file."

I felt embarrassed again and did not want to resume the mantle of counsellor. "Yes, but that file doesn't seem to have anything to do with *who* you are."

"Who am I?"

"In another time you might have been a famous poet or a visionary, a religious leader. Today, people don't know what to make of you so they give you labels."

"Schizophrenic. It's not a very pretty word."

"No, it isn't. I think it's just a word to use when someone acts differently, when someone has stronger feelings, when their understanding of the world is different from what is comfortable."

"Words can work for you or they can work against you. It all depends on who's using them. I keep a journal, too. I keep track of everything. Words have helped me heal more than any doctor. I have several volumes. I began a new one the day I met you."

"Why?"

"New beginnings. New story. Who knows where it will go?"

"Can I read it some time?"

"I think so. But not right away. Later. We need time first."

"Sure. We've got all the time in the world."

I realized the others in the room were watching just then but I didn't care. I had no enemies here. I had only family. They all knew how I felt about Gloria, and not one of them cared about the so-called rules of professionalism that I should have been abiding by. "Gloria, I'm not sure which one of us should be the client and which one the counsellor. I think you'd be better at this job than I am."

"Thanks for the compliment, Alex. I have some insight that most people don't have, I agree, but you're the healer."

The word came as a bit of a shock. "Counsellor" had felt awkward but eventually comfortable. But "healer" was something else. "Gloria, I don't feel like a healer."

"But you are. They all know it. Henry Sinclair knows it. And that was what yesterday was all about. It was part of the healing process. What you did was helping to heal a society with no compassion. Chuck Lawrence knew that, and that's precisely why he attacked you. I was watching. I could see something happening between him and you before he touched you. It scared me. I was afraid you were really hurt, but then when I saw you on TV, I understood how it had all worked out."

"Phew. Gloria, come on back down to earth. I love the thought of being some kind of martyr for Canadian TV, but I didn't really *do* much of anything."

"That's where you're wrong. You should have heard the commentaries. I think people across the country had felt like victims for so long, and when the minister of finance actually took a swipe at you, they identified with you in a big way. Then when they heard what you said, the way you spoke to him there on the steps of the police station, they were ready to elect you prime minister."

"I don't want to be prime minster."

"I know. All you want to be is a good healer."

"Your words, not mine."

Gloria touched my hair and then my cheek. I felt my breath catch in my throat and my eyes begin to go funny again. "Go talk to Henry. He's waiting for you. I've got another poem I'd like to write."

"What's this one about?"

She closed her eyes as if looking for the information. "It's about stars, that's all I know."

"Make it a good one."

I tapped gently on Sinclair's door and the glass rattled in its frame. "Come on in."

"It's me."

"The hero returns," Sinclair said but I could not quite get a reading on the tone of this voice.

"Not exactly."

Henry shook his head and smiled. "I knew there was something unusual about you, Alex, the first time you walked in through the door."

"Look, I was more victim of circumstance than anything. Don't get the wrong idea that I'm a crusader or something."

"Modesty. I like that."

"Thanks. But I don't really believe any of what happened yesterday is gonna do anybody a bit of good."

"Well, you might be right there, but you had your Andy Warhol — your thirty seconds or whatever it was of fame — and it *should* be good for something. I stayed here last night until about nine o'clock, and even then people kept calling. Seems nobody could track you down, but they knew where you worked."

I cringed. "Sorry about that, chief."

175

"No problem. It was actually pretty interesting . . . as a learning experience for me. But I should tell you, another security guy from the federal government arrived unannounced and walked into my office. Very shiny shoes, black-rimmed glasses. Said he was pretty sure you were clean, that it was all a misunderstanding, but he wanted to know if you had a drug problem or if you were a homosexual. Then he wanted to know if you were a good employee."

"What did you tell him?"

"Told him you were clean but that he had no right to concern himself with your sexual preference, that it had nothing to do with federal security. Then I told him you were the finest employee I had ever known."

"Did you tell him I was working for free?"

"I didn't think he needed to hear that. But he didn't stay long. He seemed satisfied and he left. That's when the media barrage hit again. Bunch of phone calls. It was still early in BC, and apparently you were good copy even on the West Coast. You were smart to stay wherever you were, although Canada was gravely disappointed that you weren't available. I guess you don't care for that sort of thing."

"No, not really. I just needed a little breathing space."

"A wise move. You want to take the day off to decompress a bit more?"

"No, I'm okay."

"Good, I was hoping you were going to say that, and if you hadn't I would have talked you into staying anyway. We're going to have company in about half an hour."

"More media stuff?"

"Nope. I think the media has already decided that yesterday's story is yesterday's story. Some big demonstration today in Toronto with striking workers or something. You're a has-been."

"Guess that's better than a never-was. Then who's on the guest list?"

"Provincial deputy minster of social services. His boss watched the TV. I think it reminded him that we were still in existence."

"Oh, shit."

"Oh, shit is right. Our funding has technically run out, but we're coasting because of some bureaucratic error. Mind you, we'd already been cut way back, but we had enough to pay for lights and phones and transportation for our clients. The guy who owns this place has been off in the Cayman Islands for three months and hasn't been handy to give us the boot. It was a nice string of circumstances in our favour."

"Until I ended up on TV and they traced me to New Dawn?"

"Not your fault, Alex. I'm not blaming you."

"But now what?"

"Now, Lance McCully — the deputy minster — is coming to check us out. I guess I don't have to remind you that he and Chuck belong to the same political party. Federal, provincial, they all wipe each other's bums when necessary. All I can figure out is that if he comes and doesn't like what he sees, he's going to blame it on you — lunatic fringe and all that — then use you as a good reason for closing us down. If he likes what he sees, then he might give us some special status and keep us going as goodwill and a further apology for what happened yesterday. Maybe make the party look a little more compassionate as well. I'm guessing here, but look at the timing. It could swing either way, depending on which direction would make his party look good."

"I hate this," I said.

Sinclair flattened his hands on the desk in front of him, then scratched his jaw in three different places. "Come on, Alex, I'm counting on you. I have no idea why Lance McCully is coming here, but deputy ministers don't usually come a-calling for no reason. I expect the worst, I can't lie to you. McCully is political. You made one of his role-models look bad. I just don't think he's gonna like us. All I've got is you out there in the work room with people doing what? Taping cardboard boxes and making copper trinkets? We're not high tech. We're not cutting edge. We're nothing."

"Henry, I don't want you to lose this place. *I* don't want to lose this place. New Dawn and everyone here mean a lot to me. I haven't had much of anything good in my life in the last ten years. I *need* this place."

I felt nauseous and wobbly, and not just because of our discussion. Whatever happened to me up on the mountain yesterday was not something I could pretend didn't happen. For a brief instant I felt as if I would throw up.

Henry leaned across his desk. "You all right?"

I gulped. "Yes. I'm fine. It's just . . . well, what I said. I don't want to lose this place."

"Neither do I, dammit. So we put a truly brave face on, lad. We tell everybody working today what's up, and we impress the hell out of McCully. If it looks like he's going to give us a bad report card by the time he leaves, we beat the shit out of him."

Twenty-three

I have never been very good at being tested. Written tests in school or university were often painful experiences for me, and graded classroom presentations were even worse. I had always been among the legion more fearful of speaking in public than of outright death. Amazingly, I had performed my little thirty-second speech outside the police department with dignity and courage, but I did a poor job of trying to explain the gravity of our situation to everyone in the work room. What was it I was asking of them, anyway? To work harder, to give their own little sermons in praise of New Dawn to McCully? No, in the end, my best advice was to be themselves and try to be polite.

Scotty and Cornwallis didn't like the intrusion of another asshole in a suit, and they let me know it. Cornwallis said, "You know what being polite got for my father in Africville, don't you? And you know how I feel about this particular government. I'll be doing real good if I can keep from spitting in his face."

"Don't spit," I said. "It would look bad."

"I hate all the bloody bastards," Scotty said. He used to be a union hell-raiser in his longshoreman days. Having these two old guys together during a government visit was like leaving the matches by the kerosene, but all I could say was, "I'm counting on you to be cool."

"We be cool," Cornwallis said, but I didn't like the look in his eyes.

When Lance McCully arrived, he was wearing a dark business suit and he had three suck-up cronies with him, but he did not look like a man about to close us down. Maybe he'd had a good enema the night before or had just discovered that his pension had been pumped up by the province, I don't know. But he was a man with a glow, superficial for sure but kind of infectious.

"Got any gum?" Roger was the first off the mark.

Lance didn't, but his outside man produced a full pack of Spearmint, making Roger the happiest ex-cop in the history of the Montreal police force.

We were off to a good start. That's when Rebecca gave Jules the cue to play music. It wasn't exactly "Pomp and Circumstance," but it was a tarted-up version of "Ode to Joy," and who could resist a little lift with that in the air? Henry Sinclair raised an eyebrow at me. The music had been Gloria's idea, not mine, but I thought it couldn't hurt. McCully was smiling. He leaned over and asked me if Jules was really playing or if it was just a recording.

"It's real," I said in my most mannerly voice. "Everything you see here is the real thing. We may be small, but we like to think we're on the cutting edge of work therapy for those with special needs."

The henchmen were impressed and Lance seemed more than a little curious.

"It's part of a program involving music, writing, art and occupational upgrading. Productivity is up, results are good all around. Once we have our latest raw data processed, we expect to sell the training package to similar institutions in the States and in Europe." Way out of my depth, I gladly dived into the murky waters of pseudo-political bullshit. Sinclair placed his hands together in front of his face as if he were praying, although he had declared to me that he was both a humanist and an atheist and that these two concepts made a perfectly logical marriage.

"Where do they go once they've graduated from this program?" Lance asked. "How many of them find jobs?"

I knew there was no sensible answer to this question. Hell, as far as I could tell, no one graduated to go anywhere. This was an end unto itself. Work, friends, a safe haven in which to spend days, learn skills, be productive, explore. Sinclair was terribly afraid I was going to open my mouth so he spoke first.

"Mr. McCully, New Dawn has been in existence for eight years now. We have received Burnside Industrial Park's award for community achievement three times. We subcontract with three of the biggest firms in the park. We're more interested, however, in creating jobs right here rather than sending our clients out to compete for places in an already overcrowded workforce."

This workforce tour-de-force duly impressed McCully. Everyone else in the room seemed uncomfortable, but as Jules played his final chord and returned to the bench by Rebecca to package computer software, I felt confident that things were going to be okay. Rebecca introduced herself, and McCully spoke to her as if addressing a small child, shouting and enunciating every syllable.

Doris and Steve had continued to simply stare out the window, pretending none of us was there at all. Now I saw Doris open Steve's favourite book, Steven Hawking's *A Brief History of Time*, and begin to read aloud.

Jeff was packaging today as well, performing his task smoothly and automatically. He wore his Walkman and was mouthing the lyrics to a Red Hot Chili Peppers song.

"What's his situation?" Lance whispered to me.

"He's blind," I said matter-of-factly.

"But he's a fine driver," Rebecca chimed in, having overheard our conversation. McCully looked baffled.

"It's a standing joke," Sinclair said.

As we made our way around the room, I despised the way this visitation felt like a test. Everyone was supposed to perform for the guest in some way or other. Why exactly was he here, anyway?

Scotty and Cornwallis looked surly but kept quiet when I introduced them to McCully.

"It's good to see that you include people of colour in your program," Lance said with fashionable political correctness.

Cornwallis cleared his throat and picked up the hot soldering iron by his hand, but Scotty immediately snatched it away and pretended to be soldering down a connection on the inside of the dismembered VCR before him.

Gloria was perhaps the unhappiest of all of us. She hated being inspected. "She's a fine writer," I said to McCully. Gloria glared at me.

"What are you working on today?" he asked, again as if addressing a small child.

"It's something private, I assure you," she said, her voice hard as ice.

McCully took the hint and we moved on. "And the reason *she* is here?" he asked Sinclair, a bit too loudly for my liking.

Henry swallowed hard and in a low voice said, "Schizophrenia. She's come a very long way."

When I looked back at Gloria, she had venom in her eyes. These outside agitators had suddenly created a new barrier between us. There were only professionals and people with problems in this room. I had chosen my side, as necessary, and I didn't like the feeling at all.

McCully and his flunkies retired to Henry's office for coffee, and I was left to do damage control with my friends in the work room.

"I'm sorry, Gloria," I said. "I hated that."

Gloria was silent.

182

"Can you read to me what you're writing?"

"Here," she said, "read it for yourself."

She handed me the notebook and I saw only a blank page.

"It's about the meaning of life. What do you think?"

McCully's visit injured Gloria in some very private way. Now was not the right time to try to re-establish contact, but I made a grave mistake. In my professional voice, I said, "I like it," and I handed her back the notebook. Instead of taking it, she let it fall to the floor. She turned away from me and pulled out a volume of the *Encyclopedia of Religion*. "I'm going to read for a while, if you don't mind."

"I don't mind," I said, but I felt rotten. "Gloria?"

"It's okay. Alex. Not now. Now is not a good time. It's my problem, not yours."

But I knew it was my problem, too, and it was breaking my heart.

As soon as McCully left, Sinclair called me into his office for a debriefing. "How did we do?" I asked.

He threw his hands up. "Hell if I know. McCully never said anything about the oversight that we were still getting funding. He seemed impressed with your 'cutting edge' motif. Now we have to draw up a program to show him, but that's no big deal if it'll save our bacon. I did the verbal dance around federal cutbacks and involvement of the private sector, and I did it well. But he's keen on mainstreaming special needs people of all ages, and you and I know that this means simply cutting them free, letting them sink. Take us right back to where we were before we had any social programs at all. I don't know what to think."

"But if there was a test to be passed, did we pass it?"

"With flying colours. We played the game very well. I just

don't know if we were playing the right game, or if we played by the rules, or even if there are any rules any more. I was thinking we'd be screwed without Connie here. She used to charm the pants off those government types whenever they showed up. I was never sure why she was willing to play up to them because most of the time she didn't seem to care about this place, but whenever someone from Social Services would come — and it was always a man — she'd be as sweet as sugar and hang all over those guys. Connie was a mystery to me. I told her she shouldn't have to degrade herself like that, but she said it was all for a good cause.

"But we did all right without her. Thanks to you, Alex. Whatever happens, I'm here to the bitter end. They'll have to haul me out of here with a backhoe. This is where I make my stand."

"Me too, Henry. Truth is I don't have anywhere else to go. I think you know that."

"Don't sell yourself short."

Gloria went home early that day, and I took Jeff for a drive around the parking lot, but, by mid-afternoon, I was exhausted and nauseous again. I felt uneasy all over and weak. I toughed it out until four-thirty but then drove home to Brenton Street. In the mirror I looked awful. On my old Radio Shack answering machine I heard a voice I had not heard in a long while. "Please call, Alex. It's your mother. Please call me back when you get in." But I didn't have the energy to speak to her then. I didn't have what it would take to return to the task of being her son and all the heavy baggage that would go along with it.

Instead, I fell down on my bed with my clothes still on, and I plunged into sleep.

Twenty-four

My mother had seen my face on television. The whole thing shook her to the roots of her being, for we had always been a family of no significance, small people who did not ever, ever attempt to disturb the universe. My father's rules of order had prevailed even after his death. They said one of his lungs had collapsed and the other was not strong enough to pull oxygen into his bloodstream. There had been awful breathing problems towards the end. My father had never expected a long life or an idiot's idea of a happy retirement. He expected to suffer, and suffer he did. He lay dying over a period of two months in the middle of a summer when the very air of Saint John seemed unbreathable to all of us.

At first I was numb to my father's death because I had run myself dry of rage years before when Karen died. I wish my father could have lived out his life towards the end with some sort of pleasure, some kind of fun. Dumb as it sounds, I always wanted my father to have a hobby. I wished he could whittle, or play spoons or guitar, or cards even. For he was a man bereft of pleasure. He was a believer from an early age in a short, hard life, with no surprises from any serendipitous force that would provide him with good luck. He blew a hundred dollars on 649 lottery tickets when his illness was first diagnosed and did not win a cent. In his own mind, that helped to seal his fate.

My father's only winning gamble had been at life insurance. The Irving company had sent in a man one day to sell life insurance to the employees at the pulp mill, and my father finally found a bet he could win. There had never been much money to speak of from the house and land at Lepreau, but when my father left the pain and troubles of this world behind, he should have had a big smile on his face for at least one thing. He had invested a little over two hundred dollars a year. K.C. Irving had meted out some of his own as part of an employee benefit package. And if ever I prayed for the existence of an afterlife, it was the day the cheque arrived. I wanted my father to know about his gift.

It was the only way he could be generous, you might say. Stiff, stubborn and negative in this life but, once dead, a giver. Enough money to allow me to fumble through university and graduate studies and then move on to Halifax. My mother had as much to live on, or maybe even a little more, than she ever had. She said she would stay on in the grey little upstairs flat. She was not about to move again in her life. Our Lepreau house had long since been levelled. Saint John was her home, for good or ill, and she would not budge. I had departed with her blessing, first to the States and later to Halifax, because she knew there was nothing, nothing for me to stay home for.

"Will you come home for a visit?" My mother's plaintive voice echoed through the phone receiver.

"Yes. I was planning on it. Are you all right?"

"I'm not bad. I could give you a list of aches and pains, but I won't run up your phone bill. I'll tell you when you get here. It's nothing of significance, so don't start worrying about me. It's me who's worrying about you."

"You can't believe what they say on television."

"You looked hurt."

"Stunned. A man in a suit knocks you down, it comes as a surprise. I'm sure the whole fiasco hurt him more than me."

"Still, can you come visit? I want to see with my own eyes that my boy is okay."

It was a Saturday morning. My hands were full here in Nova Scotia. My life was full here as well — full of wonder and worry. I was afraid things would fall apart if I left the province. "I'm on the road in ten minutes, Mom. I'll be there by this afternoon."

"Thanks, Alex. You're sweet. Be sure to wear your seat belt."

"It's the law. I will."

There was no answer at Gloria's house, and I got her answering machine with the wind chimes and her New Age voice saying, "I may be out or on a spiritual quest, but please leave a message." I was going to invite her along, but if I wanted to get there to visit and return by Sunday evening, I'd have to be on the road soon. I hung up and, after a hurried job of packing, tried once more before I went out the door. I drove across the A. Murray McKay Bridge and headed to New Brunswick.

With a sense of happy irony I heard on the CBC that the nuclear generator at Point Lepreau had been shut down for what was first thought to be regular maintenance. Turned out that the cooling system had significant salt water corrosion and they might be "off line" for many months. My friend the King of Fundy getting back at the bastards.

I saw a hitchhiker near Shubenacadie, a young Native man with a black pony tail, a guitar case and a green garbage bag. "Mi'kmaq luggage," he explained later.

He reminded me of Tony Christmas, the artist I had met in jail. I jerked the car onto the shoulder and came to a stop. The hitchhiker was a guy with a million dollar smile and aspirations to be a country singer. "Got a gig in Moncton. You going that far?"

"You got yourself a first class ticket to Moncton," I said, happy to have some company.

"Haven't I seen you somewhere?"

"Dunno."

He leaned over and studied my face. "TV. You were the guy wrestling with Lawrence. Cool."

"Thanks. But it wasn't intentional."

"That story has legs, my friend. People everywhere were watching you and maybe thinking they'd like to take a crack at the jerk."

"I never threw a punch."

"Well, you should've. I'm gonna write a song and include you in it. Is that okay with you?"

"Sure. Thanks. What's your name?"

"Dwight. At least that's my stage name. Like Dwight Yoakum. On stage I'm Dwight Lightnin'. My real name's Jeremy Marshall, but I'd appreciate it if you'd call me Dwight. This is my first really big gig, and I gotta get used to people callin' me by my stage name."

"Where you playing, Dwight?"

"Feeny's Tavern. Just down the street from Crystal Palace. I'm hoping maybe somebody from a record company'll be in the crowd. A lotta them types hang out in Moncton, I hear."

"You never know. You got a back-up band?"

He looked sullen all of a sudden. I had asked the wrong question. "Nah, just me. Think the audience will be disappointed to see one lone Indian with a guitar?"

"Shit, no," I said with the greatest conviction. "Look at Buffy St. Marie. Heck, look at Bob Dylan or Johnny Cash. They all got their start with just a guitar, playing places like Moncton."

"Moncton's pretty big, eh? And it's bilingual, too. I got some French words in my tunes."

"Moncton is gonna love you, Dwight."

"They say that sometimes if you're trying to build up a following you hire people to sit in the crowd and cheer for you. Then everybody who doesn't know who you are thinks you're hot."

"You don't need that. That's just for losers who don't have real talent." I always felt funny when the word "loser" slipped out of my mouth. It was a word that my father seemed to have invented. I hated the word and everything it meant and wished I could suck it back in, chew it up and spit it out the window onto the side of the highway.

"People think I have talent. Everyone in Indian Brook believes I'm going to be a big success."

"Gonna sell out and go to Nashville?"

"I won't sell out. I've got integrity. But I will go to Nashville. Look at Rita MacNeil. Even she went to Nashville and came back."

"What are your songs about?"

"About the land. About people. About fishing. About fighting for what's right. Some songs are just about trucks, though, and women with, ya know, really knock-out bodies."

"It's a good mix."

"Country songs gotta be down to earth. Not a lot of big words and mixed up, complicated chords and stuff."

"I can appreciate that."

"We're gonna shoot a video at Indian Brook. Everyone in the community will be in it. It's gonna start out at a hockey game, see, and then include a lot of shots of little kids and trucks with dogs in the back. I love any video with a dog in it. We'd put horses in it but there's not many horses around. But we've got some women with really fine bodies who'll be in it if I can persuade them that it's gonna be on the Country Music Channel. It's gonna be a really fine video."

189

Dwight was maybe five years younger than me, and I liked the guy immensely. He had a youthful, naïve optimism that had passed me by. I had been young, but I had never really believed in beautiful, impossible dreams. I was a dreamer, but a dreamer without focus and with low expectations. I could dream of far-away places but not with me in the picture. I could dream of fame and success, of being a movie star even, or a rock singer, but it was never *me* in the picture. Dwight rooted around in his "Mi'kmaq luggage" until he found a harmonica. He cupped his hands over it and released a loud, raucous pair of notes, took a deep breath and ran a scale up and down, then played a short, sweet, sad melody.

"You have words that go with that?"

"I do. But they're only in Mi'kmaq."

"I like foreign languages. I'd really appreciate it if you'd give me a sampling."

Dwight smiled. "Funny you call Mi'kmaq a foreign language. That's what my father said about English." I got the point, but there wasn't a bit of hostility in his voice. "Anyways, here goes."

He hit a few more introductory notes on the blues harp and then closed his eyes, rocked slightly, and sang something that was neither pop nor country. The words spilled out of him, and I did not know what they meant, but they gave me a chill down my spine as I drove on past Truro and made the turn onto the Trans-Canada, west towards New Brunswick. When Dwight finished, he didn't open his eyes for a full minute after his tune was over. I had never heard anything in Mi'kmaq before, and I liked it.

"I like it. What's it about?"

"It's about where we come from and where we're going. It's about the land. We come from the land and the rocks and the trees and the sky, and we go back into those things. The

Creator put Mi'kmaq people here in this place. All my ancestors are still back there in Indian Brook. They never went away. And that's where I go, back into that place. The song says you can't ever own the land, it's part of you and you're part of it. It's the song of the land. Not everybody feels that way, but I do."

I was thinking of my home again at Lepreau, about the forest and the shoreline. Once we had been forced away from that first home, I never truly knew who I was again until I had found my way to New Dawn. "I think it's a great song. They're gonna love it at Feeny's."

Dwight/Jeremy laughed at that. "I ain't gonna be a dumb enough Indian to sing *that* for the people drinking beer at Feeny's. I just shared that one with you, man, 'cause of what you did to Lawrence. 'Cause of that song, though, I can't go rushing off to Nashville for a full-on career as a country singer. I want to travel, but I gotta keep my roots back near the Shubenacadie River."

"I understand. Makes sense to me. Thanks for the performance."

"No problem. Hey, you stop at the Irving station, I'll buy you one of them big cappuccinos, okay?" Dwight rooted through his green garbage bag again until he found his wallet. He seemed to be smiling for no reason at all.

"Let me get this straight," I said. "A country singer who sings songs in Mi'kmaq and drinks cappuccino?"

He laughed. "Maybe the world isn't ready for me yet. Maybe I'm a little bit ahead of my time."

As I pulled off the highway into the Irving station for gas and cappuccino, I told Dwight that I thought he *was* ahead of his time, but that the world needed to hear from him.

"Go for the extra large," he said. "On me. We'll have to stop and pee before we get to Moncton, but there's a great place up ahead with a big birch forest I want to show you. We drink our coffees and then go pee in the woods. It's an old Mi'kmaq ritual."

"Extra large," I said. "I'll fill up on gas and you score the caffeine."

"You're on."

Twenty-five

Before I said goodbye to Jeremy Marshall, I went into Feeny's and downed a single glass of draft Moosehead with him. Inside the tavern, a nondescript dingy hall with a sticky floor and a few rheumy-eyed afternoon drinkers at the bar, Dwight was not greeted with much enthusiasm from the owner and was reluctantly given permission to do the sound check on an antiquated PA rig that might have been purchased at a military auction. Taverns in the afternoon are depressing sanctuaries for men and occasionally a few women who have settled into their small addictions to beer and cigarettes as an alternative to the uphill, losing battle of day-to-day living.

In that cave of swaddled despair, Dwight's sound check was like a bolt of lightning, or so I thought. Instead of singing, however, he took the microphone and began a long, rambling, impromptu comedy routine. At first he drew only catcalls and scowls, and it looked as if the owner was about to yank him off the stage. This isn't what he'd been hired to do, after all. It wasn't even time for his show. Here was this long-haired Indian from out of province making fun of the customers in Feeny's. I almost wished I hadn't stopped in to see what would happen next.

But as Feeny (or whoever had taken over the tavern from Feeny) was making his way to the stage, Dwight asked him over the microphone, "Did you hear the one about the two nuns on bicycles?"

Feeny stopped dead in his tracks. The rheumy eyes turned from their beer to look up at the stage.

Dwight delivered the story and then the punch line, and it caught us all off guard. Somebody at the bar started to laugh, then cough, and somebody set down his cigarette long enough to bring two hands together in a ragged applause. Feeny waved as if shooing away a fly. Then he went back to his station behind the bar. Dwight finally pulled out his guitar and sang "Wabash Cannonball" in a voice borrowed from Hank Snow.

I was out the door before he finished and walked across the street to a little patch of public land designated Tidal Bore Park. I looked down at the muddy waters of the Petitcodiac River, where each day the Fundy tidal surge pushed a small brown wall of water up into the land. The few tourists seemed disappointed to see "the highest tide in the world" rise in a river with water the colour of raw sewage. I got back into my car and drove out of the city and down a long highway that made my bones ache. There are highways back to powerful emotions, and that leg of my trip, from Moncton to Saint John, is one of them.

Driving into the city of my youth, I looked on that empty hill where the old hospital had been torn down a short while ago. It had been an eyesore for many years until it became a public embarrassment, and finally the citizens of the city cheered when it was blown up in classic Hollywood fashion and put out of its misery. I took the turn-off that led me downtown and towards the harbour where I had grown up. The pigeons still bobbed their heads as they walked in the gutters, and I saw at least two dead birds on the streets, their bodies compressed into the pavement by the uncompromising traffic of the Loyalist City.

I did not knock, but walked in through the squeaky wooden door, down a narrow hallway and into the kitchen flooded with afternoon light. The radio was on, and some CBC announcer was talking about a brewery that was soon to close down, more jobs to be lost in the wake of free trade with the Americans. My mother was peeling potatoes, a study in solitude.

I said nothing and waited for her to look up. Brief surprise was ambushed by genuine joy and eclipsed by something even larger, all in the space of a few seconds. She stood up and embraced me, the small paring knife still in her right hand, safely pointed away from my back. "You looked heavier on TV. I thought maybe you had put on weight."

"No. Still skinny as ever. What's for dinner?"

"Thought I'd boil some potatoes, cabbage and carrots and maybe do up some corned beef."

"I always liked your corned beef. I'm sorry I haven't called."

"You were busy with your job and all. Sit down."

I sat and she turned the radio off. There were kids shouting out in the street, traffic somewhere in the distance, and the sound of machinery running down at the dock, but it was peaceful and quiet in my mother's kitchen.

"Everything okay with you?" I asked, suddenly feeling guilty that I hadn't brought her some small present to show that I had been thinking about her, that she was still special in my life.

"Okay, I suppose. I was worried about you, but I can see you're okay. More than okay. I can see life in Nova Scotia is good to you."

"It is. I've got a job, a girlfriend . . ." The word tasted funny on my tongue. It was the word a kid in grade six would use for someone he had a crush on, someone he passed notes to during third period English class.

"Girlfriend, eh?" The knife concluded a swift, perfect circumnavigation of a small potato, and the skin spiralled into a pot. Eyebrows raised.

"It's not like before. This one isn't a vampire."

My mother pursed her lips. She had helped to pick up the pieces after the Nagasaki of my college romances. "Wisdom comes with age," was all she said.

I wished that I had a picture of Gloria to show her. I did feel like a sixth grader with a girlfriend, but I certainly didn't want to hide her from my mother. I wanted the two of them to meet. I didn't know how to tell my mother that Gloria was a client in the workshop where I was employed. "Gloria is like . . . sunshine. She's creative and funny and beautiful." I was gushing.

"You got it bad."

"The worst," I said, smiling. "She'll come with me next time I visit. I promise."

"You got someone. And that's important. Don't never let go of her." There was suddenly a sternness in her voice. I recognized an octave of pain in the way the words caught in her throat.

"I won't."

She walked over to the garbage can, dumped the peels, set the potatoes in the sink, turned on the tap, and, looking straight at the wall, said, "I don't think I want to live here any more, Alex. I'm thinking about moving into a home."

"What?" It came as a full frontal shock.

"An old people's home."

"You're not that old. You're only sixty-three."

"Sixty-four."

"But I thought you never wanted to move again."

She was still staring at the wall as silence filled each province of the lonely nation that my mother had inherited. I had noticed for the first time that her hair was fully grey. There had always been grey hairs among the black, but now the lighter colour had won out. I realized, too, that she was wearing an old dress — an around-the-house, kitchen-work dress — the same one she had worn the day I first went out the door to university. Maybe it went further back than that. It was a garment of timeless, faded quality. My mother had never given in to changes in fashion, for she had never had any notion of it or care for it in her life. "I can't live alone any longer. I don't care where I live now, as long as I'm around people. Even strangers. I don't care. Since your father died, I don't even know who I am any more."

She turned around and I put my arms around her, smelled the garden smell of my mother's hair and held her tightly to me. "I shouldn't have moved away," I said.

"No, Alex, that's not it. I'm not blaming you. It's me. I was never any good at adapting to changes. I was never strong."

"No, you're wrong. You were always the strong one. You kept the family going."

"No, your father was the strong one. He kept us together. He never let go even when things were awful."

I hadn't fully reconciled all my memories of my father. He was a simple man, but that was not excuse enough for his cold tyranny. He was a man who begrudged the smallest of pleasures to himself or to any of us. "He was never very nice to you."

My mother turned around, and I could see there were tears in her eyes. Tears and anger. "You wouldn't understand. You shouldn't say such an ugly thing. We grew up in a different time. People didn't show affection the way they do today."

"I know. I'm sorry. I always had a hard time understanding him. I swore I wouldn't be like him. I wasn't even sure he cared about me — about us. Karen worshipped him and I never understood why. But she was just a little kid." As if that explained away a foolish love for a parent.

"Karen," my mother said, as if it was the first time she had spoken the name out loud in many years. "We both loved Karen. He had a hard time showing his feelings, I know. And he had to work. If he hadn't worked all the time, where would we have been? Out on the street, I suppose."

"He killed himself with work. I never understood why he stayed with those rotten jobs. He could have done something else. He didn't have to kill himself at it."

"Hard work was all he knew. He figured it was all he deserved. He didn't have an education like you. He didn't think he was worth anything."

"And he tried to pass that philosophy on to his kids." My own lack of self-worth had an origin and a name, and it was Father.

"Alex, after Karen died, your father cried every night in bed. He would wake up late at night and cry until his pillow was soaked. I'd have to get up and change the pillow case and then cradle him like a little baby until he went back to sleep."

"I have a hard time believing that's the same man I knew."

"Your father never let anybody really get to know him, not even you kids. But he was a good man."

197

I said nothing. My father was no doubt a "good man," one who could not break out of some mindset that caged him from an early age. Part of me hated him for having had such a limited view of himself and the world, yet part of me had become him, even against my will. And for that I could not forgive him. "You were the one who held the family together, Mom."

"But now I have no family, and I don't have anyone to hold me together. Alex, I need to get out of here now. And I hope you'll understand. It's a place called Pine Ridge. It's not exactly a nursing home. I don't need that yet, but it's a place for old people like me who don't have anyone to live with."

An only son feels tremendous guilt at a moment like this, and the guilt nearly smothered me. "I could move back here."

"I wouldn't allow it," she said, defiant and out of character. "You have a life to live, Alex. Don't try to be your father."

The irony of that statement caught me off guard. She was right. Punishment and self-sacrifice was the game the MacNab men played, whether it did anybody any good or not.

And then my mother did a very strange thing. She set the pot of potatoes on the electric stove to boil, opened a cabinet and brought forth a bottle of Bright's Sherry with two stemmed glasses.

"I've never seen you drink in your life. I don't believe this." It was not criticism but unabashed amazement.

"I haven't quite figured out how to be a proper alcoholic yet, but I have decided to cultivate this one small vice." Even the language was radically out of character. She poured the russet liquid into the two glasses, each about the size of a thimble.

"You know how they say on the TV shows, 'Get a life?' That's me, Alex. I don't have many clues, but I'm trying to get a life. Cheers."

She tossed off the tiny splash of sherry and set the glass

down. I followed. It was sweet and foreign to my taste buds, and having a drink with my mother shocked me in some deep preserve of my being.

"I never drink more than two of these, and I know the dangers of drinking alone," she said.

"And that's why you want to move into some building with a bunch of old ladies."

"Ladies and men. And you said sixty-four wasn't old. They're just like me. And they have cocktails at three in the afternoon, every day, whether they want to or not."

"What did you say they call this place, Club Med?"

"Pine Ridge, silly."

"What else don't I know about my own mother?"

"You know all the rest. I still have dreams about our old life on the shore. There were mornings when I hugged myself just because I was so happy to be alive. It was never easy, that life, and it was bloody hard on Alex Senior. But it was always ours. No one should ever have been allowed to take it away."

I tried to take another slip from my glass, but it was empty. "I got a story for you, Mom."

"That's gonna require a refill." She poured seconds for us, and I noticed the price sticker on the bottle. Probably the cheapest bottle of anything in the New Brunswick Liquor Commission.

"I'm glad you splurged on the good stuff."

"Nothing's too good for my family."

Her words had a sweet, sweet irony that I savoured. It was the sort of thing a TV father or mother might say, but it was nothing that anyone in my old home would have said, seriously or in jest. We had always settled for just what it took to get by. That was part of the definition of who we were.

My mother sipped her drink this time and made it last over

the telling of my story about Karen and me and the protesters of Lepreau. I said the names of Joe Woods, Muriel Dorworth and Ben Milligan with the same reverence that I had used whenever Karen and I had talked of that day. My mother listened wide-eyed as she carefully brushed her grey hair out of her face with her hands and then traced her fingers down to the tips of the strands. "He couldn't even understand what they were doing there, could he? He thought they were a bunch of radicals with some selfish purpose, didn't he? I bet Karen and I would have been in big trouble if he had known we were there that day they got arrested."

"Your father knew all about it," my mother suddenly said.

I shook my head. "Not only have you started drinking, but it looks like you've learned how to fib as well." I could not believe in my wildest imagination that she was telling the truth.

"It's true. Clarence from down the road had been there. He'd seen you kids, and you know what kind of blabbermouth Clarence LeDare was."

"You're telling me straight?"

"As straight as I can tell you. Your father hated himself for not being able to fight back, to protect us and save our home. You're right, he didn't like those protesters. He didn't trust them one bit, but when he found out you kids had gone over there, he didn't know what to do about it. So he did nothing. It was his way."

I pressed my fingers into my forehead and followed the creases, east to west. "Got any cookies to go with the pop?" I asked.

My mother took another molecular sip and produced a brown bag of chocolate chip cookies.

"So nothing is absolute. Nothing is necessarily as it seems. Not even him."

"Fancy idea. You learn that in some philosophy class at UNB?"

"No. I just learned that now from my mother."

"See, little boys should listen to their mothers more often."

"Then I never really knew him either, did I?"

My mother bit into a cookie. "No. I don't think anyone in this world knew your father because of those walls he had built up around himself. No one but me."

"Thank God he had you."

"Thank God I had him."

"Jesus, Mary and Joseph."

"Alex, I want you to take me for a ride around the city. In your car. I don't get out."

"Where do you want to go? One of the new malls?"

"No, thank you."

"Reversing Falls? Bet you haven't been there in a dog's age."

"No."

"Where, then?"

"I want you to take me to see the hospital."

"It's gone, you know that. I sure wish I had been here when they blew it up."

"I saw it on TV, and it went down some nice."

"But why would you want to go there? Nothing but a pile of bulldozed rubble now."

"I think you know."

I looked directly into her eyes and she held me fixed in hers. I took my last tiny sip of sherry. "Okay, Mom. But you got to put some coffee on. You got me all boozed up here, and now you want me behind the wheel of a car."

"All I got is instant. Decaf."

"I'll take it," I said, hoping it might somehow locate the cappuccino caffeine still floating around in my bloodstream and reactivate it.

There was a throbbing in my head and a slight feeling of nausea as we drove north to the site of the old hospital. It was neither sherry nor coffee but something else playing games with my system. I would not show my discomfort to my mother on our pilgrimage, but I was troubled by her desire to go to the hospital. We drove up and away from the harbour and found the street that brought back a flood of memories. The driveway no longer existed, and we stopped by the curb and peered through the chain-link fence.

"Let's get out," my mother said.

The fence had been busted down by vandals in one place, and my mother was the first to step over it. I had no choice but to follow. "It looks like there's been a war here," she said.

"That's the way I'd always felt about this place. It was a battleground, and it was the place where this family always lost. I hated this hospital."

"No one was ever unkind to us here. I can't remember a soul who was unkind."

Twenty-six

My mother held onto my arm as we walked out across the rubble that once was the largest hospital in New Brunswick. I wished I had been around to cheer this building to its dramatic death. Most of those who worked here had been both competent and kind, but hospitals, at their best, provide few happy memories, and this one, built near the edge of a jagged cliff, had always looked stark and forbidding. Now it was nothing but blasted concrete, brick, twisted rebar. Fragments of glass laced the colossal mess, capturing the intermittent sunlight — square nuggets of safety glass from those old metal-frame doors, long deadly scimitars of glass, pockets of glass minutia.

"I remember coming here the day Karen was born," I said.

"How can you remember that? You were so young."

"I shouldn't really remember, should I? Four years old. Maybe I just remember you telling me about it, and then I sort of filled in the blanks."

"Maybe. I remember your father was very good about the whole thing."

That wasn't in my memory bank at all, but I would not intrude on my mother's happy delusions.

"I also remember coming here when Karen died," she said, and I suddenly realized exactly why we were here.

A robin came to rest on a finger of metal sticking up out of this devastation. We both stopped and looked at him. He sang out loud and clear, and I wondered why he was here. No lawn. No flowers. No worms in this horrific landscape. Not far behind him a pair of rats raced from shadow to shadow. They frightened the bird and he flew off.

I leaned over to look into the debris at my feet as if I might find clues to the meaning of my life and some long-lost knowledge about my family. *Karen was why we were here*. I found a greenish penny and a faded fragment from a cover of an old *Time* magazine. April 1952, well before I was born. Pieces of anybody's past. I picked away at small, chipped pieces of concrete and dug a small hole.

"What are you looking for?"

"I have no idea. I kinda wish you hadn't brought me here, but now that we're here I feel as if I'm supposed to be looking for something." I felt like a little kid in a catastrophic sand-box, surrounded by destruction in some morbidly imagined child's game. There were broken pieces of bottles, and eve-rywhere there was dust, dust, dust. Pulverized cement and stone, and then this: a small cracked amulet with a picture of the Virgin Mary. The chain was still attached. I laughed, picked it up and handed it to my mother. "We must have been the only family in New Brunswick that didn't go to church or have some sort of religion," I said. "I never knew what to put down on those forms at school where they asked for your denomination. So I left it blank. I lied once or twice though and said I was a Baptist."

"Your father wouldn't have approved of that."

"Lots of things he didn't approve of. But didn't he believe in God at all?"

"Alexander's belief was that you lived, you worked and you died. It was a sort of duty — to be born, to endure. Death was just the end of living. No heaven, no hell. Nothing. He wouldn't allow me to bring any religion into the house."

"And he died here. This same place. Karen and then him. This hospital took them both away from us. So when he was dying, he believed he wasn't going anywhere at all."

"I tried to convince him there had to be something beyond this world, but he told me to save my breath. The last time I saw him, with those tubes up his nose, with that irregular, awful breathing and those machines, I swear he had a sense of humour about it all. He had finally given up being angry. For him it was all over. Nothing more to come. He'd paid his dues and could call it quits. It's not much to go out with, I would say, but it was him. I loved him for what he was. I don't think he ever fully understood that."

"Why is it some people try so hard to be unhappy?"

"Don't know. But I know it's infectious. It infected you like a virus from the time you were little."

"Yeah. But I've finally gotten over it." I sat down again and poked around in the ruins like a little kid. "Her name's Gloria."

"Then you're blessed."

"That's a funny way of looking at it. I thought we were all atheists."

"No. I was a believer. I'm not sure what I believed in except him and you kids as a family. For some of us that's all we need."

"Karen was never, ever infected by his way of thinking."

"No. You protected her from that, didn't you?"

"Yeah, I did. And I knew I was doing it. I *had* to do it. I was protecting her from him — not that he would hit her or hurt her. I just didn't want her poisoned by that way of seeing the world." The two rats came closer to us, and one stood up on his hind legs and sniffed the air, sniffed our presence. He reminded me of pictures I'd seen of a prairie gopher.

My mother wet her thumb and rubbed the grime off the little charm of the Virgin Mary. "I thought about getting involved with some church after he died, but each time I tried, I found that if I was going to believe in God, I was going to end up hating him. Better to believe in something you love than something you hate."

"Even if it's an illusion?"

She looked up at the sky. "Now you're talking college talk again. You know I can't keep up with that." But she knew what I meant. She just didn't want the conversation to go further. It didn't matter. In the space of ten minutes, my mother and I had communicated more truth to each other than we ever had in all our years together.

"After Karen died, you wanted to bring me here for some tests or something, didn't you?"

"You weren't well for a long time after your sister's death. Yes, I wanted to bring you in for tests."

"Why?"

"Like I said, her death hurt you deeply."

"No, it wasn't just that, was it?"

"Alex, I don't remember all that clearly. Yes, I did want you to get looked at, that's all."

"But he said no. Why?"

My mother seemed very uncomfortable now. "Your father didn't trust the hospital, I guess, didn't trust the doctors or the medicine. None of it. Karen was dead. He was all broken up inside."

I was missing a piece of the puzzle and I knew it, but I would not push her on this point. "If you don't believe in God, then you have no one to blame but yourself."

"Is that how you felt after Karen died?"

"No," I said.

"How did you feel?"

"I can't remember. I can remember missing her awfully. I can remember thinking about her all the time in years after that, but I can hardly remember anything about that year."

"You were fourteen years old."

"I remember I didn't want to be fourteen years old. I wanted to be a kid again. A little kid. I wanted to be back on the Fundy shore with a house and a sister. I wanted the world to perform some great, magical time-transformation trick that would allow me to go back. And I swear I almost thought I could do it. I remember that much. But that's about all. I think my sanity was saved by the escape into books — mostly science fiction and fantasy novels. The reading room of the library saved me."

"You don't remember being sick?"

"No. Was I?"

"I thought you were. But your father said it was just the way you were. No tests. No doctors."

"Well," I said, taking a deep breath and then pitching a small, jagged piece of concrete at one of the rats, "I'm still here. And Karen would have been twenty-six if she was alive now."

"Funny that you can even say that. I never allowed myself the luxury of thinking about *what if*."

"Mom, as I recall, you never allowed yourself the luxury of anything."

"My family was my luxury. I was never alone. That was plenty."

"Come on, let's go. I'm hungry. I haven't had a home-cooked meal in a long time."

The sound of our feet crunching across the hospital grounds stayed with me for a long time. I had crossed a bridge of understanding with my mother that we had never ever even dared to approach before. She still clutched the locket of the Virgin Mary. I was convinced that it had once been held by someone who had been dying here in the hospital or a Catholic son or daughter praying for someone about to die. How could a thing like this, lost perhaps in a piece of stuffed furniture, have survived the blast, the bulldozers and the weather? I imagined the layered stories of grief beneath my feet. Maybe there were happy endings here, but I didn't see any evidence. And I wondered, too, how many exulting moments of hope had turned, over the succession of weeks or months, into defeat. You might walk out of a hospital once or twice or a dozen or a hundred times in life, but the sad fact of the matter was that one time you'd go in and you wouldn't come out. The ending would always be the same.

I helped my mother over the broken fence. To anyone driving by just then, we might have appeared like a couple of homeless vandals sneaking away from the scene of a crime. I drove slowly back to our old wood-shingled row home near the harbour. I tried in vain once more to focus on the events of that crushing year of my life, but they were buried in my own mental dust and debris. A wave of nausea swept over me and an almost indistinguishable agitation in my chest, and then a grey mist settled into my head. My mother was not saying a word now, and I allowed my imagination to pretend that Karen was alive, twenty-six years old and sitting in the back seat.

I began to tell the story of teaching Jeff to drive. I pretended I was sharing it with both my mother and Karen. I could see by my mother's expression that she thought I was making it up. I almost spoke out loud to Karen just then. "Tell her," I was about to say to my dead sister. "Tell Mom that I'm not lying." But I said nothing, and I wondered why my befuddled brain had imagined Karen with me there in Nova Scotia, sharing in Jeff's youthful triumph of driving blind for the first time.

I nearly missed stopping at a red light and apologized to my mother for our abrupt halt. "Hope you didn't teach him to drive like that," she said.

"Jeff's a good driver," I said. And I added, "Isn't he, Karen?" but only in my head. And then, as if my dead father was there with us as well, I heard his ancient advice rattling in my brain: "It's wrong to give a person too much hope. It's bloody wrong."

Twenty-seven

My mother and I watched TV long into the evening, and then I slept soundly and happily there on the Saint John chesterfield of my childhood. Soon my mother would move into Pine Ridge and take up a social life, become a different woman from the lonely, kind-hearted soul who healed the wounds of her children and led a dedicated, dreary existence. She had been my father's prisoner as much as I was, I realized, as she had administered to us both out of love and duty. With my father long gone, it was finally my turn to set her free. At Pine Ridge Manor, breakfast, lunch and dinner would be provided, and there would even be a cocktail hour in the afternoons. Her days would be golden if she could learn to adapt to a life without work or worry.

My Saint John home would be rented to someone else. A young couple, perhaps my own age, would move in and wonder at the arcane linoleum on the floor, the ugly lime-green paint on the walls and the ancientness of everything that had been part of my life here. It would all be erased, and, even though I had many reasons to hate this house and this town, I grieved to let it go.

There was a highway to lead me out of the city back to my own new, wonderful world, full of its own tribulations and misery. But it was, after all, my world, the cosmos of New Dawn, of Gloria, of my friends who were called my clients, of the impending financial doom and my new-found celebrity as the man slugged by the not-so-honourable minster of finance.

But first, there was this other road, certainly one less travelled than the Trans-Canada. But it was one travelled again and again in my memory, and it was time to go there in the flesh.

"I'm driving down home. Our old place. Would you be up for going along?" I asked my mother after a solid breakfast of oatmeal and eggs.

My mother stood at the sink, scouring an old black frying pan with a Curly Kate. "You mean you really want to go back there?"

"Yeah, I do. So many things in my life are left unfinished. I know it sounds foolish, but I want to go there. I want to smell the air by the shore. I want to be there."

"But it's all gone."

"No, it isn't," I said. But I couldn't say one more word for fear that my voice would crack.

"I'll go just to keep you company, if it's something you feel you need to do."

"Thanks."

And so on that Sunday in late June, we drove south out of Saint John, past the Reversing Falls, on through Greendale, Purdy's Corner and Island View Heights and on to South Bay and Musquash, where we turned off on the little road to Chance Harbour and then Dipper Harbour. On a map, our old house would have been located between Dipper and Maces Bay, but we had never thought ourselves to be a citizen of either. We lived at Point Lepreau, or, more rightly, we lived "on the shore."

The Bay of Fundy was blue and flat, as if it had been ironed smooth. Not a trace of wind. I stopped by the gate of the nuclear power plant, and the security guard surveyed me from his glass-walled booth. It was here that my friends the protestors made their stand on my behalf and lost their battle with law and progress. I got out of the car and popped the hood. Behind that fence, I knew, workers were undertaking some sort of repair work on the coolant pipes. I surveyed the domes of the structure, the ugliness of it all, the sharp contrast with the blue sky above and that flat blue bay in the distance. I checked the oil level in the engine, pretended to fiddle with something under the hood until the guard came over. He was friendly enough.

"Problems?"

"Not really. Just overheating a little."

"Tell me about it," he said, rolling his eyes and nodding towards the power plant.

"Right, I heard. Make you nervous?"

"Sometimes. But hey, least I got a job."

"I know what you mean."

"Sure you don't need any help?"

"It all looks okay," I said and slammed down the hood. "Just being cautious, I guess."

"Take care."

I got back in the car and smiled at my mother.

"This all used to be a big field," she said. "Over there was a bog where we used to pick cranberries, and that there had been forest right up to the shore. Makes you feel old to see it all wiped out like this."

I was thankful that the guard had been nice. I could tell from his accent that he was from around here. The power plant had probably saved him from having to move into Saint John. Or maybe it saved him from living half his life on pogey. "Maybe some good comes from bad things," I said to the windshield.

We drove on further, and it came as a shock and a surprise

211

to find our old driveway still there. I turned the car and drove right up into what used to be the old yard. There was not a trace of a house, and alder bushes had returned to claim much of the back yard.

"It's like they forced us to move out and then never used this land for nothing," my mother said.

"They had to buy up all the land around the plant. In case of an accident, I guess."

"But they always told us an accident was impossible."

"Nearly impossible," I reminded her. "Accidents can happen, and if they had some sort of meltdown or something, then we'd get radioactive poisoning."

"It still doesn't seem right. They made us move and then they didn't even use this land for anything. They haven't even had an accident since they built the place, right?"

"Minor accidents, I think. No Three Mile Island or Chernobyl."

"Think about it, then, Alex. We could have stayed here. Stayed in our own house, all them years. Right up to now. Everything might have been different. Makes me bloody mad. Silly bastards made us move out, and they didn't need to do it at all. We wouldn't have had to put Alexander through all that mess with lawyers and the frigging government stealing our land for next to nothing. What a waste of time."

In a way she was right. Had my father played it cooler, and had we been allowed to stay, he probably would have landed himself a job as a maintenance guy at the damn plant itself. Might not have been any worse than whatever it was that killed him. At least we would have been here by the bay.

"Let's get out and walk around," I said.

I helped my mother out of the car, and we surveyed the alders along the driveway, noted the crushed Keith's beer cans and empty Captain Morgan rum bottles and junk tossed here by locals. Our old back yard had become the place to sit in your car, drink booze with your girlfriend and get way from the world for a while.

"Disgusting," my mother said. "Look at all the garbage."

We walked straight to the small mound of debris that had once been our house, our home. I saw the look on her face and suddenly realized that I might have made a big mistake. "I don't think I was ever afraid of dying until just this minute," she said.

"What are you talking about?"

"Look at this place, Alex. It's like we never lived here. Nobody would ever care nowadays about who had lived here or what our lives were like. It's all been erased. After we moved to Saint John, I could still *see* this yard, still see you and Karen playing on your sleds in the winter. I could see it plain as day. Now that I'm here, all I can see is a big alder patch and piles of garbage somebody heaved here. Nobody cares."

"I still care. I still care about you, about Karen and Dad, too. I loved our life here, even when it was hard. This was our place."

"And they took that away from us. I want to know, who gave 'em the right to do that?"

"I don't know."

"It's gonna be the same thing when I'm gone, isn't it, Alex? A few people will notice and then, after a little bit, it's like you never even existed. That's the way it was with Karen and it was the way it was with your father. And if it was only me and you still caring, all we had to show for it was pain, Alex. Frigging pain right here in the heart."

"Let's walk over to the shore."

"At least the water's still here. The tide still goes in and out, you reckon?"

"Yes. I used to think it was all done by some big guy underneath the sea."

"The King of the Bay of Fundy, right?"

"How'd you know? I thought that was just Karen and me and our little games."

"Karen told me about him and about the others who you thought lived in the forest. She told me in the hospital. I told her it was all true."

The water seemed to go on forever. A few puffy clouds drifted like dreams above it all. You could not see the power plant from here. You could not hear it. You could see a few scallop boats way off and gulls swooping down and around. The tide was full up and the water was so clear today you could see grey, smooth stones on the bottom. But not a wave, not a ripple.

"Alex, you had some special gift, but I don't think you ever figured out how to use it once Karen was gone."

"Yeah, I did. I lost it for a while but it's back. I just figured it out. My job. The people I work with. It's who I am. It's funny standing here with you like this looking out. I can remember how it felt on a summer day all those years ago. And then we were shoved out and everything went bad, and it was like my life was put on hold until just this year. All because I had stopped caring about anything but me. Now I don't worry about me so much. I care about the people I work with back in Halifax. And I care about you. That's why I'm glad you're moving to Pine Ridge and you'll learn to play decadent card games like strip poker and sip gin or whatever they do there." I picked up a flat, oval stone and soared it out into the air and then watched as it dropped into the sea, watched the perfectly circular rings disturb the tranquil surface.

"I guess I don't really mind dying when the time comes," my mother said. "It's just that I think I'll probably die not having figured out really what life is about. It's as if I know about all the pieces of living day to day. I just don't know

214

how they fit together." She turned around and faced the place where our house once stood. "There was something there that I lost, and I could never quite get a grip on it again. And now it's all just like a dream, none of it was real at all. Aside from you being here with me, Alex, as a kind of anchor, I don't really even know who I am."

"I know that feeling."

"But you've found your place in the world and proven them all wrong."

"What do you mean?"

She seemed uncomfortable and looked away from me and up into the sky at the circling gulls. "Nothing, really. It was a slip of the tongue. It was one of those silly things I'd been carrying around in my head for such a long time, and now I said it in a very stupid way. Forgive me."

I tried to make light of whatever it was she was trying to tell me. "It's okay. Remember, I'm a big boy now. I can handle whatever people said about me in the past."

"Well, it certainly wasn't that you were stupid or anything. Your father was no great thinker, but you were always a whiz, and — all them books from the library. I thought someone would've given you a medal or something."

"Then what was it?"

My mother closed her eyes for an instant, and when she opened them, they had a far-away look. "Your father knew for a long time that he had health problems. His father had died young, and there was a history of heart trouble. In those days, people just made the best of whatever they were born with. When Alexander figured out that it was something he had passed on to Karen that killed her, he hated himself. And then when the doctors said you should be tested — x-rays and all that stuff — your father refused. I told him he was wrong, but he had this idea stuck in his head: it was a conspiracy against him and against us. He was downright crazy about all this, but he never spoke a word of it when you were around."

"I remember the doctors saying something about tests. It was because of the way I was feeling in school."

"It was all just stress. That's all it was."

She glanced back at me. "Look at you now. Healthy. Happy, even. Guess you proved them wrong. Guess your father knew what he was talking about for once, after all. How has your health been? You look just fine."

"I've been doing great. Never better."

"I guess it's a good thing to come back here, now that I think about it. Put the past in the past. It doesn't hurt to get a fix on it, on who you were, on who *we* were back then."

"It was a fine place to be a kid."

"You didn't need much back then, just each other. I can still see everything as it was."

We were quiet on the drive back to Saint John, and I pondered the intersections of my life. Lepreau, Saint John, Halifax. I could fix myself in each of those worlds, but I had a hard time seeing the linkage of one to the other. It was as if I had lived independent lives, each segment of existence parcelled up, one separate from the next. No logic, no cause and effect. I was convinced that who I was now had almost nothing to do with who I had been as a kid in Saint John. And as a result I was certain that the talk about my own childhood health problems had been paranoia on someone's part and a fallacy.

As I said goodbye to my mother, I promised to visit often, and I knew as I said the words I was lying. It was hard enough to visit her in her own home. It would be even worse to visit her in the retirement village, but I vowed to myself I would spend lavishly on long-distance calls. I could not say that any single thing troubled me on my long Sunday drive back to Halifax. I determined to let the miles consume the volatile cocktail of emotions and knowledge that had come from this voyage into the darkness and light of my past. By Hampton, I had satisfied myself that my mother's move to Pine Ridge was a wonderful idea. By the time I connected with the Trans-Canada in Sussex, I was sure that nothing, absolutely nothing, could have changed the history that was the destruction of our homestead at Lepreau. Petitcodiac saw the diminution of all my fears about my health, for I felt a certain exultation in leaving southern New Brunswick behind me and the pull of my tires drawing me back towards Nova Scotia.

Moncton to Memramcook was filled with Acadian music on the radio and an almost unaccountable blind optimism about the future. And there was a mutable and workable mental geography to the Tantramar Marsh that led me on to Nova Scotia in the midst of a tourist tide — Winnebagos and travel trailers, cars full of Quebec families on vacation, bikers with girlfriends straddling their motorcycles, cars with windsurfers on top, and camper trucks with bicycles roped on front and back. As I crossed the border at the Missaguash River, I remembered that the only reason I had any money at all right now to even pay for gas was my father's life insurance policy, and I silently thanked him.

Then, slowing down to slip past the tourist centre welcoming me to "Canada's Ocean Playground," I rolled down the window and let the sweet smell of salt hay sweep through the car. I breathed deep, sensed the warm sun through the windshield and felt as if I had just been let out after a long prison term. I was invincible, fully charged and alive. I would live forever, my life was just beginning.

As the highway twinned, I pushed the pedal closer to the floor, passed a string of trucks and airstream trailers and, with each breath, filled my brain with the image of Gloria.

Twenty-eight

Everyone was standing in the parking lot at New Dawn Workshop when I arrived. It was a damp, chilly morning, the kind of morning that leads you to believe winter never really gives up in Nova Scotia, just gets lazy once in a while.

They were all looking at me except Gloria and Rebecca, who were huddled around Roger, conversing in a frenzied, animated way. I wanted to speak to Gloria before talking to anyone else, but so intent was she on Roger that she didn't look my way. Then everybody started to talk to me at once.

Henry Sinclair stood by the door. He looked up at the sky and then down at the pavement and then stared at a set of keys in his hands. I excused myself from my good friends and went to talk to the boss.

"Henry?"

"We're locked out. I got a phone call last night. I should have called and told everyone not to come. I had some sort of hope that the landlord would back off. Or give us another month, another week."

I felt sick again and a little dizzy. I tried to read hope into Sinclair's announcement, but there was not a trace. "We'll go someplace else," I said. "It's only a building. There are lots of buildings."

"And lots of regulations. I called five churches last night, asked for a temporary home, even if just for a week until we could sort things out."

"And?"

"Pick a religion. Any religion. They have committees that have to meet first. They have fire regulations. They have insurance problems. The province can legislate us out of existence with good-intentioned regulations. I thought I had a nibble with the Baptists, if you can believe that, but then I had to wrangle with the fire marshall. They don't call him a marshall for nothing."

"But I thought things were looking good with the province. The little visit from the deputy minister. I thought we had Social Services in the bag."

"Past tense. We didn't have a prayer."

"But you led me to believe that we'd be able to hang on."

"I led a lot of people to believe a lot of stuff, Alex. I'm sorry. It works ninety-nine per cent of the time. Times get tough and I put a good face on things. My little theory about ignoring some hard facts. It worked okay while we were semi-invisible. But once we were out there in broad daylight, some bureaucrats found us too embarrassing and too expensive."

"It was that skirmish with Chuck Lawrence, wasn't it?"

"It backfired. The bastard wanted revenge and had plenty of friends in the provincial government."

"Oh, shit. Then it was my fault."

"Yes, no, maybe. It was nobody's fault. Time was running out. Shifting sand and all that. You became a kind of naive national champion after what you said on TV, and everybody in Canada loved that. But then the public forgot about you the next day. Guess the political assholes didn't. Politics is the business of getting even. Don't lose any sleep over it. There's nothing anybody could have done. I just wish you'd gotten in one good slug for me."

"I still feel like I made things worse."

"Forget it. You were very good for New Dawn while we lasted."

"What do you mean?"

"I mean it's over. I'm tired, Alex. I've been keeping this thing from unravelling for over a year. The writing was on the wall. Almost all the other sheltered workshops like ours disappeared long ago. We were a dinosaur from the age of compassion. Now we need to let it go and find something else to do with our lives."

But I did not want to let it go and seek alternatives. I wanted my world back. "What about them?"

"That's the really hard part."

"They know, right?"

"They know we have a problem. They don't know what kind." Sinclair studied his keys again, leaned over and shook his head. "I couldn't bring myself to tell them the truth. I was hoping, well, you know."

"Henry, I don't know if I can."

"I understand that. I just know that I *can't*."

Everyone was watching us now. Cornwallis gave me a sad, knowing look. He knew. He had enough experience to sniff out real trouble without being told. I think Rebecca must have figured it out by now, too. Someone had led Jeff to my car, and he was studying it with his hands. The guy loved just touching automobiles, fixing the feel of door handles and headlights, grillwork and wheel covers in his head.

Without Rebecca to keep him occupied, Jules had sat down on the pavement and was playing silent music on the damp asphalt surface. Was it Mozart, Rachmaninoff or Claude Debussy?

"I just told them it was a problem with the lock," Henry conceded.

"Why don't we go down to the Legislature and protest? These guys will be great."

Henry rubbed the dampness on his forehead and heaved a great sigh. "In order to keep this place going, I fudged a lot of numbers. I borrowed money from the bank and made it appear that I had collateral I didn't have. I created a nice little paper wall to protect this place, but it was just that, paper."

"You did what you had to do."

"Yeah, and what I had to do some folks might call fraud."

I felt awful for Henry Sinclair, one of the most likeable human beings I had ever met on earth. "What would R.D. Laing do in a situation like this?"

"Hallucinate, I suppose, his hallucinations being legitimate experiences of an alternate reality."

"I'm all in favour of alternate realities. I just don't think it's going to help these guys right now. So I guess the big protest is not a wise move."

"It could be embarrassing, and I might go to jail sooner rather than later."

"They wouldn't put you in jail for juggling the books."

"I don't think they call it juggling. I think they call it cooking the books. But it's important for you to know that I did it for New Dawn, not me. I haven't been drawing pay, my house is mortgaged to the hilt, and now I'll probably lose my wife along with the family homestead."

"Shit."

"Shit hits the fan, it has to go somewhere. Go ahead, Alex, tell 'em for me, please, and get this over with. They think we're waiting for a locksmith. I don't like to keep the lie going. It's bad mental health."

In the short time I'd know him, I had come to believe Henry Sinclair was the greatest mentor I had encountered in my befuddled life, one of the eminent ones who embodied compassion, vision, and, I had thought, enough down-to-earth common sense to create something of genuine value in a world addicted to trivial excess. I would not think less of him. His glasses had beads of fog as did his hair. We were all enshrouded on this sad morning in a salty blanket of mist. In the muted light, everything glistened with an other-worldly quality, including Cornwallis and Scotty walking towards us.

"We're fucked, aren't we?" Scotty asked.

Sinclair blew air out between his teeth in a kind of whistle, wiped the drops of moisture from his glasses and looked away, up toward a streetlight that had stayed on into the dismal daylight.

Cornwallis shook his head. "Scotty, man, have some dignity. Wash out your mouth. This is the brass here." He cleared his throat. "What is it, Doctor Sinclair? Are we standing here in the fog waiting for a new set of keys, or have we come to the end of the muddy road?"

"We got a problem, Cornwallis," I said. "A big problem."

Cornwallis rolled his eyes and Scotty kicked at the pavement.

I was prepared to launch into something vague and optimistic, something about small setbacks and technical problems, any kind of gentle delusionary bullshit I could pack in. Instead I said, "Funding's been cut off and we can't pay the rent. So we're locked out of the building. Everybody's gonna have to go home today and wait until we get things sorted out." There. The news was delivered.

"In other words, we're fucked," Cornwallis said.

"Yeah, Cornwallis," Henry echoed. "We're fucked."

I desperately wanted five minutes alone with Gloria before

I told everyone else, but that would not happen. Instead, I gathered them all together and studied the faces. Steve looked hopeful, although I think it was just today's curious contortion of his facial muscles. Doris held his hand as they sat side by side in wheelchairs that gleamed with jewel-like droplets. Rebecca held Jules's hand. Jeff walked cautiously toward our voices. A few of the others looked nervous. Gloria was still talking to Roger, and Roger kept shaking his head. And then I told them all the truth. Henry looked embarrassed and weak beside me, and, when I had finished, all he could say was that it was all true and he wished it could be otherwise. And then he finished by saying, "I love you all," which smoothed a blanket of silence over the morning and left a Last Supper echo in my own head.

"Time to get everyone home," I said.

"Scotty and me will go catch the bus," Cornwallis said.

"I'll take Doris and Steve and couple of the others in my van," Henry said. "We'll make two trips if we have to."

"It's not right," I heard Jeff mumble. I had never seen the guy angry before. He had a right to be angry, but I also knew that he was young, he was smart, and he probably had more opportunities awaiting him than most of the others.

"We're gonna work on it," I said, but the words fell with a hollow thud on the pavement.

Jeff said nothing else, and his eyes moved back and forth behind his eyelids, expressing a rage he could not fully vent.

Sinclair began to load people and wheelchairs into his van. I was surprised that no one really wanted to talk further about anything. Gloria spared me only the slightest eye contact. She was holding onto Roger's arm now. Roger looked as if he was about to explode. Somehow he had known what was going down here before anyone else. Despite his injuries, he still had good cop instincts. He wasn't easily fooled. Gloria hung onto him as if she was holding him back from doing something nasty. I saw hurt and fear in her eyes as well.

"Gloria?"

"Alex, why didn't you tell me?"

"Sorry, I didn't know it would come to this."

"I don't think Roger's taking this too well."

"Roger," I said, "I'm sorry about this, pal. Want a piece of gum?" I fished in my pocket for some, but there was none there.

"No," he said, shaking his head and shifting his weight from side to side. I was trying to find a way to get inside his brain and figure out what he must be feeling. The rage of an eight-year-old in the body of a man, I was sure, was a formidable, dark force.

"Roger, it's going to be okay, man. We're going to work this out. Just stay cool."

"Stay cool," he repeated sarcastically.

"Let's get you home," Gloria said and tried to move him towards my car.

Roger suddenly twisted away from her and walked off, looking around as if someone was about to attack him. He had a crazed animal way about him, and I pulled Gloria back when she tried to follow him. "Roger, it's going to be all right. Honest." I said.

"Do something," Gloria demanded. "He's really scared."

"Roger?"

Roger had gone to the corner of the parking lot and picked up a chunk of rock that must have weighted at least forty pounds.

"Roger. Put it down," Rebecca called out to him. Jeff started walking towards Roger. "Roger, take it easy," he said and was nearly knocked over as Roger slipped past him carrying the rock.

It wasn't exactly that I was slow, just that I was intimidated by the look on Roger's face. I took one step at a time and kept talking to him, but he was much stronger than I had anticipated. As I tried to take his arm, he elbowed me aside and hurtled past, then, without letting go of the rock, smashed it through the glass door of the building. Glass shattered, Gloria screamed and an alarm went off inside.

Roger let out a loud howl. He dropped the rock now. His hands were cut and dripping blood. He looked at them, horrified and trying to come to grips with the sight of his own blood and the pain.

"Easy, Rog," I said. I looked him straight in the eyes and saw the rage diminish into fear, pain and defeat.

"We gotta get him out of here," Jeff said.

Roger was trying to bring his hands together, but I could see three pieces of glass jammed into his palms. I gripped his wrists and didn't lose eye contact. "Gloria, help me."

I held onto Roger and spoke soothing words as Gloria pulled out the shards of glass and dabbed a scarf at his hands. Rebecca came to assist Gloria, wrapping each hand carefully to stop the bleeding.

"We gotta get him to the hospital," Rebecca said.

"And we gotta get out of here," Jeff repeated.

"Let's go," I said. "Roger, you're going to be okay."

"Am I going to be okay?" he asked.

"You're going to be okay."

"I'm not going to get any gum any more, am I?"

"I bet they have gum at the hospital."

"I don't want to go to the hospital."

"Yes, you do," I said. "They'll have gum there."

Roger tried to hold up his hands. "I'm not going to be able to take the wrapper off."

It was a snug fit in my car, but we made it. Jules remained amazingly calm, as if he didn't notice that anything was out of the ordinary. Jeff seemed more worried about getting caught by the police than the fact that Roger was injured.

"Turn left," Rebecca said as we came to Windmill Road. She was directing me to Dartmouth General.

Blood was dripping onto the floor and Gloria was pressing on the makeshift bandages. Roger looked at his own blood and asked, "Where's it coming from?"

When Roger's wife arrived at the hospital and discovered that her husband was already bandaged and not in any real danger, she turned on me. "This is your fault," she said poking a finger into my chest. "I should sue you and Sinclair and that stupid workshop that does nobody any good at all."

I was unprepared for the insult, and it was Gloria who intervened on my behalf. "I think you should take Roger home," she said matter-of-factly.

She looked at Gloria and just kind of snorted the way a horse would. She didn't have to say what was on her mind about taking advice from a whacko.

Twenty-nine

"I only want to see beautiful things," Gloria admitted to me later that morning. She invited me back to her small apartment near Bedford Basin. It was the first time I had been inside, and as I entered I felt as if I were stepping into another world, another century. There were no hard edges anywhere in the place, just drapes and dangling scarves of many bright colours, hand-made wool hangings, macramé, and soft, dewy paintings of suns and flowers, unicorns, stars and lush vegetation. It was like entering a fantasy cocoon.

"You did pretty good with Roger."

Gloria looked at me briefly and then folded herself into my arms. We had entered the kingdom of soft, and I was a very willing captive. "If I try to stay focused, I really can live in a place where nothing is ugly. Only good things happen."

"That's one escape route. You've been there before, I take it."

"You might call it escape, but translate that into something else. Everything we experience, we edit and select what we want to keep. Some people can block out pain. I can do that. So can you if you want to."

"Henry Sinclair would say it's bad to block out anything. Better to confront it all head on. Admit to the harshest truths." I realized the irony of this even as I said it. So maybe Henry S. had a tough time practising what he preached.

Gloria pulled away. "Japanese tea?"

"Sure. Do I have to use chopsticks to drink it?"

"Would you prefer English tea?"

"No. Green tea is fine."

"If it's green, it means it still has some life in it, vitality. It's not dead yet."

Gloria was being obtuse. I detected barriers between us and wanted to tear them down. I felt an ache deep inside and so powerful that it seemed my bones would break. I wanted to kiss her and hold her in my arms and make love to her here and now. But this was not the nature of our relationship. We were working on something else. There was a bond, half-forged. "I guess I'm no longer your counsellor," I said, trying to put a positive spin on a very bad situation.

She set a tea kettle on a small electric stove. "Alex, did you

227

ever feel like there's something just an arm's length away, and you know it's the most wonderful thing, and you want to reach out and touch it, take hold of it. You try, but you can't grasp it. You don't even know what it is."

"You try to touch it and then it's gone, right?"

"How did you know?"

"I know. I feel that way about something in my past. I feel that way sometimes about you. I feel that way about New Dawn slipping away and losing touch with all these good people."

"I don't like categories and labels, do you?"

"I hate them."

"But language is labelling things, making categories. I try to get away from it in my poetry, but I can't. I want to live without structures or artificial order. But it's a childlike thing. I want things to be natural, to be full of life and to be beautiful. If I keep focused, like when I'm writing or sketching or meditating, it can be that way."

"I guess in some ways you're luckier than the rest of us because you can do that."

"But it doesn't help anyone but me. Look at poor Roger. You saw me talking to him. I was trying to calm him down, trying to help him, but it didn't do any good."

"But at least you tried. That's all any of us can do."

"I don't know. Sometimes I think that if I really concentrate I can make everything better. Me. Roger. Everything around us. Everything. But I know it's just an illusion. A pretty illusion. Crazy, huh?"

"Nothing wrong with idealistic notions."

"Now you sound clinical again."

"Sorry. I don't want to be clinical. I want to break down all the walls. I want to know everything about you." I felt like I was moving into dangerous, uncertain territory. I knew a necessary balance had to be achieved here. I would have to give as well as take when it came to deep, dark longings and secrets and beliefs.

The tea kettle shrilled, and Gloria poured hot water into an earthenware pot over loose green tea leaves. She was smiling. "How do I know I can trust you? "

"You can."

"How do I know you aren't using me as some sort of guinea pig? Gonna write some article for *Psychology Today*?"

"I'm not that ambitious."

"Okay. Fair enough. I want us to go to the next level," she said. "But you have to answer a few questions first."

I knew there would be a price, but Gloria was acting more playful than serious, and I loved sitting here talking to her. Here, in her silky cocoon, we were truly apart from the world. It was hard to believe that we were in a room on the edge of the industrial park. A busy highway was only twenty feet away. Trucks rolled by delivering gasoline and drywall and cement and boxes and boxes of the junk that keeps commerce alive. And here I was in the realm of the forgotten, in a place outside of time with Gloria, and I was deeply, deeply in love, half fearful that she was all an illusion.

"First question," she began. "Do you believe in God?"

"Go for the big ones first, right? Well, all I can say is yes, no, maybe, all of the above. My parents never went to a church. I read the Bible but didn't like most of it. I am opposed to the idea of a vengeful God like the one in the Old Testament, yet a presence like that sure helps to explain all the rotten things that happen on earth. I believe in spirit, but I don't know if I'm a part of it or separate from it. I believe in free will, not a big puppeteer in the sky. I like the idea of reincarnation, but I sometimes would like to lose my agnosticism and believe in something hard and fast. Like those fundamentalists who have it all figured out. You either go to

229

heaven or go to hell. Nice and easy. But it's gotta be bullshit, right? There. What about you. Are you a Catholic or a Protestant? Buddhist or Hindu?"

"I'm a believer in Wicca."

I was caught off guard and thought she was kidding. "Like the furniture?"

She smacked me with a pillow. "Wicca, silly. Earth religion. I believe in the spirit of the planet. Some people associate it with witchcraft."

"You don't look like a witch." I was starting to giggle but stopped when she gave me a look that would fry meat. "Sorry."

"Wicca is an ancient religion, a pagan one. We celebrate the earth, the Mother Earth. It's a very caring and compassionate form of belief. A believer in Wicca does nothing to harm anyone, and he or she works to protect the earth. We believe in the spirit of everything on this planet."

"Okay," I said. "I'm cool with that. And in the old days, they misunderstood your kind and burned them at the stake or drowned them by dipping them for extended periods into New England ponds."

"Yes. There are many intolerant societies."

"Do you have, like, secret ceremonies?"

"No, Alex. No secret ceremonies. I don't even belong to anything. I just read and meditate. I do it on my own."

"I like that. I never trusted organized religion. They always end up starting wars."

"I wouldn't be good at war. Tea?"

"Thanks. Next question."

She reached out and held her hands over my head and then closed her eyes.

"What?" I asked.

"You'll laugh if I tell you."

"No, I won't," I said, sipping my tea from a tiny clay bowl with no handle.

"Promise?"

"Promise."

She held out her hands again and closed her eyes. I closed mine too and thought I could feel the power of her hands, some sort of energy coming from them as they hovered above my head.

"I'm trying to touch your aura. I know you think this is all very New Age, but I can feel the energy coming from you."

"Is this good?"

"Mostly. I can see people's auras. Sometimes, not always. Some are red, some yellow, some bright, some dim. You have a strong yellow aura, and I can feel the energy coming from you. Great inner strength but a tremendous amount of uncertainty. Does any of that uncertainty have to do with me?"

"No," I said. "I'm uncertain about almost everything in my life, always have been. When it comes to you, though, I'm certain. I love you, Gloria."

She opened her eyes and seemed to have a hard time focusing on my face. "You're brave, too, Alex. Brave to make that commitment with words. Have you ever been hurt before? In love, I mean?"

"Yes. Twice. The one I fell for the hardest was named Donna. It was in graduate school. I was just a convenience and I didn't know it. I wasn't very experienced and didn't have much to go on. She was much smarter than me. She was pretty. I should have suspected something was wrong. She built me up and then dropped me." I snapped my fingers. "Just like that. It made me believe that that kind of happiness was false. I vowed never to fall in love again. Not like that. I didn't want to take the chance on all that pain."

"But you just said that you loved me."

"I've changed my mind, as you can see. With you I'll take the chance again. I've spent too much of my life as a loner, doing what loners do — spending their time all alone. You end up like a big tree without roots."

"No nourishment from Mother Earth."

"Something like that. Maybe all I needed was the right kind of witch to cast a spell."

"Don't make fun. This is serious."

"I know. Question back at you. I know you've been hurt before. Hurt in a way that goes so deep I don't know if I can even understand. Aren't you afraid of taking a chance on me?"

"Yes, I am."

"And you know that it scares me to think that I could, in some way, let you down or hurt you badly. What if I don't mean to but go ahead and do it somehow? Unintentionally. You're a complex person, Gloria. I don't know if I can fully understand you or take care of you."

"Maybe you can't, Alex. Maybe you can't fully understand or take care of me, but I would like it if you tried."

"I can do that. I can try." I reached out and put my hands over her head. She closed her eyes and I closed mine. Did I connect with her aura? Who knows. There was so much energy swimming around in that room, so much power and love racing though my own head that I felt something, something amazing. It was tangible, electrifying and real. I could attach those labels to it. And it was all part of who Gloria was and something we were becoming as the cool foggy morning outside gave way to a very warm, fine afternoon.

Thirty

The police report said that Roger had stepped out into the street in front of the truck. A cement truck to be precise, one of those great bloated beasts that roll down the road with sand and cement and stone sloshing around and around inside the revolving gut of steel. Roger died almost instantly. I missed the gruesome footage that showed up on TV that evening. An MITV news van had been in the neighbourhood and picked up the ambulance call on a scanner. The driver of the cement truck had used his two-way radio to call for help.

Despite the impact, Roger made a handsome corpse for the nightly news. The driver of the truck was still on the scene for the cameras, sitting on the curb and crying. Then, when a policemen checked Roger's identity by opening his wallet, he discovered that the victim was a former cop, and he, too, started to cry. The TV people put an ironic and melancholy spin on the story, and I'm glad I wasn't in the habit of watching television.

Instead, I had spent a most magnificent afternoon with Gloria as she had led me willingly into the labyrinths of Wicca wisdom, goddess worship, guiding spirits, aromatic oils, dream catchers, and gemstones imbued with primal energy. It was wonderful to let her become my teacher of bright, occult mysteries and beliefs. I was willing to follow her anywhere she wanted to take me, and if she had told me that God was a stump in the woods at Point Pleasant Park, I would have believed without question. In her private world were art and beauty, poetry and spirit. Spirit in all things. Only once did she refer to "entities of darkness," but she assured me that there were so many good guiding spirits that

233

no one need fear the dark ones unless you harboured "ug-liness in your heart." And all that time, we had not talked about New Dawn. We had pretended that everything was going to turn out all right.

When I left Gloria's house I had more than a mild case of euphoria. I drove back to my apartment, parked the car and went walking around Halifax in the early evening. I talked to the statue of Robbie Burns across from the Public Gardens, and I gave change to every panhandler I met. When I ran out, I went into Tim Horton's, ordered a coffee, asked for another pocketful of change and gave out more. But I did not sleep well that night despite my new dream catcher hanging in the window, framing the full moon. My breathing seemed unusual, and I experienced a heaviness in my chest. I broke out into a sweat at around eleven o'clock for no apparent reason, and everything seemed out of sync inside me. None of this was new. I had been a rotten sleeper all my life. My mother said it was because I was sensitive.

The phone rang at six-thirty in the morning, and, even before I opened my eyes, I lifted the receiver and heard Henry Sinclair's voice: "There's no one to blame, Alex. Don't even begin to try to make sense of it. It was an accident."

I swallowed hard and pressed a thumbnail into my finger to test to see if I was in the middle of a nightmare.

"Henry, I don't know what you're talking about."

Henry Sinclair sucked in his breath. "Sorry. It's Roger. He died last night."

The driver of the truck would say Roger walked directly into his path. It was intentional. One second Roger was stand-ing by the side of the road. The next thing he smiled at the driver, looked right at him, raised a bandaged hand as if in some kind of salute and then stepped directly into the path of several tons of unstoppable inertia. He never screamed.

All morning, alone in my room, I made an elaborate ceremony of laying the blame upon myself. I traced invisible lines in the happenstance of my own life that had brought about Roger's death. It began with the protesters of Point Lepreau. Joe Wood, Muriel Dorworth and Ben Milligan. The idea that you could change government — change anything with sheer will power backed up by strong conviction — that was all wrong. Then there were those misadventures of my own muddled career, leading eventually to New Dawn and the Chuck Lawrence protest. A fist in the face, national notoriety backfiring, some scrutineer from Social Services finally hammering down the coffin lid on New Dawn. And Roger realizing there was no place left for him. Roger's return to childhood had ended that day. I went out and bought a copy of the *Daily News* and studied the picture of him. Ruggedly handsome, that movie star look. The front page of the paper wore him well, and his story — the tragedy in Montreal and the "accident" yesterday — tugged at the heartstrings of Nova Scotia.

I sometimes think that nonviolent people have a monumental handicap when confronted with their own rage. I am one of those people. A young man learns his father's response to injustice, inherits it like crooked teeth or dark hair. I had inherited my father's inability to scream and kick at the indignities of life. I thought I had outgrown the lessons of my youth, but I was yet my father's son. The world was a terrible place, and some of us victims willingly wore name tags. As I sank back into my bed I mustered enough gumption to tear my dream catcher down from the window and crush it. I laughed at the great illusion I had mustered of myself as some kind of healer, counsellor, improver of lives.

I felt far more sorry for myself than I did for Roger or Roger's wife or for my friends at New Dawn. But I was sure that Gloria deserved all the concern and attention I could provide. When I knocked on her door, however, she opened it halfway but would not let me in. Her apartment was dark except for one small candle. The curtains were all drawn tight. "This should not have happened," she said. "I told Roger yesterday that the locked doors were a mistake. I told him you and Doctor Sinclair would sort things out."

"Gloria, you were his friend. You tried to help." My voice sounded weak and helpless. I reached out to touch her hand, but she pulled away and looked towards the light from the candle sitting on a small table in the middle of the room. "Can I come in?" I asked for a second time.

"No. Not now. I need to be alone. I won't be at the funeral. You go. Go for both of us. It's important that you're there for everyone else, too. Be strong. Be strong for all of them, especially Doctor Sinclair." Her voice was cool and level, but then it took on a harsh edge. "Tell them everything will be okay, that it will be like it was before. Lie to them."

"Gloria, I think you need some kind of help with this. I think we all do."

She laughed. "Grief counselling, is that what you recommend?"

I didn't respond. I felt vulnerable and exposed. If I kept standing here, she would say something to hurt me. I could feel it coming and I wasn't ready for that.

It's true — a man's death is more the affair of the survivors than his own affair. As I turned to leave Gloria, I felt a twinge of jealousy for old Rog, who had taken the quick way to the end of the freeway, leaving to the rest of us the noisy traffic of living, the suffering through endless stoplights and detours, the agonies of a journey fraught with bad drivers and sloppy road repair.

I tried to find her eyes and make her understand I would be there for her. I would give her time, forgive her for any cruel thing she might say to me. I wanted to admit I had already assigned the blame to myself, but I did not know where to turn for punishment. Roger's death had made us all less than we were. I was diminished by Roger's death, and I was also angry at him for leaving us. Like Gloria, perhaps, I was angry at anything that perverted the view of the world as a place of beauty.

The funeral took place in a bright, airy, modern chapel that smelled of Lysol and fresh lilies. Henry Sinclair looked devastated and did not get up to speak. All of the people from New Dawn except Gloria were there, but Rebecca was the only one among us to have the courage to go up to the front. She signed as she talked. Rebecca spoke in a loud, clear voice that must have sounded odd to those unaccustomed to hearing a deaf person speak. She talked about Roger's kind, playful nature, about his eagerness to learn and his appreciation of his teachers, about the workshop and about what a good friend he was. After she finished speaking, she continued to sign for several silent minutes, and I wondered if she was catching up on her translation or if she had a secret message for anyone who could understand. Jules certainly. Henry perhaps. I comprehended almost none of it except the unmistakeable hand motion over the heart for the word "love." Rebecca had decided that some things should not be said with sounds.

A generic minister spouted nonsense from a fill-in-the-

blank funeral routine. His attempted sincerity felt professional and false. Anyone who has ever attended such a service
would forgive the man, but I felt the ceremony was doubly
marred by the presence of a dozen or so policemen. Although
they probably had never known Roger personally, since he
had moved here from Montreal, they had learned he was an
ex-cop and came to show support for a fallen brother. A
young, short-haired man who looked like he scrubbed himself each morning with Dutch Cleanser said, "Those of us
who risk our lives for the common good grieve over the loss
of this fine man. We dedicate our lives to honour those who
give their lives to keep families safe, and we honour the
memory of any veteran who has worn the blue uniform of
service to his community."

I had a fleeting urge to stand and ask this unblinking
bonehead how Roger's decision to step in front of a cement
truck had helped to keep anyone's family safe. I wanted to
tell him that Roger, the adult child, had been in some ways
better than most of us, not because he felt any sense of duty
but because he had rediscovered a sense of wonder. Maybe
that was Roger's legacy.

But I wasn't bold enough to say a word. I stewed in my
own juices as my father would have. When I looked over at
Roger's wife and she turned and looked at me, I felt as if I
had been caught cheating at something. She was not crying
but was studying the faces of others in the room, as if search-
ing for some connection, some semblance of reality in this
awful sanctuary.

The starched, grim policemen were the ones to lower
Roger's casket into the grave. Inside the now-closed box he
was wearing his old Montreal uniform. As the preacher said
a nondescript prayer, I fingered a pack of gum in my pocket.
When the prayer was over, an awkward moment of silence

fixed us all in our own mediocre mortality. I thought the crowd was about to break up when Roger's wife stepped forward and tossed in a jumbo pack of Doublemint. It rivetted the attention of the mourners and, as I looked around, I almost expected to see a dozen other people toss in packs of gum as well. But the point had been made and there was an audible sigh of relief. Scotty laughed, but a poke in the ribs from Cornwallis quickly sobered him. The police contingent glared down at the packet of gum and then marched away.

Henry Sinclair tried to speak to me after the service, but he was having a bad day with language. "Of course," he said in a hushed voice, a kind of Shakespearean aside as everyone was walking away, "of course, there will be a certain amount of confusion and uncertainty. No one is ever prepared for this inevitability. Closure is the important thing. Everyone will go on from here, closing this chapter of their lives."

"Henry, they don't need closure. They need us. We need to keep New Dawn open."

"That's impossible. Yesterday, I heard from Social Services. I heard from the bank, and I heard from our friends in blue. There's a court order on New Dawn. It can't be reopened. I'll lose my house, and it looks like my wife — well, she's had it. She says she's not sure she can live with a man who has no integrity. Those were her words. But I think she means she can't live with a man who has no assets. And I mean none. They can't fine me for my crimes of compassion because I'll have no money left. There's some talk of actually putting me in jail, but I don't think it will come to that. But what I can't do is try to come up with anything that involves our clients. Social Services will be contacting each one with . . . alternatives."

"You know there's nothing for them out there."

Henry shrugged, then leaned against a tree, removed his

glasses and rubbed his eyes. "Alex. You were with me to the end. I'll always remember that."

Rebecca came over then and hugged both of us. Jules followed in her wake and did the same. As I looked into his distant eyes, I desperately wished he had been allowed to play his music at the funeral. I wished we all had done something together, with Gloria, someplace away from here — a pagan ceremony for the death of our friend. Jeff, Cornwallis, Scotty, Doris and Steve were there with us, waiting for Sinclair to speak to them. But he couldn't do it. He opened his mouth, then stopped himself, turned and walked away.

I knew it was my job to say something, anything, but all I could conjure were false hopes and lies. I saw pain and despair in the faces of these, my friends, and I had no healing words, not a shred of counsellor's wisdom. We had all been evicted from the safe haven of New Dawn Workshop and issued passports into foreign, unfamiliar territory. I wanted to say something bold and brave, something brilliant, but like my first in command I had nothing to say.

I stood my ground and bowed my head, and eventually everyone began to leave. Doris and Steve were rolled away by Jeff and Rebecca. Cornwallis put a stiff hand on my shoulder and squeezed hard, then tapped my chin with a fist. *Chin up.* Soon I was alone with Roger and his grave. I saw the men with shovels walking towards me, and I reached down and scooped up a handful of the dark rich earth and poured it into my pocket. I did not stay to study the job of men who sift soil back in on those who have left us. I wandered off among the graves and could not even remember where I had parked my car.

When the tears finally began to flow, I sat down in the grass and cried upon a headstone made of dark marble. When my eyes cleared enough to read the names, I saw that

I was mourning on the grave of a man named Parker who had died in 1967, the year I was born. It was a twin headstone, and his wife's name, Susan, was already engraved there. Like her husband, she had been born in 1918, but the year of her death had not been inscribed yet. Thirty years after the death of her husband she was still alive, not ready yet to lie down beside him in the cold, dark earth.

Thirty-one

When I got out of bed the next morning, I was sluggish and depressed. I felt despair and hopelessness settling in for a long encampment. These familiar companions would want their rooms back in the inn that was my former self. The clock told me that it was only five forty-five. A war was going on inside me, and I was prepared to retreat into the blankets, return to the comfortable defeat of sleep. I knew I could sleep for long stretches of time if I wanted to. I wondered what the world record was for human sleep without the use of pharmaceuticals and whether it would be worth trying to break it.

I lay back down and listened to my own breathing, studied the sound of my heart, a dull, familiar throbbing in my ears. And once again I thought of Karen. I remembered how she had told me that she thought there was something wrong with her heart, and I had many times put my ear up to her chest and listened. She was nine and I was thirteen then, and I would listen and reassure her that she was perfectly normal. Karen missed a lot of school that year and looked pale and unhealthy.

The doctors eventually told us that she had a malformation in her heart but that there was nothing to be done about it. They surmised that the current problems had to do with her growth and that she "might grow out of it." But she was never allowed that opportunity.

I heard the garbage truck screech to a stop, the familiar sound of receptacles emptied and then tossed back onto the morning sidewalk. Something about the notion of working men with responsibilities, up early, taking away our refuse, pulled me out of my stupor and made me sit up, put two feet firmly on the floor. On the table by my bed was a poem Gloria had given me. It was folded in half. I opened it and smoothed it out on the table, then read it twice. It was a celebration of living in the present. And I wondered if Roger's death had completely wrenched Gloria out of her flowery Wicca world of the spirit earth.

I put on a shirt and pants, watched the red numbers change on my nightstand clock. I reread Gloria's poem, looking for a clue, a signal. I don't know why, but I was also remembering what I had learned from a UNB English prof. Swimming around in my brain were two poets: T.S. Eliot and Walt Whitman. "Prufrock" versus *Leaves of Grass*. Sink into a studied despondency and escape or celebrate and embrace. Back then I had preferred Eliot over Whitman, but now I could not see why.

That same professor, a skinny, nervous guy with thick, curly hair, had brought another poet, a living one, into the classroom one day. Alden Nowlan had driven down from Fredericton and sat uncomfortably in front of the Intro to Poetry class on a frosty Saint John morning. He looked frazzled and uncertain about why he was there, and something about his sad presence made me like him immensely. In a gruff voice Nowlan read a poem about a bull moose who had

242

wandered into a cow pasture, only to be gunned down before a crowd of onlookers. And then he read a poem about visiting a "school for the retarded" as he called it. I remember when he stopped in the middle and cleared his throat and then apologetically spit something into his handkerchief. A girl in the classroom laughed loudly enough for him to hear, and he looked very embarrassed. He finished by reading a poem about being a bird, soaring high up in the sky. It sang of sweetness and joy in being alive. It was very much like Gloria's poem.

I made a point of shaking Alden Nowlan's hand that day after class and thanking him for coming down from Fredericton. He had a hurt, victimized look in his eyes, and he tried to cover it with a false smile and an even more false laugh. Something about his eyes haunted me, and it wasn't until I had left the building and gone outside that I realized it was the look I saw in my own eyes most mornings when I looked into the mirror. Before I had left the class, the poet had started to say something to me but was cut off by another professor who had come into the room to meet him. The part I had heard was, "There's a lot of . . ." and the rest was lost in the interruption.

I had always meant to write to Alden Nowlan and tell him again how much his visit meant to me, to ask him what it was that he had said. It might have been nothing at all of significance — polite chatter — but I guessed at several options: 1. "There's a lot of pain and suffering out there. The best you can do is try to make the most of what you have." It was like something my father might have said. Or 2. "There's a lot of us, people like you and me. Don't lose hope." For his poetry was very much about victims and losers, and that look in his eyes told me he recognized me as part of the tribe. Or it could have been simply: 3. "There's a lot of pretty girls

243

here. You're a lucky lad to be in this class." But I refused to believe it was anything so mundane.

Two years later in graduate school I would fall in love with one of those pretty girls who had been in that class that day, and she would break my heart into five easy pieces and toss it into the garbage for the trashmen to haul away to the dump. I would take a long while to recover, and there would be scars.

I phoned Gloria and told her to be ready to take a trip. She sounded groggy, and I knew I had woken her up. "Wear shoes you can hike in. I have a place I'm taking you to." I hung up, not allowing her to try and dissuade me.

Gloria looked tired and distracted when I arrived and, at first, tried to talk me into leaving. "I don't feel very well," she said. "I just don't feel like doing anything."

"I know you don't, but I have to take you some place. That place I discovered."

We drove down the Eastern Shore on Highway 7 and turned onto the dirt road at Parker's Lake heading towards the interior. I drove cautiously over the potholes until we came to the trail leading up to Devil's Loft. It was only eight-fifteen and the sky was cerulean blue. The forest was cool and damp, and I let silence be our companion on the first leg of the journey upwards. We stopped at the base of a high rock wall in a small grotto beneath a canopy of towering pine trees. Bracken ferns filled the forest floor. A trio of lady slipper plants bloomed in a small clearing amidst the ferns. Gloria touched the flowers delicately, but neither of us would pick them. "Is this the place?"

"No," I said, and I pointed up the rock face. "We don't have to go straight. There's a path here."

Gloria traced her hand across the fronds of a fern in front of her and breathed in the cool earth smell of the forest. "I feel alive here," she said.

"Good. I thought you would. Something about this place makes you feel that way. Wait till you get to the top."

I decided against taking her up the littered, easy route to the summit. Instead we snaked the more difficult trail back and forth on narrow ledges of rock, bracing our feet against the granite face, leaning into it and testing various roots and branches that grew out of the crevices. It was not any dramatic test of rock climbing skill but a slow, careful, studied dance as we ascended. She held onto my hand sometimes as I tested and retested every foothold, every handhold, to ensure she was safe.

We finally rose above the canopy of the forest and felt the warm sun on our faces. I told her not to turn around for the view until we were at the very top. When we finally arrived and seated ourselves among the wind-sculpted bonsai spruce, pines and dry moss, I waved a hand out at the vista before us. The lake below rippled with an early morning breeze. A seemingly endless forest stretched to the north, partitioned by other high, bare granite ridges. Wisps of cirrus clouds garnished the sky.

"Does this place have a name?"

"Devil's Loft," I said. "It's a misnomer for sure. This is where I slept that night."

"Wow. That must have been quite an experience."

"I don't know what happened to me. I wasn't sure I'd ever be able to get back down. I was scared. I thought I might die here."

"I'm not afraid of my own death. It's the death of others that scares me."

"That's because you have to hang around and feel the loss

when someone else dies. If you die, you don't have anything to worry about."

Gloria looked wide-eyed out into the empty spaces. "I think that was what Roger realized."

"You think he was that sophisticated?"

"Yeah. I do. Roger understood. He also knew that he was deserting us, but he'd been through so much already. He knew he wasn't strong enough to put up a good front and keep going. He tried to say that to me. Roger just knew there wasn't any place left for him. I feel that way sometimes."

"I know you do. So do I. It's an awful feeling."

I pulled a sealed envelope out of my pocket. I carefully opened it and showed her the dark soil I'd taken from Roger's grave. "Roger's wife was the one to throw in the pack of gum," I said.

"Somebody had to do it. I'm glad it was her."

"Any ancient Wicca ceremonies you wanna do with this?"

"You're making fun of my beliefs."

"Not really. I don't have any religious beliefs of my own, so I'm willing to go along with anything as long as it isn't too weird. Heck, this very place was probably once crawling with all kinds of witches. You wouldn't believe the dreams that went through my head the night I slept here."

She closed her eyes and held her hands up into the wind, then ran them smoothly across the face of the rock she sat on. "I don't sense any devils or witches at all. But I do think this is a sacred place. That's why you brought me here. You made it a place of spirit."

"A place of healing. I decree it so because I believe in the sun and the moon and the stars."

"Bullshit. You said that you don't believe in anything."

"Everything and nothing. But most of all I believe in you."

Gloria had come fully back to life as I spoke those words,

and I felt that I had healed her with my words, healed her with my love. "I think I believe in past lives," I said. "I think we were together in some other time."

"You don't believe that. You're playing games with me."

"I want to believe it. Don't you feel that way?"

"Yes, I do. But I'll tell you the truth. I'm more like you than I've admitted. I try very hard to believe in things — like the Wicca stuff, the earth spirits, reincarnation. I tell myself it's all true, but I don't know if it is or isn't. It just makes a kind of sense to me, gives me some hope, and it's better than believing in nothing."

I stirred the dirt around in the envelope with my finger and realized that Gloria had just removed a veil from her personality. She was far more rational than she pretended. "You're right. And I believe in more than I've admitted. I believed in New Dawn, but that's history. I still believe in Henry Sinclair, though, and all of those people there that are like my family. I believe in Jeff driving even though he's blind, and I believe in Jules's music. And I almost believe in me — this person I am now who doesn't seem to be connected to who I was in the past."

"Don't worry about the past. It's over."

"I don't think it is."

I picked out a small amount of dirt and threw it up into the wind and held the envelope out to Gloria. She did the same. We scattered the soil from Roger's grave south, then west, then north, and finally spread what was left in a small crevice in the rock to the east of where we sat.

"You do all this like it must mean something," Gloria said.

"I guess it does. It's connecting you and me and Roger and the sky and the earth."

"That sounds very convincing. I like it."

The shadow of a bird passed over us then and I expected

to look up and see an eagle, but it was an osprey. It shrieked, swooped low over us and then descended into the valley.

"Special effects," I said.

"I like it. You were obviously a very successful shaman in your previous life."

"I was. I had a few good tricks, my rates were low, and there wasn't much competition. I did okay for myself."

And we sat in silence for several golden minutes, watching as the osprey swept down towards the lake far below. Eventually, we saw a splash where it dove for a fish. It surfaced, successful, rose above the water, shook itself to release the water from its wings, and then rose back up into the sky and headed west until it was lost from view.

"Do you think we're good for each other?" Gloria asked as she picked up several small pebbles and tossed them over the edge.

"I think you are good for me, but I don't know about the rest." Now that she had asked such a blunt question, the very one that had troubled me ever since I'd fallen for her, I was more uneasy than ever about the truth of the matter.

"That's nonsense. Besides, I think it's already too late. You've made me fall in love with you. One of your shaman's spells from that previous life. You're stuck with me."

The wind had shifted from the south to the west, and it was in our face now, sweeping up the cliff with wonderful forest smells — pungent flowery scents and the powerful green aroma of life.

"Being here alone with you makes me feel that I've made the rest of the world go away. Just you and me. Here and now."

I nodded as if I agreed, but it was far from the truth. I could not wrestle myself into the present. Something Gloria had said made me feel an almost terrifying sense of responsibility, and it took me back to New Brunswick, 1978.

"Gloria, I haven't told you about Karen. About my sister. I don't know why I have to spoil this, but I haven't talked about her to anyone for a long time. Now's the time."

I felt nauseous. I knew there was some physiological tie between the story I was about to tell and what had happened to me that night I had blacked out while sitting up here at Devil's Loft.

Gloria looked at me but said nothing.

"Karen was my responsibility. From the time we were little kids. She was born when I was four. My father worked and my mother was around but always busy, and Karen just always wanted to be with me doing whatever I was doing."

I told Gloria about the Lords and Ladies of the forests of Lepreau and about the King of the Bay of Fundy, about the protesters and about the loss of our home on the Fundy shore. "We were living in Saint John. She hadn't been well for quite a while, and it had something to do with her heart. I always believed she would just get better one day. I was fourteen and she was ten. We hated almost everything about Saint John, except for the library and hanging around down at the harbour. My mother had gone out to visit with a sick friend, and I was supposed to stay home with Karen. Instead I went down to the library to get some science fiction books to read. I spent more time there than I meant to. I loved all those stupid books, I loved the dusty smell of them. I loved just reading the back covers. I stayed longer than I should have.

"And then I came home and she was in bed, not breathing. I didn't know what to do. I picked her up and carried her down the sidewalk until a man stopped his car and took us to the hospital. But she was dead. I couldn't speak. I couldn't even tell the people at the hospital my name or where I lived. My mother and father didn't find me until it was almost midnight. My mother said none of it was my fault, but my father said nothing at all. He just looked at me. When we went home he wouldn't talk to me for a week. I was supposed to take care of Karen, to protect her, and I had failed. I could never forgive myself and I still haven't. I've thought it through, rationalized it in every way possible. I was only fourteen. There probably would have been nothing that could have been done for her. That's what the doctors said. But I still feel my father's eyes piercing right through me. And that's not the worst of it.

"I've felt alone ever since she died. I used to think it would go away, but it keeps coming back. I guess some things can never heal."

Gloria listened intently, but when I stopped speaking she looked away. "I know. Some things don't heal. But we go on living anyway, right?" She scooped up some fine grains of the soil we had sprinkled in the crevice of the rock. "Responsibility never stops. I guess I learned that. Better to learn to cope with the pain than to create more hurt. It's never going to be a beautiful world, is it, Alex?"

Thirty-two

It was an easy hike back down from Devil's Loft, but my head was acting weird. I was confused about everything and I didn't know why. Despite the beauty of the day and the mountain forest, I felt as if something was wrong, as if I didn't belong there. I was cold and my heart wanted to jump out of my chest. Gloria, on the other hand, was relaxed and enjoying the descent. When we stopped for a break in the grotto of lady slippers, she looked at my face and touched my forehead. Then I pulled her to me and held onto her tightly, as if she was the only thing familiar in a place that suddenly seemed unreal, alien. But I was afraid to let her know about this terrible sensation.

I closed my eyes and heard the voice of a raven echoing against the rock cliff. Gloria's arms were soft, her hair smelled wonderful. I could not comprehend what was wrong with me, and I wondered why I had been so foolish as to return here to this place after my dreadful night on the top of this rocky cliff.

But I tried not to show my fear or my confusion. I was certain that whatever was happening to me was psychological, something wrong in the head. I didn't want to talk about it. I trudged on, down the erratic path, stumbling every few steps now over roots and rocks.

Gloria was telling me about flowers, I think, or herbs. Something to do with Wiccan customs. I could not concentrate on what she was saying in spite of her enthusiasm over cinquefoil, horsetails, coltsfoot, sage and thyme.

My hand was finally opening the car door, and I wasn't sure I could drive. And then I felt the pain rip through my chest, I felt my lungs unable to collect the air. I heard Gloria's voice, and I tried to speak but couldn't. I lost my grip on the car handle, fell to the ground, and stared up at the sun as I lay upon my back. I was shocked that the sun seemed to be disappearing, turning to black before my eyes. It never even occurred to me that I was passing into unconsciousness. I heard Gloria call my name, heard her feet moving on the stones of the road, and then I was swallowed by the darkness and stabbed by another hot knife of pain in my chest. *Make the pain go away,* I begged silently. And it did.

I awoke in a hospital room at Dartmouth General two days later. Confusion filled my brain. My chest felt sore, I could hear blood pounding in my ears. I don't know why, but I experienced a powerful sensation of sadness and loss as I awoke. I tried to remember how I got here, but I couldn't. There was a tube in my nose, and as far as I could tell it was providing me with oxygen. I had hazy, blurry vision, but it was enough to assess that I was in one piece. Now I recognized a dull pain as I breathed in and out.

I wanted to feel the exhilaration of being alive after being "away" for all that time, but my joy was clouded with something else — something muffling my thoughts. Drugs of some sort, I tried to assure myself. I moved my head to the side and realized I was not alone. Gloria was there, asleep in the chair. With great difficulty I raised my arm, stretched out a finger and touched her arm. She awoke and leaned over to kiss me on the cheek.

I tried to find words to make language but my tongue seemed overly large in my mouth and it was hard to do more than whine like a dog. I lifted my other arm to find the tube to wrench it from my nose, but Gloria stopped me and whispered for me to just lie quietly. "Welcome back," she said. "I missed you."

Gloria got up, and I tried to speak again. "Don't leave me," I wanted to say.

"It's okay. I'm getting the doctor."

She walked out of the room, and an exquisite pang of loneliness swept my soul, more awful than anything I had ever felt before in my life. The loneliness was coupled with fear, and I longed to fall back into unconsciousness.

She was probably gone for less than two minutes. My head filled up with information, as if my subconscious mind was overly anxious to download all of the recent events as soon as I found my way back to the waking world. Devil's Loft. The demise of New Dawn. Roger's death, his funeral. I could clearly see the chewing gum on the coffin. I could see the grains of soil on the rock atop the mountain. And my battered and bruised ego was trying to tell me that something terrible had happened and I would never be the same again. Nothing would ever be as it was before. I had been privy to a short tenure of happiness in my life that would now be wrenched away. My father's voice from somewhere deep inside me was saying what I should have known all along: we came from a tribe that would never be allowed to live without considerable grief.

The doctor, a woman with dark, concerned eyes, delicately undid the tape that held the oxygen tube in my nose and then, seeing Gloria's distress, asked her to wait outside. When Gloria was gone, the doctor held a stethoscope to my heart. I tried to sit up, but she placed a palm upon my chest and shook her head. So I lay there, exhausted from even that small exertion, and I waited.

"Can you speak?"

"Yes."

"Do you know who I am?"

"A doctor."

"Yes. But call me Vergie. I come from a family that did not believe in formality."

"Vergie." My voice sounded scratchy, almost artificial.

"Your throat is dry. Here, sip some water."

As the water slid down my throat I felt as if I had never tasted such a wonderful thing before. My head felt light again, but my brain tried to register why sipping water from a straw could seem like such a miracle.

"Better?"

"Yes."

"It's good to have you conscious again."

"It's good to be, um, back."

"Do you know what happened?"

"No."

"Your heart stopped beating."

"What?"

"It stopped. Fortunately for you, it started again. For the time being, you are okay. Isn't that good?"

"Yes. Very good."

"Should I stop there for now?"

"No."

"Are you sure?"

I blinked and drank again, feeling life flow back into me. "I'm feeling better now. I'm really anxious to know everything."

Vergie picked up the edge of the rumpled blanket and sheet and straightened them. She made a fuss over smoothing out the wrinkle in the bedspread and tucking in a corner, as if she wasn't a doctor at all but the orderly whose job it was to arrange the bed linen. She picked up my chart, read it.

I was waiting eagerly for more information. All I knew at this point was that I must have come close to dying and that I was now feeling very, very tired again. She could tell I was exhausted.

"You go back to sleep. Call me when you wake up again and we'll pick up the story from there. It can wait, believe me." She showed me the buzzer beside the bed and left.

Gloria returned, and I tried very hard to remain conscious, but I felt like a drowning man. The pain was more acute now, but some part of my being seemed to drag me

254

back away from it. I was in retreat from life again. I tried to hang on. I wanted to talk to Gloria.

She sat down beside me, and I could tell she was filled with a dread she could not control. "Alex, I don't know if I can do this," she confessed. "I don't know if I'm strong enough. I was preparing myself for anything. I was preparing myself to love you and getting ready to take the chance that you might change, that you would someday lose interest in me and move on to someone else. I was making myself strong for you. But I don't know if I can handle this."

And before I could say that she did not have to be strong for me, that all she had to do was be there, I fell back into the inky darkness.

It was evening when I awoke again, and this time Gloria was not there. I still felt immobile, but I wiggled my toes, stretched my fingers. I was able to remove the tube from my nose on my own. I tried to sit up and found it impossible. But I was awake, hungry now, slightly better adjusted to being alive than the time before. The pain was not gone but diminished, and I noticed another tube with a needle inserted into my arm, wondered if it was some sort of painkiller dripping into my system. I found the buzzer and a nurse came.

"Can I see Vergie?"

"Yes, I'll get her."

"And Gloria?"

"Who?"

"She was with me."

"Oh. Sorry. She left a while ago. I'll get the doctor."

"Stronger?"

"A little."

"More questions? I'm ready if you are."

I drank water through a straw, this time holding the cup myself. My voice still sounded like sandpaper. "Good thing I'm not a singer."

"You'll get your voice back. It's temporary. Mind if I ask you a question before we get started?"

"I guess not. Looks like I'm not going anywhere important."

"Have you been treated for this before?"

"This *what*?"

"Ventricular fibrillation. Irregular heartbeats. You had something close to a heart attack but not the usual kind."

The words "heart attack" echoed in my head. "No, I've never had a heart attack. I don't understand."

"Okay, I shouldn't have used those words. It wasn't exactly a heart attack. Your heart stopped. You've had some problem there all your life, right?"

"No. This is nuts."

"There now, don't get upset. Look, we did x-rays. You've got a malformation of the lower part of your heart. You must have been born with it."

"I've always been healthy," I lied. I was prepared to deny everything. This was some kind of sick joke.

"I don't have any medical records to go on. Have you never been to a doctor for heart problems, palpitations, murmurs, blackouts, ever before?"

I tried to take a deep breath, and it hurt my lungs. "I had a problem with stress a few years ago. Panic attacks. It went away." I didn't want to tell her about blacking out at Devil's Loft the week before. I didn't want anyone to have any clues that said I was in bad shape and maybe getting worse. "Look, I've never been a star athlete, but I've been pretty healthy. I don't understand this."

"Easy, Alex. Maybe we should wait longer before we talk about this."

"No, dammit. I want to know now."

There was an awkward silence.

"Do you know what happened to Gloria?" I asked more civilly.

"I told her to go home and get some rest. She's very worried about you."

"And does she have good reason to worry?" I studied the woman's face. She had a professional demeanour and a softness about her eyes. She appeared to be not much older than me, and in another setting I might have found her exotic and attractive. I almost told her so.

"Yes. Your condition is very serious."

"Why do I keep thinking this is all a bad TV show?" I was angry, outraged at whatever or whomever had put me in this situation.

"Real life, Alex, is full of moments like this. TV makes a mockery of it, but I take it very seriously. Do you understand?"

"Yes. Tell me more. When will I get better?"

"Do you feel tired?"

"Yes. What does that have to do with it?"

"You may feel this way . . . often."

"And the pain?"

"Is it bad?"

"No, but it's there. I think you're keeping it dulled with something."

"A painkiller, that thing in your arm. It helps, yes?"

"Yes."

"Don't worry. The pain will subside. And I'm sorry that I told you you had a heart attack. I needed you to understand how serious the problem was."

"Then I didn't have a heart attack?"

"Not technically speaking. But actually a heart attack can

be treated more readily than your condition. Like I said, your heart stopped. It just stopped."

"Jesus. How could that happen?"

"It happens. Sometimes the heartbeat can be irregular. Sometimes the muscles in the lower chamber of your heart will sort of twitch, but the heart doesn't pump. Sometimes it starts right back up, but sometimes it doesn't. You were very lucky. You blacked out when your heart went into the erratic rhythm. Your girlfriend got you in the car, and I think your heart stopped altogether while she was driving. Fortunately, she got you to an RCMP station and they had paddles. Otherwise you'd be gone. You ended up here after you were stabilized."

"I didn't know she could even drive."

"She said she watched you teach a friend."

I tried to laugh but it hurt my chest. Gloria had been in the back seat a couple of times when I'd taken Jeff on driving lessons in the parking lot.

"You're going to need her. You're going to need all your friends. What about family?"

"My mother's in New Brunswick. I don't want her involved."

"The rest of your family?"

"Gone," I said. I felt like a boy withholding a secret. Why was it I didn't want her to know anything else about me or about my family?

"Any of them have anything like this? This arrhythmia, pardon the expression, often runs in the family."

"No, nothing," I lied. I believed that if I held onto my secrets, she would not be able to tie together all the facts and present me with the full picture. I just didn't want to know how badly off I was, and I didn't want to know that whatever killed my sister and maybe my father might kill me any day now. "How do you treat this? How do you fix me back up?"

"Rest first, then some physiotherapy, then some drugs, but with this condition, the drugs can sometimes make it worse. That's how you're different from a heart attack patient. There's a sort of healing that can take place from a heart attack. You have a condition that is part of the very design of your heart."

"Something I was born with?"

"Yes. I can't believe it was never detected."

I could, but I wouldn't say it. Ever since Karen had died, I'd minimized any and all contact with doctors, refused x-rays, mistrusted everyone in the medical profession. In truth, I had suspected there was something wrong with me long ago, and I had kept this suspicion hidden in the deepest recesses of my brain. It started the year before Karen died, but her death made me block it out. "Say it to me in the simplest terms possible."

"It's a defect in the heart. We don't know how to repair it."

"A bad heart?"

"Not all bad. Alex, it's amazing you haven't run into this sooner. I don't know how that could have happened. But here you are, and you've suffered once. I will not lie to you. It will happen again. You can improve your condition, you can do everything to prevent it, but it *will* happen again. Maybe tomorrow, maybe ten years from now. Maybe thirty years from now. This is a terrible fact, but I believe that you need to know. I'll get you some literature on it when you're ready. We can't even begin to predict when a problem might come up again."

"You're telling me you can't do anything about it?"

"Not much. I feel like a fool saying that. But there it is. Now rest, please."

The room seemed too small just then. The world seemed a hostile, hopeless place, and I did not want to be in it. My father had started me out with more than a bad attitude towards life. He had good reason to expect the worst for himself, although he had probably never heard of ventricular fibrillation or arrythmia, never knew that it might not be a good idea for someone with such a condition to make a living at hard physical labour. I shut my eyes and remembered that morbid, angry look on his face the day the doctor told us that Karen was dead. I think, like me, he had covered up his own physical problems all his life. I think he believed — or he knew — that he had passed them on to Karen.

Vergie tucked in the blankets again, smoothed them with her hands, smiled in a way that seemed to have nothing at all to do with being a doctor. "I was born on the island of Mindanao in the Philippines. When I was young an earthquake destroyed our village and killed my mother, father and two brothers. I was injured very badly, and I was certain that I, too, would die. I even *wanted* to die to be with my family. An old woman I had once hated took me in even though I treated her very badly. But she told me that every moment of living is sacred. She convinced me to live in the moment, not in the past. I did not believe it was possible until she gave me a kitten to keep as a pet. Along with so many of the survivors, she died of typhoid from the bad water in the village after the earthquake had ruined the clean wells. But I lived on and so did my little pet. And I could not understand why. But I learned to do as she had said. I learned to love the sacred nature of every minute. I say this to you not as a doctor but as a survivor."

She touched my forehead and then left me alone. I closed my eyes and tried very hard to forgive my father for doing this thing to both Karen and me. I wondered at the cruel paradox that both he and I felt the same responsibility for Karen's death. Neither of us had forgiven ourselves, ever, and yet he had died without talking about this thing between us.

For I had grown up in a family where we had failed to make language a true tool of our emotions.

As I closed my eyes again, I felt less alone. Terror gave way to the smallest bubble of possibility that I could eventually claw my way back to a semblance of life outside a hospital. But it was shattered into a million jagged fragments of fear as the darkness bullied the light from the world again.

Thirty-three

I awoke this time to the sound of a baby crying, a sound that travelled a great distance down antiseptic hospital hallways to find me on this otherwise quiet morning. I had drifted in and out of consciousness over several days. Complications with the heart, the circulation, the medication. I was here and then I was not. Even now I was not fully certain I was alive, the fog was so thick in my skull. But the crying of a baby, newborn perhaps, many rooms away, was so startling, so insistent, so demanding. A life, needing something: food, comfort, its mother's love. This was what pulled me back to life.

The baby howled louder, and I wanted to get up and go to it and offer comfort. It seemed as if it would not stop, and I wondered in my befuddled way if there was no one else in this hospital, no one to comfort a child new to this crazy world.

The crying stopped, but it echoed in my heart with its powerful insistence and need. I removed that damn tube from my nose and breathed only the hospital air now. It smelled artificial, toxic and raw in my lungs. I touched my face

261

with my hands and the skin felt clammy, alien. I had a beard, something rare for me, a stubbly, rasping scruff. Something about the touch of it let me know I was different. Forever different. New identity. No going back. There was a mirror in the room, but I knew that if I was to look into one, I would see the image of my father, the ill-shaven pulp cutter. Rarely as a child had I touched his face with my hand, but when I did, it had felt just like this.

I half-expected that parts of me were missing. My right hand explored uncertain territory. Two arms, two legs. Everything intact. Just a defective heart that might give out at any second of the night or day. Then I found another tube — a catheter. This discovery humbled me more than everything else. Someone had attached this thing to me. If not this time, then the next time, this is the way I would die — tube up the nose, tube between the legs. What else would they have wired or pumped into me to keep me alive? And why would I want to live at all if I was just a failing organism in a bed, taking up space, waiting for the inevitable. Death, dark and brooding and waiting in the wings, had been cheated of me once. But it was only a matter of time.

While asleep or unconscious, my brain had been chewing away at something. Roger had haunted my thoughts. Roger had perhaps been wiser than anyone had known. Roger's comprehension of his own hopelessness was what sent him out onto the road in front of a truck. Was this a kind of courage I could begin to understand? But no, I wasn't ready to off myself to ease my pain or anybody else's. That baby was crying for something, fighting to live, crying for attention, for sustenance. It's what we all wanted. I wanted to live so badly I could taste it, like the salt of Fundy seawater in my throat.

I would tear and rage and shriek at death and doctors and anyone who would continue to say my life would be short and improbable.

But I would not punish a living soul on my behalf. I would learn to care for myself, recover, and when the end came, I wanted to be alone in a room, dialling a phone perhaps for ambulance men, strangers, to find me, bring me back or let me go on. But I would not be some place where the god-awful responsibility of my living or dying was thrust upon anyone. Not my mother, for she had seen way too much of early death. Not some friend. Not even a hired nurse or housekeeper would have to put up with my demise. Above all, I would not allow Gloria back into my life.

She had already expressed her fear. I knew her history. I had no choice but to set her free, push her gently away and then stay out of her life so she could get on with it without me dragging her down.

I drifted off into a blue-grey hazy place that seemed warm and safe, and I wondered each time if this was death. Asleep or half-waking, never quite knowing which, it became familiar geography to me, and I would finally wake and find the tube back in my nose, delivering oxygen to my weary lungs. Sometimes, while in that state, I listened for my heart to stop its pulsating thud, thud, thud. I waited for the silence at the end of the drumbeat, but instead that flawed organ worked on, saving death for some other time, for some more dramatic ambush.

One morning, my eyelids half open, a half-formed memory still in my head, I tried to focus on Henry Sinclair, sitting on an orange vinyl chair by my bed. "Welcome back," he said as he traced his fingers through his thinning black hair.

"One damned thing after another," I said with as much energy as I could muster.

"Damned is the operative word there. How are you, Alex?"

"I've been better, but they say I'm recovering."

"Your doctor explained to me. Ventricular fibrillation."

"Sounds like the punch line in a bad joke, doesn't it?"

"It sounds like you're going to be well enough to get out of here soon is what it sounds like. "

"Vergie is an optimist."

"Who?"

"My doctor, the angel of mercy from the Philippines."

"She's probably telling you the truth."

"Telling me what I want to hear is more like it. It's as if I've got this one-way airplane ticket, already booked and paid for. Only problem is that I don't know what day or hour the plane is going to take off, but I've got a seat reserved and I'll be in it. Hope it's a window seat. But not right by the wing. I love to watch the clouds."

"Alex, none of us knows for sure how much longer we'll be alive. Anything can happen. Look at Roger."

"Roger was in control of his travel arrangements."

Henry removed his glasses as he often did, studied the rims, looking for the secret message. The air in the room was dense. My breathing became heavy, laboured, but after a few minutes things got better.

"How is everybody doing?" I asked.

"It's been a rough time. People don't just want to stay at home."

"I don't blame them. They miss New Dawn. I miss New Dawn."

"Don't think I haven't been trying. Churches, community halls. It's either fire regulations or a money issue or something vaguely political that I can't quite put my finger on."

I had a been dreaming of New Brunswick again in recent days. The shoreline, Point Lepreau. The house. The building of the power plant. I had dreamed of a meltdown at Lepreau and of the whole coast dead and irradiated, lifeless for centuries. But something else. "Joe Wood, Muriel Dorworth, Ben Milligan." I must have spoken out loud, although I wasn't sure the words could be heard.

"Who? What?"

I explained about the protestors of Lepreau, those gentle, almost mythical heroes of my childhood. "Ben Milligan was some kind of minister. Unitarian, I think."

"And?"

"Did you try the Unitarians? Did you ask if you could meet in their church?"

"No. But I guess it wouldn't hurt."

"Tell them about us. Tell them about me. And Ben Milligan."

"What do I have to lose?" Then he sighed, a great, sorrowful sound that reminded me of my father on the shore with Karen and me. Sadness, defeat. "Jesus, Alex. I've been wallowing in self-pity ever since we got closed down. I didn't know I was so weak. Everyone depended on me, and all I had done was create a fancy little illusion."

"What you created was a kind of sanctuary. Too bad those churches can't recognize that. New Dawn was the safe place for a lot of good people who needed it. I needed New Dawn more than anyone. That's why you hired me, wasn't it?"

"Maybe, but I should have told you I didn't have the cash to pay you."

"Guess it didn't seem important at the time." I swallowed hard, caught my breath. "Henry, have you seen Gloria?"

"Yes."

"You know, we sort of found ourselves in this . . . relationship."

"Yes. I think it was okay. Don't worry about that. Good for both of you."

"Have you talked with her? They say she's been here but not when I've been awake. I keep going in and out of this consciousness thing."

"Yes. She has been here. And yes, I've talked to her."

"I need to break it off."

"Why?"

"You know why. I've already caused her pain."

"No, you helped her. She said so. You helped her get through Roger's death. She took that very personally. He was a friend."

"Come on, Henry, you know what I'm saying. I can't put Gloria through any more than I have."

"You want my opinion as a professional or as a friend?" I studied the lines in his face. "I think I just got both."

"Don't push her away, Alex. She deserves that."

"Which was that? The professional or the friend?"

Henry just shook his head, reached into his pocket and pulled out a small notebook. "She's coming up here later. But she gave me this to pass on to you. Wanted you to read it. If you were asleep, I was supposed to leave it by your bed."

Henry handed the notebook to me, and I felt a kind of electric thrill just to touch it. "I'm off. Go ahead and read it. She'll be here in a while. You do what's best."

Henry took my hand but held it gingerly, as if he was afraid a serious handshake would injure me. "I'll talk to the Unitarians. You get some rest."

When he was gone, I opened the notebook and held it to my face, smelled the pages. *Gloria, Gloria, Gloria.* The little book was Gloria's world, her cosy apartment, her own sanctuary that she had let me into. I fought hard against reading it. I was resolute. I would do whatever was necessary to end our relationship. I hated myself just then and wondered how my purposeful compassion could feel so much like self-loathing. It did not seem logical.

Oh, sweet oblivion. A battle surged within me: which did I want more — the final beat of my ailing, traitor heart or one more chance to be with Gloria? To feel her hair upon my cheek, to touch her face with my hand, to lose myself in her eyes.

I opened to the first page. Handwriting like a small neat garden. Words formed like flower arrangements, each one delicate and precise, intentional, resonant upon the page. It was prose this time, not poetry:

> The world according to Alex. Already he has led me high up and away from who I was. I know where I am going and can have no fear of anything or anyone. The word "love" seems so small and incapable of containing this feeling. He brings me the singing sky, the wind like sweet messengers of possibility. Together we carve the precision of two souls slipping into sunrise or sunset, our touch the elastic dimension of some new universe.
>
> No limits, all possibility within each second, each glowing moment together. A fierce feeling of wilful need in me now. Not to be lost. One minute. One hour. A lifetime can expand or contract. We can compress the world into whatever we have. Time has no dominion in the place where we are.
>
> Love, a weak verb in the great expanse of our country where some other langauge must in-

vent itself for us, for our tongues to find in the days ahead.

Alex, come back to me and give us time. Grant me the chance to be with you night and day. There can never be loss or regret. Hold onto me. Just hold me. Nothing, nothing can diminish us, not even death.

There was more, but I could not read on. I closed the notebook gently, tucked it beneath my pillow. Felt more than ever the urgent need to push her away from me and save her from the futility of remaining in love with a dying man. Was it the hard-edged pessimism of my father speaking in my head? If I was weak, a victim, then why not let her love me, let her care for me? But I came from a legion of men who set duty above personal dire need. In another time, I would perhaps have gladly died on some pitted, muddy and point-less battlefield in the belief that I was saving her. Now I would do this other thing. I would impose a granite will against my own love and save her from suffering, for I knew I could not save myself. And I would make her understand.

Thirty-four

My heart stopped again that night. I was near sleep, feeling like a ship coming into a snug, friendly harbour, when suddenly I felt a hammer stroke, a steel maul pounding upon my chest, and then the searing pain I had encountered only one time before. The agony made me long for death and rage against whatever blind forces could cause any living soul to feel this way. I understood immediately how easy it is to welcome death and, in that same second of clarity, saw myself for the coward that I was. I did not want to fight for life at all. I heard the alarm go off on the monitor, saw first an orderly, then a nurse, then an unknown doctor file into the room, and, in the moments that seemed to last for hours, I wanted to beg them to ignore the machine, ignore me.

I waited anxiously for some sort of hand to lift me away from that place, but the pain did not go away until blackness fell down on me like a lead sheet — cold, hard and comfortless. I finally tried to lift a hand and fend it off, but my body had turned traitor.

I fully expected to die.

But I was in the belly of the beast, a hospital that would not allow me such courtesy.

When I awoke again it was to music. Someone had put headphones on me, and I was listening to a Rachmaninoff symphony. I opened my eyes and saw that the headphones were hooked up to a portable tape player. I recognized the sound of the keyboard, and I knew it was a tape of Jules playing the instrument. I let the music wash over me, but some part of me wanted to argue with the beauty of the sound; that same part of me was angry at the good will of whoever had brought it to me. Memories of people and places flooded back, and I wanted them to stop. I shook my head to try and dislodge the earphones, but they held firmly. A nurse saw me as she walked by the room and came in, checked the monitors, then walked out again.

"We had a crash cart right outside your room," Vergie told me as soon as she arrived and lifted the earphones away. "You were in a hospital — what can I say, we're professionals. We expected this to happen. You were in the right place and we were ready."

"Could you let me go next time?" I asked, my mouth dry, my voice barely discernible.

"You didn't appreciate our good work?"

"Thanks. I'm sorry."

"Here, have some water."

"How many more times is this going to happen before I'm through?"

She smiled, and I saw the face of a fifty-year-old woman who had seen much pain in her life. She touched my forehead with a warm hand. "It might not happen again for a long time. I've increased the medication to a level that should prevent the heart from acting like it did. If we can get you stable, we might be able to operate, but your particular problem is somewhat rare."

"Lucky me."

"Lucky to be alive."

"Did you tell anyone else?"

"You haven't told us the address of your parents, remember? Those other visitors? Should we call the young woman or that funny pair that brought you the music?"

"No. Absolutely not."

"Mr. Tough Guy."

"Doctor Vergie, I hate this. I don't think I can handle any more of it. Tell me what to do."

She sat down, touched her thin silver necklace. "Be brave," she said. "Let people who want to help you do their job. Don't give up. And don't push away people who care about you."

I didn't want to hear any of that. I turned my head towards the wall.

"You're going to sleep a lot in the next few days again. I've got to load you up with some pretty strong stuff. It's not so much to keep you groggy but to help regulate that heartbeat, keep it slow and regular. After that, we'll see."

She fiddled with the controls of the tube that was attached to my arm. I wanted to scream at her, say no. I did not want to continue to lie here like a vegetable. I was sick of living, sick of the prospects of more pain. I deeply dreaded the thought of getting well only to get worse again over and over. I can honestly say that if there was a switch for me to pull, a button to push that would have given me an end, I would have made the move. Instead, I slid down the side of a sandy wall into a deep, deep canyon. I went down, down, and my eyelids felt like heavy curtains, but somewhere I was sure I could see birds with enormous wings circling.

I know that Gloria was there the following day. She sat and read to me from a book of English poetry. I could hear her, but I could barely see her through the Fundy fog of the drugs. I could not speak to her, but there was a kind of war going on in my head. The regiment of will wanted to push her away, ignore her, build impenetrable military lines to keep her out of my life. But rebel troops were ready to fight for her, to bring

271

her back into my life, to force me to consciousness. I lay there in my medical stupor, waiting for my heart to stop again, listening to her, yearning for her, wanting to hold her in my arms.

"Alex, I want you to know I'm doing okay. I'm going to be here for you no matter what. I've learned to be strong. Nothing is more important to me than you are. I can take care of you. We've only begun to know what it's like to love each other. I think you've already healed me in some powerful way that I could not have imagined. Now you need to get better, and I know you will."

I felt an exquisite terror just then. The war in my fickle brain. My useless body trapping my spirit. I was aware of many dimensions. Life and death did not seem so far apart, steps along the way to somewhere. Gloria's words inside my head, strong and beautiful and healing me, but at the same time creating rage at my frailty.

That voice that offered me salvation: Gloria beside me reading more poetry, then children's stories — the voice of my mother, the voice of a little girl, Karen's voice, then back to Gloria, then something else I could not identify. Gloria's earth goddess, perhaps, Wiccan healer or spirit guide.

When they eased off on the dope-drip, I awoke to the music again. Jules playing Brahms with the sound of a church organ. My arms miraculously worked. I lifted the earphones from my head and opened my eyes, and the light was painful. I raised my arms, curled my toes. Aches but no pains. I placed my hand over my heart and felt it pounding slowly and naturally, as if I was in perfect health. I removed the oxygen tube and swore as I removed the catheter.

I sat up on the edge of the bed, went dizzy, grabbed hold

of a metal bar that kept me from falling. I let the planet spin for a minute, then forced it to stop. I tried to stand and found I could do it, but I still had the tube attached to my arm, still had wires tethering me to a heart monitor. I found the switch to the monitor, turned it off. No siren, no squeal. It just went dead with a satisfying click, and I felt a waft of relief. I saw the adjustment valve on the IV medication and cranked it closed. End of drip. Without pulling the needle from my arm, I saw the connection where the tube could be slipped apart. Once again I was an individual, not an apparatus.

I stood, I breathed. Every new motion was a test. I waited for my heart to do its trick. I waited for it to kill me, but it would not. I found a washbasin on my night stand and splashed some water onto my face. As it dripped down over my lips I tasted it, and it seemed like the same salty water that I once licked from my lips as a swimmer, a child on the summer shore. The room wanted to whirl again, but I trained it not to. My feet wanted to pretend they didn't remember how to walk, but I commanded them to work.

I circumnavigated my room three times before regaining my bed and falling asleep. When I awoke yet again I was attached only to the heart monitor. I felt refreshed, substantial, prepared to take whatever next step was required of me.

"In a couple of weeks," Vergie told me, "I think you can leave. You take the pills, you have a shot at staying alive. The safe thing to do would be to stay here in the hospital for another month, but there are others waiting for the bed. Cutbacks. Seems drastic, but it's out of our hands."

"I want to leave. It's okay." I was thinking that my old enemy Chuck Lawrence had unwittingly done me a big favour here.

"She keeps asking about you, you know."

"I'll talk to her."

Vergie studied my face and knew I was hiding something.

"You're going to be weak for quite a while. It'll take some time. Don't exercise. Don't drive, either. You could pass out. Take it easy and watch TV."

"You went to medical school to be able to give advice like 'watch TV'?" I was trying to sound funny, but the bitter edge of sarcasm was cruel.

"Watch your mouth or I'll pump some more dope into you," she teased. She fiddled with her necklace again, and this time I could see the small silver cross pendant. I had a feeling she was saying a silent prayer for me in the awkward interval that followed. I wanted to ask her, but it seemed a private thing, something to do with childhood and earthquakes in the Philippines. I kept quiet, afraid that I'd admit I thought religion and superstition were one and the same.

"Stay with us one more day, just to be safe. Then we give you the boot."

"Sure," I said. "Thanks, Vergie."

She handed me a phone. "I had this plugged in for you specially. Use it."

I stared at the phone and despised what it represented. A communication link to everything out there. The woolly world of semi-consciousness suddenly seemed much friendlier.

My clothes were folded into a small neat pile on the chair. I found my wallet still in the pocket, found the folded card that contained all the phone numbers of the people who had been part of my life. I dared not call Gloria. My door of escape was still open. I was determined to save her from whatever agonies our continued relationship could hold for her. In many ways, the damage was already done. All I could do was minimize it.

The same could be said of my mother. She had a happier future ahead of her at Pine Ridge Manor. I was glad I had not allowed her to take part in any of this current catastrophe. She would learn the story afterwards, and that grief would have to satisfy the ravenous appetite for suffering that propelled this inhospitable planet.

My car keys were in my pants pocket as well. Somewhere in the hospital parking lot my Dodge Shadow sat rusting away in the salty air. Gloria had followed the ambulance and then left it out there, waiting for me to get better and drive off. A car waiting for its owner to recover. Metallic loyalty. Dull, witless allegiance.

I decided to phone Cornwallis. He almost didn't believe it was me. "This is like a miracle."

"No miracle. Drugs and doctors." And then I told him I wanted him to help get me to the airport.

"You want me to do what?"

"I want to fly home to New Brunswick. To see my mother."

"Wouldn't you be better off with a taxi? Man, I still got my license, but I haven't driven in a quite a while."

"Cornwallis, I'm going to need your help to get out of here. I can walk, but I'm kind of shaky."

"Then why are you leaving?"

"They need the beds. I'm not supposed to go until tomorrow, but I have to get out of here now. I just have to."

"I think you should stay put."

"I can't. I'm being serious with you. I just can't. I need to leave tonight. Just help me to the airport."

"What about Gloria?"

"I don't know about Gloria," I lied. "I've been a lot of trouble for her. I can't do that to her any more."

Silence.

"Cornwallis?"

"Yeah, man."

"Can you help me?"

"Just tell me the truth about exactly what I'm helping you to do."

"The airport. Drive me there. That's all. Boy wants to go see his mom."

"When?"

"Tonight. About eight. I'll catch a flight out before ten."

"I don't know."

"Please?"

"Okay, son. See you soon."

Thirty-five

I never once in my entire childhood thought about running away from home. Maybe I was singular, unique in that respect. Instead, I spent much of my life running away from life itself. I hid more than I ran, really, but now I was a runner, and a runner I would remain until I ended up dead somewhere in a place far off, a place of strangers. I looked at the pills on the night stand, the medication that would help to keep my heart beating with its regulated rhythm. A medication to measure out my life. I considered leaving it there but realized that suicide was not my intention. I would die soon enough, but I would be a good boy about it. Take my pills, keep the muscle as dependable as my body would allow. Besides, I wanted to be far away and anonymous when I left this world. I refused to put Gloria through another episode of hauling my carcass back from death's cryptic door.

And I would not return home to my mother in New Brunswick. That was an even more horrific scenario. I would allow her that dream life among the morning card players and afternoon cocktail drinkers of Pine Ridge. She deserved at least that.

I considered calling the airport to see what flights were heading out late tonight but abandoned the plan. I would show up with my VISA card in hand and, trusting that I was not yet over my limit, go for whatever was available. At the very least, there'd be a flight to Toronto or Montreal. From there I would be safely on my way further west, maybe to Vancouver, or maybe I'd stay put, figure out what would come next.

Not much of a plan, but there it was. I put on my clothes and walked around the room, testing myself like a crooked old man. In the mirror, I looked pale as the Robin Hood flour my mother used to bake her bread. My wretched demeanour made me that much more certain that I did not want to drag Gloria down with me. It was the right thing to do, no matter how much it was tearing me apart inside.

"You look bad," Cornwallis said when he walked in the door. For some unknown reason, Jeff was with him.

"Bad good or bad bad?"

"I guess it could be worse," he said. "How come they're letting you leave?"

"Done everything they can do here. Now it's just up to my body to heal itself. Hey, Jeff, how you doing?"

Jeff had his hand on the frame of the door. "I'm okay, Alex. Cornwallis told me he was coming, and I asked if I could come for the ride."

"You look pretty down in the dumps," I said. I had never seen Jeff so sullen and lethargic.

"I think he's still hurting over Roger," Cornwallis said.

"It's everything," Jeff said. "Roger. You. New Dawn down the tubes. How did it all happen?"

I shrugged and was shocked that even that manoeuvre hurt. Everything about me ached, but I was going to do my best not to let on. "Shit happens," was all I could say. Bumper sticker talk. "Guess I'm ready to go."

Cornwallis frowned. He knew something was weird here. "You call Gloria today?"

"Not today," I said. "I've been enough trouble. I'll call her when I'm home in Saint John," I lied. "She'll understand."

"She's worried about you, Alex," Jeff said. "Gloria really cares about you."

"She loves you, is what Jeff is trying to say. I don't know if she'd like to hear about you sneaking off to the airport without saying goodbye."

I shrugged. "I'm not sneaking. I'll call her, honest."

"So, don't you, like, ride out of here in a wheel chair or something?" Cornwallis asked.

"That's only on TV. This is real life. I just walk out the front door."

"Sometimes even TV makes more sense than real life, don't you think?"

"Depends which show you're talking about." I took a couple of steps but wobbled a bit.

"Here, let me help you," Cornwallis said, and put a strong hand under my arm. "Man, you lost some weight. You hardly weigh anything at all."

"It's the food here," I said. "Wasn't worth eating." Truth was I had almost forgotten what food tasted like after being fed through tubes during much of my stay. I promised myself that wherever I landed I would eat like a horse.

We must have appeared an odd trio, Jeff with his hand on Cornwallis's elbow, me propped upright by the worried-looking black man. But the halls were nearly empty and no one asked any questions at the desk, where a new shift was just taking over. Then we were out the front door and into the night. Cornwallis didn't have too much trouble locating my car, and I gave him the key.

"I don't like driving at night," he said. "Why don't you drive?"

"I'm still a little shaky."

"I can see that."

"I'll drive," Jeff said. "Night time, daytime. Doesn't matter to me." But it was a goof, an old bit of the New Dawn dialogue.

Cornwallis sat down in the driver's seat and I got in the back. Jeff walked around the car and got in front.

"I don't like driving other people's cars," Cornwallis said. "Makes me nervous. Somebody always blames me if something goes wrong."

"I won't blame you."

Cornwallis started the car, then ground the starter again when he turned the key a second time. "Engine's so damn quiet I didn't even know it was started."

As we left the parking lot of Dartmouth General, I saw the lights of container ships and oils rigs sitting on the nearby waters of Halifax Harbour. It was a placid, star-filled night, and I felt as if I had not been part of the outside world for a very long time.

As Cornwallis pulled out into the street, I suddenly felt very, very frightened. I wondered if I was capable of paying the price for what I was about to do. Could I live and suffer alone, without friends, family or Gloria? I was determined that I was that strong. I would not drag others down with me. I was going to be stubborn about this. "Stubborn as an old bent nail," my father would say.

Jeff was holding out something to me. A pocket cell phone.

"What are you doing?

"Use it. It was a present to me from my parents. They think I'll be safer if I walk around with a cellular phone in case I get lost or something. I can't believe they gave me this damn thing. They sit at home waiting for me to call. But I refuse to use it." He held it up to his face and in a mock little boy's voice said, "Hello, Mom, Dad. It's me, Jeff, your son. I'm somewhere in the MicMac Mall and can't seem to find my way out. You have to come get me."

"They're just your parents."

"Yeah, and I'm grown up. I'm not stupid. Here, call Gloria. Say hi. She'll be really happy to hear from you. She's been super worried."

"She already knows I'm going," I lied.

Cornwallis caught me in the rear view mirror. Something in his eyes. A criminal look. Pissed off big time.

"You say your mother is expecting you?"

"Yeah. She'll meet me at the airport in Saint John."

"I don't think it's a good idea, you travelling there alone."

"It's only forty minutes on the plane."

"Yeah, but you never know what can happen during that forty minutes."

"Take my cell phone," Jeff added. "Please."

"No. I don't think you're supposed to use them on flights."

"Why didn't you take Gloria with you?" Cornwallis again. Interrogation mode.

"She didn't want to fly."

Suddenly Cornwallis swerved off the road onto the gravelly shoulder and brought the car to an abrupt stop.

"What the fuck is going down, Alex?"

I suddenly felt nauseous and dizzy, weaker than before. "What do you mean?"

"I mean this shit about airplane rides and lying to me about

Gloria. I talked to her today, man. She's worried sick about you. That little woman loves you, and something very strange is happening here. Where the Jesus do you think you're off to?"

I couldn't bring myself to lie further. I took a deep breath, and it seemed like hard, sluggish work for my lungs.

"Alex?" Jeff asked. "What's going on?"

I tried to act authoritarian and tough. "Look, just both of you be good friends and get me to the airport."

"Man, if you just wanted a ride, why didn't you call a freaking taxi?"

The answer was that I wasn't sure I could get out of the hospital without some sort of help, but I sat silently. We were stopped by the side of the 107 just a bit north of Burnside and heading away from Dartmouth. Cornwallis got out of the car. "I'm not driving any further. I told you, Alex, I hate driving at night."

"Cornwallis, dammit. I'm doing what I have to do. You gotta understand that."

"I don't understand. You drive if you have to. I'm not."

I opened the back seat door and tried to get out, but my muscles had turned to spaghetti. I felt weak and humiliated. "Please, just drive me the rest of the way. I'll never ask anything of you again."

"I'm not driving. Jeff, you wanna drive?"

"What?"

"Let Jeff drive, man. You taught him. Big straight highway. Let him drive if you wanna get there."

"This is crazy," I said. "Somebody could get killed."

"Drive, Jeff," Cornwallis said, his voice angry and insistent. Jeff looked puzzled, a bit scared. "Alex?"

There was little traffic on the road. A single tractor trailer raced by, making the car rock. "Somebody could get killed."

"I'm not afraid to die," Cornwallis said with such absolute

conviction that he scared me. "My guess is, neither are you, Alex. In fact, that's what this is all about in some weird way, right, boss? You're running away from all of us because you think you're gonna hurt us somehow. You think you're gonna save Gloria from something bad. Jesus H. Christ. Drive, goddamn it, Jeff! Alex'll talk you through it. He's good at talking."

Before I could wrestle words out of my mouth, Jeff was behind the steering wheel, Cornwallis was beside him. The car was in gear and moving forward.

"Ease it a little left, Jeff," I said. We were already on the highway. "Now keep the wheel straight, give it some gas. There. Fifty kilometres an hour. Just keep the wheel straight." No problem so far. But this was bloody stupid.

"How'm I doing?" Jeff asked.

"Great." A couple of cars were coming up from behind. "Better go up to sixty." Even at sixty clicks, we were way too slow for the road. They passed us: one, two. The highway was empty again. Cornwallis sat stalwart and silent. I talked Jeff through a couple of slight shifts in the roadway, amazed at his confidence.

"God, I love to drive," he said.

But then I cautioned him to slow down as we came to a merge in the highway. We had a car on our bumper and two coming into our lane from the left. There was too much information for me to tell him at once. "Just keep it steady," I said, my voice wavering.

Steady wasn't quite good enough, and one of the merging cars slowed down in front of us while the car on our bumper tried to pass. Honking horns, some skidding tires. Then both cars were past us and we were in the clear. It was a damn close call. "Pull over," I said. "Easy. Real easy."

Jeff felt the gravel of the shoulder beneath the tires, eased to a stop. We were alongside Miller's Lake. The water sparkled in the night. The moon had risen out of the forest. This was the place where a famous stump had once sported what appeared to be the head of a dragon. "Somebody's gonna get killed," I repeated.

"Like I said, I've had a good life. I'm not afraid to die," Cornwallis stated.

"What the hell is the matter with you?" I yelled at him.

Jeff sat staring straight at the windshield.

"Alex," Cornwallis continued. "Why don't we let Jeff out of the car. He can call a cab on his portable phone. Then you and me can just drive your damn car into this lake here. Do you have a problem with that?"

"Cornwallis, what are you talking about?"

"I'm talking about you, man. I figured it out. I don't know where you're going, but you're like some old Inuit going out on the ice to die, or some elephant leaving the herd to wander off and get himself killed by lions. You're running away from us because you think you're gonna die."

"I am going to die."

"So what's this gonna prove? You gonna end up some place where nobody gives a damn about you."

"It would be better that way."

Cornwallis slammed his hand into the dashboard. "Damn. Okay, I'm back in the driver's seat. Jeff, get out. Me and Smart Boy back there gonna get up a good run and see if we can find the bottom of that lake there."

Jeff got out and walked around the car. He looked scared, very scared. His hand found the guard rail, and he took a step away from the car. Cornwallis was about to slide over into the driver's seat. "No way," I said. "I'll drive."

I found the door handle this time, made it work, got myself into the driver's seat as Cornwallis reluctantly slid over to the passenger side. Adrenalin had flushed my system enough to give me strength. I just sat there for a minute and did nothing at all. I waited for Cornwallis to say something, to push me just a little bit further. But he was silent. My vision was blurry. I rubbed my eyes and finally the world came back into focus.

"Get in, Jeff," I said. "It's okay."

Jeff found his way into the back seat and I heard him click the seat belt into place. Cornwallis was staring straight ahead into the empty night. My hands were shaking and I could barely keep my grip on the steering wheel, but I drove on into the night.

Thirty-six

It was summer then. A long summer day, heat rising from the ground, warm air with forest smells wafting off the land and drifting off toward sea. The Fundy shore. Home. The sky was clear above the wet, pebbled shoreline, but we could see small squalls like cartoon ghosts off in the distance above the water. Every once in a while we heard a low boom of thunder, but it was far, far off. Above us only Easter-egg blue sky. Karen and I, wading knee-deep. Tiny crabs dancing around our toes. Karen giggling. Me, alive, happy, holding her hand. I was ten, she was six. The King of Fundy had declared a holiday.

The water was warm on our legs. Our mother was sitting on the front steps. Front because they faced the sea, yet they led up to a door that never opened. Good reason to keep the sea-windward door nailed shut. Enter by way of the landward side of the house. Less wind, less likely the door will blow off its hinges. But on this singular evening of a magnificent day, we had been transported to another place, a soft geography of family, sea and tidal grace.

Tankers squatted stolid and surreal on the horizon, muted in the soft evening light, light that painted everything with a benevolent glow. Radiance all around. Karen, luminous, holding up her bare wet arms for the sun to wash golden with light. I had a handful of wet, tiny stones and was rolling them around in my paws. Something about the feel of them in the palms of my hands felt right and good. My mother above us, smiling, shelling peas that had been given to us by a neighbour. Why we didn't have our own garden was a bit of a mystery, but my father had said the soil was no good, he'd never had much luck with growing anything other than blue potatoes, and even those always turned out wormy and blighted.

Gulls and ravens chasing each other above us, making Karen laugh. A fish jumping for a bug above the water's surface. The sea, we knew, was full of turbulent life, but the skim of the surface was calm, still as a pane of dark ice. Karen smoothed her hand across the water as if she was petting a tame animal with a soft, furry back.

"When will Dad be home?" she asked.

"Soon," I said and wondered why she wanted to break the spell.

"I wish he was home now. I miss him when he's away so long."

"I miss him, too," I said, but I lied for her sake. I was happier when he was gone because he had a way of translating every bit of happiness into something that needed worrying about or complaining over. It was as if he had a dictionary in his head in each every word had a different meaning from the ones I knew. He almost never said a kind thing. Left alone, Karen, my mother and I would have had a very happy life. Or so I fantasized. It was my father who brought us ill fortune and everyday unhappiness.

A trace of a rainbow, a mere fraction of one, appeared where one of the sea squalls diminished, and I pointed it out for Karen. She clapped loudly, as if the trick had been performed by me, and then she slapped her hands down flat on the surface of the sea, making the water jump like that fish we'd watched.

The tide was dropping, and along the shore air bubbles came up through the tiny stones and sand as if the land were exhaling. We waded ashore and had begun to walk along this stretch of beach so familiar to us when we spotted a lobster trap wedged between two rocks. I had heard the engine of the lobster boat close to shore late last night, a local fishermen sure there was a secret cache of lobsters in tight near our little beach. And then the morning's storm and the high tide must have somehow pushed this one right up onto our little home patch of coast. Now here it was, beached with twin lobsters inside to boot.

Karen put her finger right up to a claw that reached through the wooden bars, and I grabbed her hand just in time. She squealed at the thrill of having come so close to danger. Each creature was at least two feet long. These were old, wary lobsters who had avoided the fishermen all their long lives, and now here they were, tragically cast ashore and as good as dead. The rock ballast had broken free from the ribs of the trap, and that's why it had floated in with the tide.

My mother had come to the edge of the overhead lawn now and was watching us. "Looks like tonight's dinner," she said, a big smile on her face, for it had been a good long while since we'd had a lobster feed courtesy of some charitable neighbour.

Karen lay down on the wet sand and studied the lobsters, fearless and uncaring that one of these sea things might reach out with a claw and pluck her eye out. I nudged the trap away from her for safety's sake. "They're very pretty," she said. "And very sad." I don't think she had paid any mind to what our mother had just said, and already I was feeling a little tense because I knew that as soon as my father found his way home there would be a row about what be food and what be pretty sea pets.

I cupped my hands in the water and splashed some on the lobsters, wondering what it might take to keep them alive and already secretly certain that I could not eat them for dinner. Karen followed suit, and we splashed water onto our friends and poked bunched rockweed into their cage, thinking this might be something they could snack upon.

And then he arrived. Stood above on the lawn, talking to my mother. After a minute or two, he clambered down the embankment and walked to us. I could smell the sweat of him, a man who had laboured all day in blackfly-infested forests. He reeked, and I felt ashamed for him; that's how poorly I understood his daily sacrifices to keep our family going.

"Big as they come," he said. He mopped his brow with a dirty red handkerchief. "Whaddaya think, Karen?"

"I think they're cute."

My father harrumphed and spit onto a wet, bald rock. "Probably one of Henderson's traps," he observed. "That feller loses more than he keeps. Probably should tell him about this one. Think we better empty the thing first, though. Your mother'd want to cook these two fine specimens. Finally have a decent feed of something other than salt pork for a change."

Karen didn't say a word, but she looked at me with those big, hopeful eyes. I looked away from her, my own eyes darting out to sea.

Then my father heaved a long-drawn-out, end-of-the-world sigh. "Tired. Tired. Tired. Tired," he said. "How can one man be so tired?" The announcement was out of character, for it carried no flag of complaint. I even detected a small banner of satisfaction. Maybe the beauty of the evening had somehow transformed him. "Tired" had always been part of an equation involving various degrees of anger and frustration. This was different. Certainly part of it was the endless round of defeat he felt. Then he sort of collapsed onto the sand beside us. First he sat with his knees up and his elbows resting on them, his head viced between his hands, staring down at the sand, then he reached out, scooped some saltwater and rubbed it into his face as if rubbing ointment into a wound.

He sighed again and emitted something just short of a sob. It came from some deep, private, secret place, and it was an admission unlike any other. Then he looked up at the sky, clenched both his hands and pounded the sand beside him. One, two, three: just like a drumbeat. He tried to look at me but could not. He sucked back a breath as if he was taking a deep drink of beer, and then he lay down flat on his back.

"Isn't this the most beautiful day you ever saw?" Karen asked him. I was sure I knew the man's thoughts, but I did not want him to speak them out loud and ruin everything, ruin us all. My mother was still hovering on the grassy patch above us, watching us but keeping her distance.

He lay there with his head on the sand, his eyes squinting up at the sky, and I saw a tiny river run down from each eye across his cheeks. I watched as a single tear found the sand and disappeared. I wanted to ask my father a thousand questions just then, but I did not.

"Yes, Karen, it is a very good day," he said to her. Rare words, impossible words, and stranger still because my father almost never spoke directly to Karen. But I also knew that it had been a very hard day for my father. "A dirty day in the woods," as he was prone to say. But he would not speak of that part of his life tonight.

I splashed some more water on the lobsters. Karen tried to pet their shells, and as I pulled her fingers back I heard the clack of their claws. These old creatures probably still had enough strength to break a little girl's finger.

Finally my father sat up and rubbed his face again, pushing his sunburned, wrinkled skin around like modelling clay, working the wetness of tears into the wounds of his soul. "A fine day," he repeated, looking off to sea. The sun was beginning to set, and my father pointed a finger towards the south. "Looks like a water spout out there somewhere. A little tornado at sea."

Karen and I saw a thin pillar of something. Could have just been a small sea squall, but I wanted to believe him instead. "Ever see one up close?" I asked.

He nodded. "When I was a boy. Yep. Right here. Saw it lift a dory right out of the water, picked it up, twirled it about like a toy, then splashed it down a mile off shore. Just like that."

"Can it do that to us?" Karen asked.

"Could but won't," he said. "Those things are rare. Almost never come ashore. Besides, I wouldn't let anything bad happen to you. Never."

I tried to focus on the sea spout again, if that's what it was, but it had vanished. The sunset was painting the Bay of Fundy in a warm bath of yellows and reds. I stared at the oil tanker anchored several miles away, that dark, elongated smudge on the horizon. Irving's oil wanted ashore in Saint John tomorrow. Business as usual. It did not belong out there tonight. Closer to shore a couple of fish jumped for flies.

From around the headland I could hear a boat engine, an inshore fisherman. My father heard it, too. "That'd be Henderson, looking for his traps. He should never have been a fishermen. Don't have the common sense for water. I worked with him one summer. Man couldn't steer a boat betwixt a rock and a hard place."

Next he looked at the lobsters. "Now what are we gonna do with these here fellers. Henderson got lucky on these, he did. This pair probably been holding out a mighty long time, in close to shore in those deep dark clefts between the rocks. No other buddy be as foolish as Henderson to come in this close to catch 'em. Takin' a chance on tearing the hull to shreds on the fingers of rock. Now what should we do?" He wasn't asking us, just talking.

"Can we let them go?" Karen asked.

It was unthinkable. The choice was either take the lobsters to the kitchen and leave Henderson his trap, or signal to the brazen fisherman to come get his catch and maybe even wade it out to him like a good neighbour.

My father let a gust of used-up air out through his nose, flaring his nostrils. A laugh, a snort. There was something bullish about it and the twisted, fiery look that came into his eyes. Bill Henderson's boat had not appeared around the headland yet, but the engine was already a loud grumble intruding upon the peace and quiet. Without a word, my father began to drag the prisoners down the beach, and he walked right out into the water with his shoes and pants on until he was knee deep. He set the trap upon a rocky ledge and reached in, pulled out one giant lobster and held it aloft for us to see. He was holding it by its carapace, and I realized, now that it was untangled from the other one, just how enormous it was. Each lobster would have been almost a meal for the four of us. He held it with two hands as it clawed the air, and I was sure the old man with the crazed look was going to break its neck, then kill its mate and bring them both ashore for dinner. Let the trap float off for Henderson to find.

Instead, he gently set the lobster into the water and picked up the second one as well. He let both of them go and hid the trap behind another protruding rock in a such way that Henderson would not see from his boat.

Karen clapped her hands and threw sand up in the air in celebration. Some of it got in my eyes on its trip back to earth. My father started to walk shoreward but halted, turned around and dove sideways, fully clothed, into the warm sea. He stayed under in the shallows, just lying on the sea floor, for nearly a full minute before he came up gasping for air.

Karen got up to run into the water to join him, but an old instinct in me stopped her. His actions were so out of character that I didn't know what he might do next. Maybe he had lost his mind. Karen squirmed against my grip, but I did not let go. When he came dripping ashore, he hitched up his pants, just as Henderson's boat rounded the headland, travelling way too close to shore for any man's good. My father turned, gave the captain a curt little salute, and a sunbaked Bill Henderson stared at my father as if he was some odd fish that had just flipped up out of the water in the buggy sunset. But the man did not tip his cap or wave. Instead, the boat cruised on by, and the noise of its engine disturbed the dozen gulls resting one-legged on the grassy bluff west of us.

The dripping man who was my father did not say anything.

He heaved himself up onto our lawn, sat there shaking his head. Yes or no? Good or bad? Who could say what it meant.

I wiped the remainder of sand from my eyes and followed Karen to the house.

Once inside, my father took off his sopping wet pants and shirt and dropped them there on the kitchen floor, then stood there by the back door in his boxer shorts and T-shirt. A sorry sight he was, all sunburned neck and arms, skinny bag of bones for a body. A man born to hard work through hopeless hard times.

"Anything for dinner?" my father asked my mother.

"Fresh peas," she said. "Piece of pork left in the fridge, potatoes, and a tin of pears for dessert."

"S'good by me," he said. "Was a hot, dirty one in the woods today. Couldn't be much worse. Be glad when winter's back and the blackflies stop sucking me blood."

My mother looked at us, then back at my father, bronzed by a wedge of early evening sunlight. He suddenly realized how foolish he appeared, but he didn't seem to mind at all. He looked straight at Karen and made a funny face that made her explode in laughter.

Then as he walked past us he tried to cover the smile on his face and said, "It's a pretty mixed up world when an old funny-looking shore boy like me could end up with a woman as pretty as your mother."

Thirty-seven

Late at night, I returned to my bed. Tubes were reinserted, wires attached. Cornwallis and Jeff said goodbye, and I caught hell from a night nurse who told me I was a fool. Vergie had been called at home and came to check up on me, but she gave no lecture. When I woke up in the middle of the night with a tremor in my chest, I waited for my distressed heart to burst, to give up, and to kill me once and for all. But it did not. Instead I fell into a deep, bottomless sleep, and when I woke in the morning every muscle in my body hurt, every nerve seemed damaged somehow.

Gloria was there, asleep in the chair beside my bed, her hair caressed by the morning sun. I knew then that I would fight from here on, I would fight for every breath, for every heartbeat. I would demand life over death.

Gloria would be awake soon. And something new would begin. Something shaped by death but not made ugly by death. Time would be my ally, not my enemy, from here on. I would admit no enemies into my life in the days to come.